MISS SILVER

To all outward appearances she looks like a
Victorian maiden aunt – but behind the
knitting needles and the lace lurks an acute
intelligence and a pair of scanning eyes which
miss absolutely nothing. Allied to her strong
moral principles, her passion for justice and
an innate understanding of the basest human
motivations Miss Silver is a very formidable
detective indeed.

*Miss Wentworth's very endearing and shrewd
heroine is known the world over. In the USA
and in Europe she has frequently enjoyed the
enviable position of being a bestseller. These
are samples of her acclaim from the British
critics:*

'Miss Silver is marvellous' – *Daily Mail*

'Just the thing to keep you warm with
excitement' – *BBC*

'Fine melodrama . . . very good value'
– *The Observer*

**Also by the same author
and available in Coronet Books:**

The Watersplash

A Miss Silver Mystery

Patricia Wentworth

CORONET BOOKS
Hodder and Stoughton

ISBN 0-340-15950-2

Chapter 1

THE VILLAGE OF GREENINGS LIES ABOUT A MILE AND A HALF from the country town of Embank. Some day the town will swallow it up, with its picturesque old church set about with the graves of so many generations, its village street, its straggle of cottages, the Georgian Vicarage which replaced the one burned down in 1801, and its couple of small late eighteenth-century houses originally built for relatives of the Random family. But that day is not yet, because Halfpenny Lane, which connects it with Embank, does not really lead to anywhere in particular and is interrupted just beyond Greenings by a watersplash. The village is, in fact, extremely rural. A visiting artist once referred to it as "a haunt of ancient peace". But into the quietest backwater a stone may fall, disquieting ripples may spread. Sherlock Holmes has exposed the myth of country innocence.

Greenings had had its share of happenings that would not bear the light of day. But things do not remain hidden for ever. A chance word, an unexpected move, the working out of an unseen plan, and the buried things are buried no longer. When Dr. Croft got a letter from Clarice Dean he had no idea that it would lead to anything of a disturbing nature. Miss Dean had nursed Mr. James Random during his last illness a year ago. She had also nursed him some years previously through an attack of influenza. A pretty, bright girl, and extremely efficient. She wrote to say that she had been out to Canada with a patient and had only recently returned. She had loved being at Greenings and would like very much to find work in that neighbourhood. If he knew of some chronic, elderly case, perhaps he would be so kind as to recommend her.

5

It did not, of course, take him any time at all to think of Miss Ora Blake. She enjoyed ill health, and her nurses never stayed. Clarice Dean wouldn't stay, but she would tide Miss Ora over and stop Miss Mildred ringing him up three times a day and buttonholing him every time she met him in the village street. At least he hoped so. He rang Miss Blake, and listened to what she had got to say with as much patience as he could contrive.

"Nurse Dean? My dear Dr. Croft! Do you know, I always did think she was setting her cap at poor Mr. Random. Such a high colour—but all these girls make up nowadays——"

He laughed.

"Well, I think Miss Dean's colour was natural."

"Men always *do*," said Miss Ora in her comfortable purring voice. "So easily taken in. You say she wants to come down here. Now I wonder why."

"She has been out to Canada with an invalid who went on a visit to a daughter and unfortunately died there. It was quite natural that she should write to me for a recommendation."

"Oh, *quite*. Especially if there was anyone in the neighbourhood whom she wanted to see. Perhaps it was not Mr. *James* Random in whom she was interested. There is Mr. Arnold Random, and Mr. Edward——"

Dr. Croft chuckled. When he did not have too much of her he could enjoy Miss Ora Blake.

"Now, now," he said, "you mustn't forget we're on a party line. Suppose the Hall is listening in."

"Arnold Random would be very much flattered," said Miss Ora with what he was convinced was a toss of the head. "He's quite a catch now—coming in for everything after his brother died. And he can't be more than sixty—he was much younger than Mr. James. He'd be the one to make up to, not poor Edward. Though I don't know why I should call him poor. People don't run away and let themselves be thought dead and then come back and not tell anyone where they've been, unless they've got themselves into some kind of a mess."

. "Miss Ora——"

But her voice boomed against his ear.

"No, no, depend upon it, there was something very discreditable, and James Random knew it, otherwise he wouldn't have altered his will—not after bringing Edward up as his own son instead of just as a nephew. And all very well to say he thought he was dead, but there is such a thing as the wish being father to the thought."

"Miss Ora, do you wish me to engage Miss Dean for you?"

It appeared that she did wish it. She had not known Dr. Croft for thirty years without recognizing the point at which it was advisable to come to business. Mildred would write to Nurse Dean. But perhaps Dr. Croft would write too.

"My case—so complicated—and you can explain it all so well."

Miss Mildred wrote. Dr. Croft wrote, and told Clarice Dean as much as he thought suitable about the complicated case of Miss Ora Blake. He had once described it to Emmeline Random as an indisposition to do anything for anyone else. Emmeline was of course perfectly safe, but he would not have let his tongue run away with him to that extent if he had not been exasperated beyond bearing.

He was scrupulously careful in what he said to Miss Clarice Dean. She wrote by return, and followed her letter two days later, arriving to take up her new position just twenty-four hours before Edward Random came down to stay with his stepmother.

Chapter 2

EDWARD RANDOM EMERGED FROM THE STATION ENTRANCE AND turned to the right. If he had not stopped at the bookstall he would have seen Susan Wayne then. As it was, he did not see her until he had taken the next left-hand turn, now plainly marked by a signpost which said, "Greenings 1½ miles." The signpost was new, or at anyrate new to him—but then last time he had come down Jack Burton had given him a lift and they had come in from the other side. And before that—in the days before the deluge—well, you either knew where Greenings was, or you took your chance of not finding it at all. When he thought how long it was since he had got out at Embank and walked this way his face darkened.

He turned by the signpost and saw Susan walking along the lane in front of him with a suit-case swinging from an ungloved hand. The glove and its fellow had been thrust into the pocket of a blue swagger coat. She walked well, and she pleased the eye in the sort of impersonal way that it is pleased by any other agreeable feature of the landscape. A purely surface impression, but definitely pleasant. It was not until a minute or two later that the personal element began to intrude, not with any degree of insistence, but as a vague feeling that he had seen that straight fair hair before. It was very straight except just at the ends, and it was very fair and very thick, and it was cut in a page-boy bob. When nearly every girl you saw had curls all over her head, you were apt to remember the one who hadn't.

Across a five-year gap he remembered Susan Wayne—seventeen and a good deal too fat, or at anyrate what she thought was a good deal too fat. He had no rooted objection to curves himself, but the Susan he began to remember had certainly been on the plump side, with apple cheeks, round grey eyes like a kitten's, and that very thick, very fair bob. Quite a nice child. He lengthened his stride and came up with her. If it wasn't Susan, he would just go on, but if it was it would be rather absurd to stalk past her and then run into her again at Emmeline's.

She looked round at him as he came up, and for a moment he wasn't quite sure. And then he was—just like that. She wasn't fat any more, but the eyes were the same, only now that her face was thinner they looked larger, and the lashes had darkened to a golden brown. She probably did something to them, but the effect was good. After all, why go through the world with white eyelashes if you didn't want to? He frowned, and said in his abruptest manner,

"Are you Susan Wayne?"

Susan's eyes opened to their fullest extent. There was soft dust in the lane, and she hadn't heard him coming. She had been thinking about Professor Postlethwaite on his way to America, and what a pity it was that the money wouldn't run to her going too, not only because she had always wanted to go to America, but because it was practically certain that he would get his lecture notes mixed up if she wasn't there to keep them straight. And then in the twinkling of an eyelash the five-year-old past had risen up, and there was Edward Random glowering at her in the middle of Halfpenny Lane.

No one knew why it was called Halfpenny Lane, but it was. And no one knew how the past could suddenly rise up and hit you where it hurt, but it could and did—at least for a horrid moment. Just for that moment she was seventeen again, much too fat, and in love with Edward Random who was in love with Verona Grey. It was frightful, but thank goodness it didn't last. Five years ago was five years ago. Nobody can make you live things over again. Not she, nor Edward. Oh, poor Edward! A tide

of warmth and kindness flowed in. She dropped her suit-
case and put out both hands to him.

"Oh, Edward, how nice—how very nice!"

Afterwards he was to reflect that Susan was really the
only person to take this point of view about his return.
No, that wasn't quite fair. Emmeline, who was his stepmother, had done so, and quite whole-heartedly. But as in
her case affection and relief had taken the form of a perfect
deluge of tears it had not been very enlivening.

Susan did not weep, she glowed. If there was a faint
moisture in her eyes, it merely made them brighter. She
held his hands for a moment in a warm, firm clasp, then
stepped back and said all over again,

"Oh, Edward—how *nice*!"

Well, it was. He had actually stopped frowning, but the
line where the frown had been remained. The thin, dark
face showed other lines, and none of them happy ones. It
was stamped with endurance. There had been pain, bad
pain, but it hadn't broken him. There was a certain wary
alertness, a touch of bitter humour. Susan's soft heart was
stirred. It was Edward himself who had once told her with
scorn that her heart was as soft as butter that had been left
out in the sun. She had gone away and cried dreadfully,
and her eyes had swelled right up. She would have given
anything in the world to cry becomingly like Verona—a
tear or two, eyes like wet violets, long dark lashes just becomingly damp. How awful to be seventeen and fat, with
swollen eyelids and a broken heart.

Susan gave a backward glance at the horrid picture and
laughed.

"How nice to meet like this!"

The emotion of the moment was over. He considered
that she was overworking a rather tepid word.

"At anyrate I can carry your suit-case."

"Oh, no—you've got one of your own."

"It's quite light."

"So is mine." She picked it up as she spoke.

"Do I protest?"

"I don't think so—waste of time. I've got a box coming up by the carrier, so this is only things for the night."

She had taken up the case with her right hand. As he fell into step beside her, it was twisted out of her grasp so quickly and dexterously that she had no chance to resist. She really did feel angry as she reflected that Edward had always liked getting his own way and been rather ingenious over it. Whatever else had changed, he seemed to be just the same about this. Her colour brightened and she laughed.

"You really haven't changed!"

"What a pity, but while there's life there's hope. You're not still living in Greenings, are you?"

"Oh, no. Aunt Lucy died while I was at college. I work for Professor Postlethwaite, but he's gone to America on a lecture tour."

"Five years in a couple of sentences—how economical! What does he profess?"

"Oh, literature. He's gone to lecture on all the different people Shakespeare might have been. So when Emmeline wrote and said your Uncle Arnold wanted someone to catalogue the library at the Hall, and would I come and stay with her and do it, I said I would."

It was ridiculous to feel nervous, but she did. A glance at Edward's face did nothing to reassure her. It looked bleak. He said,

"How amusing."

"What is there amusing about it?"

"I don't know—it just struck me that way."

She thought *struck* was the right word. To change the subject she said,

"I suppose you are staying with Emmeline too?"

"Just for the moment. It will give Greenings something to talk about, if nothing else."

Susan looked steadily in front of her and said,

"Why should it?"

"Return of the outcast. You know, I've only been down once since I got back."

"I don't know anything—except that everyone thought you were dead——"

He said in a light, brittle voice,

"And I wasn't. My mistake. Never come back from the dead—it is a social solecism."

"You shouldn't say that. When Emmeline wrote and told me you were alive she said, 'It is *too* much happiness!'"

"Yes, I believe she really was pleased. There has to be an exception to every rule, and it rather adds to the general humour of the situation that the one person who didn't mind my being alive should be a stepmother. What else did she tell you?"

"Well, you know Emmeline's letters. There were bits about the cats—Scheherazade had just had a very plain family, and she was a good deal upset about it in between being all up in the air about you, but I gathered that you were taking a refresher course in land agency. And when she wrote the other day, there was a bit about Lord Burlingham telling her that you were going to come to him, and how nice it would be to have you so near."

She saw him smile.

"Lovely for everyone! Especially for Arnold!"

Susan hated people who beat about the bush. She plunged.

"Look here, Edward, what is all this? Why shouldn't your Uncle Arnold be pleased? Because if there has been a lurid family quarrel, I had much better know, or I shall be sure to put my foot in it."

"Both feet, I should think! It's not so much a Row as an Awkward Situation, and as you'll be right in the middle of the Random family you had better be put wise." He swung the two suit-cases and stuck out his chin. "Well, here you are—we'll start with a little potted family history. In the last generation there were three Randoms—my Uncle James, my father Jonathan, and my Uncle Arnold. James lost his wife and child and never married again. Jonathan married twice when he had tried most other things and failed at them, after which he died, leaving a son, me, a widow, Emmeline, and a considerable number of debts which Uncle James thought it his duty to pay. He had a very strong sense of duty. He put Emmeline in the south lodge and brought me up regardless."

"Yes?" Susan's voice made a question of it.

He laughed.

"It wasn't 'Yes', my dear, it was a thundering 'No'. We had an epic row, and I cleared out."

Susan remembered the row. It was about Verona, because Edward was ragingly in love with her, and James Random had taken the line that if he wanted to marry her he could go right ahead and do it, only he would have to foot the bill himself, because his allowance would automatically come to a full stop on his wedding day. A more dramatic version preferred by some credited James Random with the remark that he would rather see Edward in his coffin, but bearing in mind Mr. Random's dignified personality and temperate manner of speech, Susan, even at seventeen, had not really found herself able to believe in it. With these things in her mind, she thought it best just to go on looking interested. It was always safer to say nothing than to chance what you said being wrong, only usually she didn't think about this until it was too late.

Edward swung the suit-cases and went on in that light bitter voice.

"We now skip four and a half years. I have been dead for about three of them—quite credibly and circumstantially dead. Uncle James has naturally made a new will. Even if I haven't been formally disinherited, you don't leave the family possessions to a corpse. So Edward being dead, and James being dead, dear Uncle Arnold scoops the lot. That's the set-up. Didn't Emmeline tell you about it?"

Susan shook her head.

"I don't think so. There was a squiggle down in the corner of the last page which I couldn't quite read, but I thought it was only some more about one of the kittens which had turned out quite unexpectedly good so she had changed its name from Smut to Lucifer. Edward, you don't mean to say your Uncle Arnold didn't do anything about it? When he found you weren't dead?"

"He did not."

"But couldn't he be made to? Mr. Random would never have left you out of his will if he hadn't thought you were dead."

"And how does one prove what a dead man would or wouldn't have done? We had had a colossal row, and he did change his will. Those are facts, and the law has a stupid affection for facts."

"When did he change it—when you went away, or when he thought that you were dead?"

Just for a moment he looked at her with anger. Then he laughed and said,

"Never you mind, my child! And I'm not washing the family linen in public either. It may be dirty, and I think we'll keep it at home."

It was so much what he might have said to the schoolgirl of five years ago that it took her aback. She ought to have remembered to go on holding her tongue, but she hadn't, and he had snubbed her. And instead of really minding, it felt quite natural. She coloured, but she laughed too, and said a little ruefully,

"I'm sorry—it just slipped out."

All at once there was a warm, comfortable feeling between them. He remembered that there had always been something rather comfortable about Susan. It might be boring in the long run. He wondered whether it would be. It might, but then on the other hand it mightn't. He found himself saying,

"You really haven't changed a lot."

"Nor have you. I said so at once."

The frown had come down again.

"Most people would say I had changed considerably."

She shook her head.

"I don't believe people really do. Sometimes one bit comes to the top and you see more of it than you used to, but that isn't really a change. Apples don't turn into pears, or raspberries into plums. People have their own special flavours, and I think they keep them."

He said,

"Sour grapes and rotten medlars! Perhaps you are right. I must warn you that I am definitely in the medlar category. Even your blameless reputation may be damaged if we arrive practically hand in hand. You see, I haven't been able to account at all satisfactorily for those four and a half years, and I understand from Emmeline that there are a number of exciting stories going round. It distresses her, I'm afraid, but there isn't anything I can do about it."

"You could say where you were."

"I'm afraid it doesn't bear talking about." The brittle voice again.

Something hurt Susan at her heart. Brittle things break. But he went on.

"The favourite theory seems to be that I was in prison under a false name, but there are some quite good variants in which I fly the country because I've killed a man in a duel, or have been turned out of my club for cheating at cards."

Susan said, "I wish you would talk sense!" Her tone was downright and a little angry.

"Too much trouble. Burlingham's a brave man, isn't he? He really is offering me the agency, you know. And that's not a confidence, because if he told Emmeline, everyone within twenty miles or so will have heard all about it. And that means my Uncle Arnold—which is probably why Burlingham did it."

She said, "That sounds—horrid."

"Just a plain sequence. Arnold loves me—Burlingham loves Arnold—how pleased Arnold will be to know that Burlingham is giving me a job that will ensure my being right under his nose. Since the estates march, there's quite a chance of Arnold running into me any day of the week, even if I don't stay on with Emmeline."

Susan said bluntly, "You mean Arnold doesn't like you, and Lord Burlingham doesn't like Arnold."

Edward burst out laughing.

"You've got it in one!"

Chapter 3

EMMELINE RANDOM WAS GIVING A TEA-PARTY. WHEN SUSAN Wayne came in the room appeared to be already quite full of people, but then it was so full of other things to start with that there wasn't as much space for the human visitor as there might have been if Emmeline and her drawing-room had been different. For one thing, it wasn't really a drawing-room. It had begun life as the front parlour of the south lodge at the Hall, and when Emmeline was left a widow her brother-in-law, James Random, installed her there. He gave the parlour a bay window, and since she had always been accustomed to a drawing-room, it never occurred to her to call it anything else. The bay window certainly let in a good deal more light. It had also made it possible to admit the cottage piano with green silk flutings which she had inherited from her grandmother. But it did not really increase the wall space, which was a good deal taken up with ancestral portraits of a rather dark and forbidding nature. There was an Admiral whose features could hardly be distinguished from the maroon curtain against which he stood. There was a lady in black velvet and black ringlets whose features could not really be distinguished at all. They were Emmeline's great-grandparents, and she was very proud of them, because the Admiral had served with Nelson and was reputed to have had a better command of forcible language than anyone in the British Navy either before or since.

Jonathan Random, her late husband, whose portrait occupied the place of honour on the jutting chimney-breast was neither dark nor forbidding. He smiled upon the room in the same charming manner in which he had smiled his way through life. He had been fifty when Emmeline married him, and he had never managed either to make or to keep any money. If he had lived a year or two longer, Emmeline would not have had any money either. As it was, there remained a pittance, and the hospitality of the south lodge, where she had now been living for so long that she quite felt as if it belonged to her.

She was a small, slight person with a quantity of fair hair which was turning grey and a sweet inconsequent manner. Her finely arched eyebrows enhanced the effect of a pair of misty blue eyes. When Edward was about seven he had once remarked, "It's there, but she sees through it." Pressed as to what he meant, he had burst out indignantly, "The mist of course! It's there, but it doesn't stop her seeing things!"

A great deal had happened since Edward was seven years old. James Random had gone the way of Jonathan, and Arnold reigned at the Hall in his stead. There had been a world war, and an air raid which had killed Mr. Plowden's prize pig and a cherished cat belonging to Dr. Croft's housekeeper. Edward grew up, and when the war was over he took a course in estate management. Then he fell in love with Verona Grey, had a furious row with his Uncle James, and was seen no more in Greenings. He did not come back, and according to the postmistress he did not write.

Emmeline cried a good deal, and comforted herself with
cats. She would rather have been making believe that
Edward's children were her own grandchildren, but you
must have something, and kittens were better than not
having anything at all. At least there were always plenty
of them.

After what seemed like a very long time there was a
report that Edward was dead. It was quite circumstantial,
and James Random believed it. He told Emmeline that he
had talked with a man who had seen Edward lying dead,
but he wouldn't tell her anything more than that. He said
it would only distress her. And then he went away very
grave and shocked, and made the will which left everything
to his brother Arnold. He had been dead six months when
Edward Random came back, walking in upon Emmeline
in the late dusk of a winter evening and telling her nothing.
She cried a great deal, but she didn't ask any questions—
she didn't really want to. He had been away and he had
come back, he had been hurt and he must be comforted.
It was enough. She was therefore able to meet the storm
of questioning that broke upon her with an invariable
"My dear, I really don't know." And since this was a
bedrock fact, it did ultimately put the questioners to silence
—that is, as far as Emmeline was concerned.

They naturally went on talking to one another. Edward
had been in China—he had been in Russia. Mrs. Deacon
who did for Miss Blake, and whose daughter was house-
maid at the Hall, was quite sure that Mr. James Random
had been saying something about Russia the day his solicitor
came down and he signed his will. Doris had heard the
word quite plain when she was going past the study door,
which wasn't quite shut. "Russia."—that was what she
heard, but nothing more that she could swear to. It was
not much, but like the kittens it was better than nothing.
Some very interesting and dramatic stories were built up
on it.

And then the great China myth came into circulation.

Someone had a cousin who had a friend who had seen—
actually seen—Edward Random in hospital at Shanghai.
Or was it Singapore? Eastern names, you know—all so
very much alike.

Edward did nothing to resolve the rumours. Everyone
was interested and sympathetic. Arnold Random would
certainly have to do something for his nephew. He would
never have come in for the property if his brother James
had not believed that Edward was dead. The least, the
very least, that he could do was to hand over the estate and,
well, half the money. And when Arnold did nothing of
the sort, there were some very harsh things said about his
conduct. It was not as if he had not enough money of his
own, because he had, or as if there could have been the
slightest doubt as to James Random's intentions. And it
wasn't as if Arnold had a wife and family. He had no one
but Edward, and the least he could do . . .

Edward had been back for a month or two, when a more
sinister rumour began to go round. Nobody knew where
it had started, and most of those who passed it on were
careful to explain that they didn't believe it themselves.
But of course there is no smoke without fire. People don't
disappear unless there is a reason. Possible reasons for
Edward's disappearance crept into the news. It was at
first hinted, then introduced as a matter of speculation, and
finally whispered as a fact, that he had been in prison.

It was when these rumours reached Lord Burlingham
that he came across the High Street at Embank and, join-
ing the fish queue, told Emmeline at the top of his voice
how glad he was to have been able to offer her stepson the
job of land agent. He was a large, energetic person, and
his voice was an extremely carrying one. "Old Barr is
retiring. He has only stayed on the last six months to
oblige me. Edward can take right over. I told him he had
better have a refresher course—latest up-to-date methods
and all that kind of thing. Must produce more food for
the nation—everyone's duty. Always liked the boy—been

away too long. Always glad to do a good turn to a neighbour. Tell your brother-in-law I said so." At which he
burst into hearty laughter and went back across the road
to buttonhole old Mr. Plowden, leaving the ladies in the
queue to pause, gasp, look at one another, and then rush
into asking Emmeline a great many more questions than
she could answer.

Lord Burlingham was a self-made man. He had run
barefoot, he had sold papers in the streets. He had acquired
a fortune, bought a country estate, joined the Labour Party
and been wafted to the House of Lords upon one of those
occasions when the Tory majority there was proving more
than usually irritating. There may have been other reasons.
It was said that he did not bow very complacently to the
Party yoke, and that he was developing an inconvenient
habit of getting up in the Commons and saying what he
really thought. There may have been a feeling that it
would be safer to let him say it somewhere else.

He stood in the village street polishing his face with a
red and green bandanna and telling Mr. Plowden that
Edward Random was going to succeed old Barr.

"And someone had better tell Arnold Random before
we all meet on the Bench next week, or I shall do it myself,
and perhaps I had better not! He might have a fit! Hates
my guts, you know—thinks I'm common! And so I am!
What's wrong with it? Common sense, common law, the
common people of England—what's the matter with any
of them?"

His voice with its broad accent and occasional uncertainty
over an aitch rang out vigorously and reached the ladies in
the fish queue. Old Mr. Plowden's quavering "Certainly—
certainly, my dear fellow," was carried away by the wind.

That was a little time ago. And now Emmeline sat behind her gimcrack table and counted heads. "The Vicar
and Mrs. Ball—Mildred Blake—Dr. Croft and Cyril—four,
and myself five—and Susan should be here at any moment,
only of course she may have taken the later train—six—or

·is it seven? Then Edward——" Impossible to say. So nice if he and Susan could have met and come up together. But on the other hand Edward wouldn't be at all pleased about the tea-party. Such a pity, because they were all so kind—even Mildred, though of course she could be very trying too. But it wasn't good for Edward to shut himself away, and of course the more he did it, the more talk there would be. You couldn't expect anything else— "Seven cups—but I seem to have eight on the tray—oh dear, there's another little crack, and I must have done it myself, because nobody else touches this set!"

She said, "Oh dear no, I don't think so," to Miss Blake, who was complaining of the increasing lack of manners amongst the young, but she had heard it all so often before that her real attention was given to considering whether the milk would go round. Of course it must be made to—but would there be any left over for the cats?

Fortunately, only two of them were present. On the window-ledge Scheherazade the matriarch, a magnificent tortoiseshell. On the top of the piano Lucifer, who was turning out so well that she had dropped the plebeian name of Smut. His coal-black fur fluffed out, his fire-opal eyes ablaze, the tip of his tail just twitching, he followed the exciting play of Cyril's fingers as they rushed, glissaded, and scrambled from one end of the keyboard to the other and the black keys and the white keys kept jumping up and down. Since he was not yet six months old he might so far forget himself as to pounce. Emmeline gazed at him fondly. It would be very hard to resist him if he came and mewed for milk. She could do without any herself, but Scheherazade must come first.

She began to count all over again, and the numbers came out quite differently. There always seemed to be a cup too many or a cup too few, and if Edward—— She sent a bewildered look across the room and saw Susan Wayne come in, her fair hair shining and her face fresh and rosy.

Chapter 4

THE ROOM WAS HOT AND WAS GOING TO BE HOTTER. EVERYONE was pleased to see Susan. Even Cyril spared a moment to wave a large bony hand in her direction before going on with a piece which appeared to consist entirely of shallow glittering runs. Dr. Croft looked over his shoulder and said in an exasperated voice,

"Now that's quite enough! I don't like music with my tea! If you can call that music! More like a dog with a tin can at his tail!"

Emmeline smiled her sweet, vague smile:

"Oh, Dr. Croft, but I asked him to play, and I'm sure he does it very nicely indeed. He must have very strong fingers. But he will want his tea. And perhaps, Cyril dear, you wouldn't mind handing round the cups."

She began to count them again. "Susan—Cyril—Dr. Croft—Mrs. Ball—the Vicar—Mildred—that makes six—but I have another cup on the tray——"

Miss Blake's long, pointed nose was seen if not heard to sniff. She bore no resemblance to her plump, fair sister. Her complexion was dark, her nose aquiline, and, a little too close on either side of it, there gleamed a very bright dark eye. Emmeline remembered her as a passably handsome young woman in her thirties. There had been a time when she had feared that she might be going to have her as a sister-in-law. Arnold Random had paid her some attention, but nothing had come of it. Certainly no one would call her handsome now. She never spent a penny if she could possibly help it, and had worn the same dreary clothes and dowdy hat for at any rate the last fifteen years. She looked quite angrily at the tea-tray and said,

"Really, Emmeline—I suppose you are going to have a cup yourself!"

"Oh, yes, my dear. Let me see—yes, I believe you are right. Perhaps if I just pour out and Cyril hands them round. . . . And the scones, Susan—while they are still hot——"

Mildred Blake turned to Mrs. Ball and said in a voice which she hardly troubled to lower,

"Really, Emmeline is becoming too absent-minded!"

Mrs. Ball always agreed with everyone unless her conscience intervened. It did so now. Miss Blake was inclined to be censorious—she must not be encouraged. She said in her slow, pleasant voice, "Mrs. Random is always so kind," and then felt that she had been weak. She did try to love all her neighbours, but she found it very difficult to love Miss Blake. One just had to go on trying. She took her cup of tea and said,

"I do hope your sister is able to enjoy this lovely weather."

Miss Blake bridled.

"Really, Mrs. Ball, you are very easily pleased! I should not call it lovely myself. We have scarcely seen the sun all day, and there is quite a chilly wind."

Mrs. Ball's round cheeks became even more like rosy apples.

"But it has not rained."

"As you say, it has not actually rained. But the air is full of a clinging damp. The English climate can be very unpleasant in the autumn, or indeed at any other time of the year. But as far as my sister Ora is concerned it makes very little difference, since she moves only from her bed to the sofa and back again."

"I know. It is very hard for her—and for you. I hope you are pleased with the new nurse. I haven't met her yet, but she isn't really a stranger here, is she?"

"She nursed Mr. Random in his last illness—Mr. James Random."

"So Mrs. Random was saying. That was just before we came here. Miss Dean, isn't it? I think I saw her in the street this morning—a pretty girl."

"She is an efficient nurse," said Miss Blake in a voice which made it quite clear that her interest in Clarice Dean did not extend beyond her professional duties.

Mrs. Ball sighed. It was being very hard work.

The Vicar and Dr. Croft were talking about cricket. Emmeline was putting down a surreptitious saucer of milk for Scheherazade. Cyril, having finished handing round the cups and the cake-stand, sat down by Susan.

"Nobody told me you were coming. Why didn't they?"

If he had said that to Clarice Dean, she would have sparkled at him and asked why anyone should suppose he would be interested, after which you knew just where you were and could go right ahead. He had a date with Clarice for the evening. There was quite a good picture at the Royal in Embank. The bother was he would have to pay for them both, and it was going to be a pretty near thing. He wasn't sure he wouldn't rather have been going with Susan, who always paid for herself. But then Susan was different.

She laughed and said,

"I didn't know I was coming myself until two days ago. Mr. Random wants me to catalogue the library whilst my Professor is away. It ought to be rather fun. I believe they've got some good books."

Cyril made a face. He was a long, gangling lad with straw-coloured hair and a lot of bone. He said,

"Girls do think the oddest things are fun! A lot of mouldy old books!" He edged nearer. "I've got lots to tell you. I've had it out with my father, and I'm not going back to school."

"Oh, Cyril!"

He gave an emphatic nod.

"Well, I'm not. I failed for that beastly exam, and it would have meant another year's grind, and perhaps crashing at the end of it again. And then five years at the medical, and probably a whole lot more, because if an exam can be failed at, I'm the one to do it. I ask you, what's the point? Well, I put it to him, and of course he blew up. Parents always do! You would think by the time they were as old as that they would be able to talk a thing over calmly, but they never can! And can you tell me why? After all, it's *my* life!" He jerked his chair nearer again. "Why shouldn't I play in á dance band if I want to? I can get a job to-morrow. I'm good, you know, and the money is good too. Now, don't say, 'Oh, Cyril!' again, because I've got it all planned. I'm eighteen next week, the Royal wants a pianist, and I can put in the time there until I'm called up for my military service. I'd make my keep and a bit over. Then when I'm out of the Army, I can look round for something really good. Now you'd think my father would see that was quite a sensible plan."

"I don't know——"

Cyril edged his chair forward again.

"Of course it is! But is he reasonable? No, he isn't! And what do you suppose he wants me to do?." He made a really hideous grimace. "He wants me to stay in the Army and make a career of it! Susan, I *ask* you!"

"Well——"

"Exams—absolutely no end to them! Worse than the medical, because once you're qualified you don't actually have to take any more, but nowadays in the Army they practically never stop! If it isn't courses, it's the Staff College, and you go on having promotion exams until you've got one foot in the grave! Well, I told him flat out that I wouldn't do it and he couldn't make me, so there was another row. At the moment we're having a coolness, but I expect he'll come off it any day. He blows off steam, you know, but he's not much good at keeping up a feud. You'll put in a word for me if you get a chance, won't you? He always says you're such a sensible girl. I say, that sounds foul, doesn't it? It's meant as a compliment, only by the time you get to his age I suppose you don't remember how to pay them." He jerked his chair until it collided with hers. "I should think a girl would hate to be told she was sensible."

"She does," said Susan crisply.

Cyril's large pale blue eyes goggled at her.

"Well. it wasn't me, so you needn't look at me like that. I admire you like anything—you know I do."

Admiration is always gratifying, but Susan had now moved her chair back four times without managing to get any farther from Cyril's bony nose and the unwavering stare of his pale blue eyes. She had begun to feel that she would almost rather he went on playing the piano— almost, but not quite—when a diversion was created by Lucifer. The saucer of milk had lured him from the piano, where the black and white notes no longer bobbed entertainingly up and down. Dropping lightly to the floor, he did a stealthy jungle crawl in the direction of the tea-table, where his magnificent mamma lapped languidly from a blue and gold saucer. She may or may not have noticed his approach, but the moment his nose appeared over the saucer's edge and a pink tongue curled greedily towards the milk she dealt him a resounding box on the ear. He shrieked, spat. and fled back to the piano top, where he sat growling to himself. Some day he might stand up to the maternal tyrant, but not yet. There was a baleful glow in his amber eyes as he licked a paw and washed the insulted ear.

"Really, Emmeline—those cats! " said Mildred Blake.

Chapter 5

SUSAN WENT DOWN TO MRS. ALEXANDER'S GENERAL SHOP NEXT morning to pass the time of day and to get a picture postcard of the church with the six-hundred-year-old tunnel of yew which led up to it. The Professor would like to have one. She was turning over the postcards and waiting for Mrs. Alexander to serve Dr. Croft's housekeeper, who could take as long to buy a tin of shoe-polish as a girl who is choosing a dance-frock, when Clarice Dean came into the shop and fell upon her with effusion.

"I've been longing to see you! Miss Blake came home from Mrs. Random's and said you had come! You are going to catalogue the books at the Hall, aren't you? I wish I had a nice easy job like that, but"—with an exaggerated sigh—"we poor nurses have to work!" She lowered her voice, but not much. "Now do tell me, is Edward Random here? Someone told me he was, but Miss Blake says he wasn't at tea. Did he come by the later train?" She dropped her voice just a little further. "Or did he shirk the tea-party?"

She might sigh, and she might complain about being hard-worked, but she appeared to be in very good spirits. She had a bright, dark prettiness made up of vivid colouring, brown wavy hair, and dancing hazel eyes. She had run out in her cap and a highly becoming blue uniform with short puffed over-sleeves of white muslin.

The voice in which she asked about Edward was not really quite low enough. It had a sweet carrying quality. Mrs. Alexander and Dr. Croft's housekeeper both looked round.

Susan said,

"You had better ask him. I am buying postcards."

Clarice laughed,

"How discreet you are! But he is here now?"

"Oh, yes."

"We were quite friends, you know. Oh, years ago—I had only just finished training. I nursed Mr. James Random when he had influenza, and of course I saw quite a lot of Edward. That's how I came to be here last year when Mr. Random died—he wouldn't have anyone else. And we all thought Edward was dead! Dreadful—wasn't it? I'm longing to see him again and hear all about everything! Miss Blake says he won't utter, but I think he'll tell me!"

Susan said, "I don't think——" and then stopped. Edward would have to deal with Clarice himself.

Dr. Croft's housekeeper said in her slow, heavy way,

"Well, it's no fault of yours, Mrs. Alexander, and I'm not saying it is, but I do say and I won't go from it, that things aren't the equal of what they were before the war. Nobody won't get me from it that they're not—not the boot-polish, nor yet the leather you have to shine with it. Nothing's the same as what it used to be, nor won't be again, but I'll take a tin of the black and a tin of the brown and just make the best of them like we've all got to nowadays."

Mrs. Alexander had a fat, comfortable laugh. She said, "That's right, Miss Sims, and better put a good face on it. Not but what you won't find the polish is all right, for I use it myself."

She moved over to the other end of the counter. The warmth in her voice was for Susan.

"Well, my dear, you're back again and welcome. What can I do for you?"

Susan bought postcards, and Clarice matches.

"I don't know where they go to. And Miss Blake said to ask if you had ripe tomatoes—and oh, two pounds of the cooking apples Miss Ora likes. She said you would know."

Mrs. Alexander looked gratified.

"Why, yes, of course—off our own tree, and I don't know

the name, but it's a good one. My father always give it a
hogshead of water first week in July to swell the apples, and
we've kept right on doing it. But you'd better have the
dozen pounds like Miss Blake always do. Two pounds
won't go no way with Miss Ora—no way at all."

Edward Random walked down the village street without
looking to left or right. As he passed Mrs. Alexander's
shop, Clarice Dean ran out and stopped him. She had a
basket full of apples in one hand and a paper bag of ripe
tomatoes in the other. Her colour was bright, and so were
her eyes. She held out both hands—basket, bag, fruit and
all—and cried,

"How wonderful to meet you like this! But I don't suppose you even remember me—Clarice Dean! I nursed your
uncle—do you remember?"

Edward remembered without sentiment. A boy and girl
in a garden a long time ago. The girl had been pretty and
flirtatious. He said,

"Oh, yes, I remember. How do you do?"

"I'm nursing Miss Blake—Miss Ora Blake. Do you remember what you used to call Miss Mildred?" Her pretty,
high laugh floated down the street. She leaned towards
him to whisper, "Miss Mildew! Shocking of you, wasn't
it?"

"Schoolboy manners, I'm afraid."

She laughed again.

"You were a very nice schoolboy—and you were nearly
eighteen! We used to play tennis in the afternoons when
your uncle was resting, and you did so improve my game!
But I never get time for it now—at least hardly ever, and I
expect I've gone back a lot. I have to take my time off in
the evenings now. We could do a flick if you'd like to. The
Royal gets quite good films. Nursing's a pretty dull job.
Do say you will!"

"Well, I'm going to be rather busy taking over from Mr.
Barr. Look out—you're going to spill that fruit!"

She laughed and sparkled at him.

"I'm stupid, aren't I? It's being so glad to see you again! You're going to be Lord Burlingham's agent, aren't you? Well, you can't be taking over all day and all night. Look here, let's leave it a day or two, and then I can ring you up and we can fix something!"

She ran back into the shop, flushed and smiling.

"That was Edward Random! So he did come after all!"

Susan said, "Yes."

Clarice laughed.

"Tactful of you not to come out and spoil our little reunion, my dear! You know, I really did know him quite well, and I'm so pleased to see him again. We are going to fix up an evening to go to the pictures! Goodness—I must fly, or Miss Blake will be ringing her bell out of the window! Do you know, she did actually do that once when she thought Nurse Brown had stayed here too long gossiping with Mrs. Alexander!"

Edward walked on down the street. Clarice had changed very little indeed. She was still pretty, and still flirtatious. She seemed very pleased to see him. The warmth of her greeting had actually induced a slight surface glow. He supposed that life with Mildred and Ora would make you pleased to see practically anyone. Clarice dropped out of his mind as suddenly as she had invaded it.

The Miss Blakes lived in one of the late eighteenth-century houses. A bow window on the upper floor was supported by stone pillars set flush with the footpath and commanded an extensive view. From her couch Miss Ora Blake could see everything that went on from eight o'clock in the morning, when she left her bedroom at the back of the house and was transferred to the sitting-room in front, until after the evening meal, when she went back to her bed again. The move had to be made betimes in the morning, or she would have missed the arrival of the post, which wouldn't have done at all. She had excellent sight and was able to follow the postman's progress from one end of the village street to the other. She knew just when Maggie Ledbetter's young man stopped writing to her, and when young Mrs. Harris had all those letters from abroad. They made quite a lot of talk, until it came out that she had an aunt in Vancouver. Or at least so she said. Her husband came home from the Malay States soon afterwards, and she left Greenings, so of course it was quite impossible to know whether there really was an aunt or not, but the Miss Blakes continued to have their doubts.

Clarice Dean ran lightly up the stairs, leaving the apples and the tomatoes with Mrs. Deacon, who was Miss Blake's daily and a very good cook. She found Miss Ora very much pleased and interested.

"Now don't tell me that was Edward Random! Or perhaps I should say don't tell me it wasn't, because I could see that it was, and when you ran out of the shop like that I thought—I really thought—you were going to drop all those apples!"

"So did I!"

"Did Mrs. Alexander lend you the basket? It wasn't one of ours. And what did you have in the paper-bag? . . . Tomatoes? Well, I hope they were ripe. That was one of the things Nurse Brown used to be so tiresome about—just took whatever they gave her and never thought of looking to see if they were ripe. Well, well, why do you go on talking to me about tomatoes, when I want to hear about Edward Random? You seemed very pleased to see him."

"Oh, I was!"

Miss Ora Blake had a large round pink face, large round blue eyes, and a lot of white fluffy curls surmounted by two bows of blue satin ribbon and a little frill of lace. .She gazed solemnly at Clarice and said,

"When I was young a girl wouldn't have said that."

"Why not? We saw a great deal of each other when I was here before."

"Seven years ago."

Clarice laughed.

"We were very friendly, you know—and I don't forget my friends."

Seven years ago! .Miss Ora began to make calculations. Edward couldn't have been much more than a schoolboy— eighteen at the outside. Because he wasn't more than twenty-five now. She remembered him in his pram. Yes, he would have been eighteen when Miss Dean came down to nurse James Random through that attack of influenza. And she was already trained then. She might look young, but she must be several years older than Edward. That bright colour of hers was deceptive. Miss Ora decided to her own satisfaction that Clarice Dean might quite easily be as much as thirty.

She said tartly,

"That was a very large basket of apples."

"Mrs. Alexander said——"

"Mrs. Alexander wants to sell her fruit. But my sister Mildred won't be pleased—she won't be pleased at all. She will think we have been extravagant. She does not care for fruit herself, and we shall have to be tactful. You had better tell Mrs. Deacon to put the apples away out of sight and return the basket when she goes to her dinner."

Chapter 6

ARNOLD RANDOM WALKED DOWN THE SOUTH DRIVE UNTIL HE came to the lodge, where he paused for a moment before lifting the latch of the wicket gate. He was a man of medium height with a spare frame and features of the family type. Most of the Randoms had these features— dark and straight, with brown or hazel eyes. But they could be worn with a difference. In James Random they had been permeated with benevolence. Jonathan had not had them at all, having inherited the fair Foxwell strain .from his mother—fair and foolish, as local gossip went. In Edward the type had reappeared, emphasized, if anything, by its temporary eclipse. In Arnold it was, as it were, refined. He had the distinguished turn of the head, the upright carriage, and the beautiful hands of the aristocrat. He could, as Lord Burlingham had once remarked, have won a prize for looking down his nose against any man in England. He looked down it now at Emmeline's garden. Then he lifted the latch, took a few steps along the narrow paved path which led up to the door, and looked again.

The garden was a rectangular patch cut out of the park— flower-beds and roses on this side, and vegetables at the back. It should have been meticulously neat and tidy—a lodge garden should always be tidy. In point of fact it never was, and never had been since his brother James had let Emmeline have it. Arnold frowned at the recollection. It was not that he had any objection to flower-beds as such. He could recall a very neat and tasteful arrangement of scarlet geraniums, yellow calceolarias and blue lobelias, never a dead bloom, never a leaf out of place. But that was in old Hardy's time. Ever since Emmeline had been here things had been going from bad to worse. Great sprawling Michaelmas daisies and sunflowers. Pink and white anemones. Snapdragon and mignonette growing among the roses. And a lot of other half gone-over things whose names he didn't pretend to know. And the roses! The place was fairly smothered with them! They certainly throve—the air was quite heavy with their scent. But how unpruned, how completely out of hand! They would certainly have to go. The place was a wilderness. And the climbers on the lodge must be drastically reduced.

It was at this point that something stirred in the undergrowth and Lucifer, late Smut, emerged, walking delicately, black tail uplifted, eyes glowing like jewels in the sun. Mr. Random did not like cats. He said, "Shoo!" Lucifer

sprang, did an exciting kind of twist in mid air, came down
at right angles, and made off like a flash of black lightning
with his tail in a double kink. Scheherazade sunning herself on the windowsill watched unmoved, but Toby, a very
ugly cat with abnormally long hind legs and only one ear,
jumped down and vanished into a tangle of mint and
lavender. He had been kicked and ill-treated in his youth
before Emmeline rescued him, and he did not quite forget
it. When people said "Shoo!" he shoo'd. There were
three other cats in sight, but they did not take any notice.
Arnold Random looked bleakly at them and let the knocker
fall rather hard against Emmeline's front door.

She had quite a small kitten in her arms as she opened it.
Its mother, a pretty grey half-Persian, walked beside her,
mewing in a plaintive manner. Emmeline wore a blue
smock. Her fair hair was not as tidy as it might have been.
She had been turning out her little back room, and that
had meant moving Amina and her kittens. Amina didn't
like it at all, and one of the kittens had crawled under the
tallboy which had come to her from the same great-grandmother as the piano, and wouldn't come out. Amina was
rapidly becoming distracted, and it was really a most inconvenient moment for Arnold to call. She would not, of
course, have dreamed of letting him know this, so she
smiled her sweet, vague smile and said,
. "How kind of you! Do come in!"

Amina's basket was, quite temporarily, in the middle of
the drawing-room floor. A small shrieking kitten scrabbled
at the edge in a frantic effort to escape. Emmeline pushed
it back, gave it the one she was holding for company, and
carried the basket through to the kitchen, followed by
Amina, who walked processionally with her tail stiffly erect
and mourned in a really piercing manner.

The noise died down, and Emmeline shut two doors and
made her apologies.

"I am so sorry, Arnold. She doesn't like the kittens
being moved."

"So I observed."

Emmeline had long ceased to expect warmth from Arnold, but he was not always quite as bleak as this. He was going to be difficult, and she would never get the back room done, to say nothing of the kitten under the tallboy. Trying to look on the bright side, it occurred to her that it might get tired of being there and come out. She folded her hands in her lap and gazed attentively at her brother-in-law. Quite impossible to look at him without seeing that he was put out. Men were rather easily put out by house-cleaning and things being out of their proper place. Even her dear Jonathan, who was always so good-tempered—— Her thoughts broke off, because Arnold said,

"I am told that Edward is here."

"Oh, yes."

"I am informed that Lord Burlingham is giving him the agency."

"Oh, yes—so kind of him."

"Indeed? It had not struck me in that light. If I had to find a word to describe Lord Burlingham's behaviour I think I should have used the epithet 'impertinent'. But there is no need for us to discuss the matter. It merely occurred to me to wonder what arrangement Edward intended to make. I understand that Mr. Barr is to retain the agent's house, and I must say I should not consider it at all suitable for Edward to lodge in the village, even if there were anyone able and willing to take him in."

A pretty pink colour came into Emmeline's cheeks.

"But, Arnold, he will stay with me. *Of course.* I have never thought of anything else, and nor has he—at least——"

"That is a pity."

"Oh, no!"

Arnold had remained standing. He walked now to the window. Another of those accursed cats lay stretched among the cushions of the low, broad seat—a yellow one this time, and probably shedding its hairs all over the place. Even if he had felt any slight weakening—and Emmeline's eyes had done some heart-melting in their time—the sight would have stiffened him. The place was positively insanitary! He turned and said coldly,

"I am afraid I must ask both you and Edward to make other plans."

She gazed at him.

"Other plans?"

"Yes. I do not wish to inconvenience you in any way, but Fullerby is quite past his work. It has been obvious for a long time, and I have now given him notice. The gardener whom I am going to engage has a family, and will have to be provided with a cottage. James was only able to offer you this lodge because Fullerby owned his own house in the village."

Emmeline looked quite bewildered.

"But, Arnold, I've been here for sixteen years. I never thought——"

"Perhaps you will do so now. If you are in any doubt about the legal position, let me reassure you. You had no agreement about the lodge, I believe, and you have never paid any rent for it."

"No," said Emmeline. Then, after a little pause, "James was a very kind brother."

He remained where he was, silhouetted against the sunny garden.

"You had no agreement, and you paid no rent. The furniture, such as it is, was, I believe, put into the house and lent to you by James."

"Some of the things are my own."

"No doubt. But you cannot claim an unfurnished tenancy. You cannot, in fact, claim a tenancy at all. James allowed you to reside here because he did not require the house for a gardener. I do."

Emmeline's hands had remained folded in the lap of her blue smock. Her eyes maintained the wide puzzled look

which he found so absurd in a woman of her age. It was
almost as if she did not understand what he was saying.
He raised his voice.

"As I said, I have no desire to inconvenience you. You
will probably want to look round before you settle again.
I would suggest that you go into rooms in Embank or anywhere else that may suit you——" He stopped because she
was shaking her head.

"No, I should not care about that."

"Well, of course I have no wish to dictate."

She looked at him very directly and said,

"It is not because of Fullerby and the new gardener—is
it, Arnold? It is because of Edward. You do not like
Edward to be here."

"I do not think it at all suitable that he should be here."

"It has always been his home, Arnold. It would still be
his home if James had not believed that he was dead."

His cold composure broke.

"Burlingham has given him this agency for the express
purpose of making things unpleasant for me! It is, I suppose, his vulgar idea of a joke! Take the black sheep of
the family and set him down at your neighbour's gate!
One doesn't expect anything from a pig but a grunt, but I
must say, Emmeline, I am surprised that you should lend
yourself to such a discreditable manœuvre! Since you
appear to have an affection for Edward, you ought to be
able to see that you are doing him a great disservice by
pushing him into the limelight and raking up a lot of
things which would be much better forgotten. If you
really care for him you would do better to persuade him to
go elsewhere."

She maintained her gaze.

"And if he did?"

"It would be a great deal better for him. If he goes
where nobody knows him he can make a fresh start, and
there will be no interest in where he has been or what he
has done during the last five years. Whereas here——"

He threw up his head with a movement which brought his profile into relief. "Why should he come back here, where every second person has some fresh scandalous theory to account for the time he was away? Burlingham's motive is plain enough. He knows what I think of him, and in his own vulgar parlance, he would like to score me off. But what is Edward's motive—and what is yours? I tell you, I won't have it, and if he comes here, you must go!"

The last word was almost shouted. To anyone who did not know him very well indeed the scene would have been a surprising one. Emmeline was not surprised. This slipping of control—she had seen it happen before. Quite suddenly, as it had happened now—when a dog with which he was playing had snapped—when a horse had put his foot in a hole and let him down—when he had done something which he did not care to have known and was confronted with the consequences. She had always known that under an appearance of coolness and reserve there was something in Arnold that was unstable, something which under pressure was liable to slip. She sat looking at him now, and wondered what the pressure might be.

For his part, Arnold was aghast. The interview had got completely out of hand. He was saying all the things he had not meant to say. They burned at the back of his mind, but he had not meant to give them words. He had intended to be calm, reasonable, and dignified. He was engaging a new gardener, he required the lodge, he was reluctantly compelled to ask Emmeline to make other arrangements. There was not to have been the most distant allusion to Edward. Impossible now to revert to the calmly ordered plan.

Emmeline looked at him, her eyes very blue above the faded cotton smock, and said,

"Why are you afraid of Edward coming here?"

Chapter 7

SUSAN WALKED BACK FROM THE SHOP WITH HER POSTCARDS and a present of tomatoes for Emmeline. "My own growing," Mrs. Alexander had told her. "And I don't know that I ought to say so, but the plants come from Mr. Fullerby. Wonderful successful he have always been with the tomatoes up at the Hall—won all the prizes with them at the Embank Shows. Pity he's leaving."

"Oh, is he?"

"Well, you won't say I said so, but I did hear tell as he was. Seems he and Mr. Arnold don't rightly get on together. And maybe he won't be sorry. He's got his house, and there'll be the old age pension, and if he wants to do a bit of jobbing work, there's Miss Blake and Dr. Croft, both of them would be glad enough to have him in by the day. It's Mr. Arnold will be finding out as he's made a mistake to my way of thinking. But that's just between you and me."

Susan picked up the bag of tomatoes, but Mrs. Alexander had by no means done.

"That William Jackson will be leaving too, Miss Susan— I don't know whether you've heard. Got his notice yesterday, so I heard tell. I always did say he'd go too far one day. In the Lamb or over at Embank every night till closing time, and getting to work late in the morning. A dreadful time Annie has with him, poor thing. And what she wanted to take him for, goodness knows. Twenty years she was, with your Aunt Lucy—went to her at fourteen. And then to go and marry a good-for-nothing like William Jackson that was after her savings and the money Miss Lucy left her! Ten years younger than her if he was a day!"

Susan remembered William Jackson very well—one of the under-gardeners at the Hall. She remembered him as a boy, red-haired and ferrety-faced. She had never liked him very much. Annie had been a fool to marry him. Aunt Lucy would never have let her do it. She hoped things were not as bad as Mrs. Alexander made out, but when she said so there was a shake of the head.

"Oh, my dear, no! Poor Annie, she's nothing but a wreck. And stuck away in that lonely cottage on the other side of the Splash! No wonder they got it cheap! Downright dangerous going over those stepping-stones after dark or when it rains heavy. There did ought to be a bridge, but look what everything costs these days. Pity it didn't get seen to when labour was a penny a day back in Queen Elizabeth's time."

Susan laughed.

"A penny a day bought as much as a good many shillings do now. It paid the rent of a cottage and fed and clothed a family."

"And a pity it isn't like that now!" said Mrs. Alexander.

As Susan went back she wasn't thinking about the deterioration in the value of money, or about Fullerby, or William Jackson, or even about poor Annie. She had two pictures in her mind, and do what she would, she couldn't blot them out. In one of them she was standing in the dusty lane between Embank and Greenings with her suitcase at her feet and her hands stretched out to Edward Random. In the other Clarice Dean was doing practically the same thing in the middle of the village street. This picture was a great deal brighter and more distinct than the other. Clarice was a great deal brighter and prettier than the rather shadowy figure of Susan Wayne. She had a humiliated sense of having been outdone. Ridiculous, but there it was. She had felt warm and friendly towards Edward. She had showed it with nothing at all in her mind except that friendly warmth. And then Clarice had to do practically the same thing and do it a great deal better. There had been a sparkle—a glow of colour——

She came into the lodge, and found Emmeline in the back room lying flat on the floor trying to scoop the kitten out from under the tallboy with a dusting-brush, whilst Amina wailed from the kitchen. With every tiny claw the kitten clung to the carpet.

"Perhaps if we took the drawers out——"

"These old things are generally solid right through."

They took out the bottom drawer, which was immensely heavy because it was full of photograph albums. As Susan had feared, the bottom of the tallboy was solid oak, but right in the middle where the heaviest album had been the boards had parted and there was a definite crack. After about half an hour of the most exhausting and exhaustive pressing, poking, and levering with a chisel they had almost reached the point of deciding that there was nothing to be done that way, when the kitten, who had probably begun to feel hungry, came crawling out on its belly like a little black snake, fixed them with a reproachful stare, and yawned in Emmeline's face.

It was not until the back room had resumed its usual littered appearance, most of the things which Emmeline had intended to throw away having been reprieved, that she said to Susan in quite her ordinary voice,

"Arnold has been here this morning. He wants to turn me out. But I don't think we will tell Edward just for the present. I am afraid it would worry him."

Chapter 8

EDWARD STAYED LATE WITH MR. BARR. IT WAS JUST SHORT OF
ten o'clock and black dark when he came down to the
watersplash and got out a pocket torch to see him over the
stepping-stones, though for the matter of that his feet would
have found them easily enough with no more than memory
to guide. There had been heavy rain in the night, and the
stream was full. The stones were slippery and the big flat
one half-way across had a film of water over it. He took
them with a run and a jump, and was aware of being
relaxed, and freer than he had been during the five arid
years which lay behind him. It was not raining now—it
had not rained all day—but the air was damp, and soft, and
very mild. "East, west, home's best." The words rang in
his mind. There wasn't any place like the one where the
world had come alive to you, where you knew every stick
and stone, every man, woman and child, where you could
look around you and know that the men of your blood had
had their part in the shaping of things for three hundred
years.

He came up the slope from the splash and saw the church
tower black against the sky. A faint glow showed the
tracery in the window by the organ loft. The still air
carried the sound of music.

Everything in Edward stiffened. After all, there was one
familiar thing which had slipped from his mind. It was
Friday, and on a Friday night from nine to ten Arnold
would be in the church practising for Sunday. The Hall
made its own electric light, and its supply extended to the
church. The days when a village child panted over the
bellows were gone. The organ was a fine one, and Arnold
could take his fill of music. The village was proud of his

playing. On a summer evening the musically inclined would stand and listen for ten minutes or so before going on their way with the remark that Mr. Arnold did play lovely.

Edward felt no urge to stand and listen. His softened mood was gone. He frowned in the dark, lengthened his stride, and nearly collided with someone making a wavering course from the village. He said sharply, "Hold up, man!" and lent a hand to the process. The fellow had been drinking. He swayed where he stood and said, "Beg pardon, sir." Edward turned the torch on him. Reddish hair and a dead white face. If it hadn't been for that unnatural pallor, he might not have known him, but wet or fine, boy or man, sun, wind or rain, William Jackson's skin had never tanned. "Colour of cream cheese," Edward could remember old Fullerby saying. "And no more the matter with him than with you nor v h me, Mr. Edward." It was William Jackson all right, and quite a bit the worse for wear. Edward spoke his name, and William straightened up.

"That's right, Mr. Edward—going home—that's me—just going home——"

"Well, you'd better be careful over the stones. They're slippery."

There was an unsteady laugh.

"I'm all right—couldn't slip if I tried to. Nails in my boots, that's what does it—and over those stones four times a day reg'lar. Got the old cottage at the turn, Annie and me have. That's since your time. Matter of two years we been married—Annie Parker that used to work for Miss Lucy Wayne. Left her a nice little bit, Miss Lucy did, so we bought the cottage and I put up the banns."

The drink was more in his legs than in his tongue, but he was in a mood to stand talking, and Edward was not. He said briskly,

"Well, you'd better be getting along—and mind your step."

William Jackson swayed. He could stand all right if he wanted to—stand as steady as any of them. The trouble was, he didn't know whether he wanted to be coming or going. There was Mr. Arnold up there in the church, and what did he have that last pint for if it wasn't to get him so he could stand his ground and say the piece he planned to say? But there was Mr. Edward here—suppose he was to say his piece to Mr. Edward. There was the two of them in it—Mr. Arnold up at the church, and Mr. Edward here in the lane. He didn't rightly know—he didn't ought to have had that last pint—— He said in a doubtful voice,

"Mr. Edward——"

But Edward had already passed him.

"Good night, Willy," he said, and was gone.

There was the sound of his footsteps getting less, very quick and firm, the same as he always walked from the time they were boys together. Perhaps he did ought to have talked to Mr. Edward—but it was the other one that had the cash. He shook his head, standing there all by himself in the damp lane. Then he turned and went up through the black yew tunnel to the church.

Chapter 9

THE SEWING-PARTY AT THE VICARAGE WAS BREAKING UP. IT had been started rather humbly and tentatively by Mrs. Ball, who was interested in the Save the Children movement, but it had proved quite a success. Friday evening found most of the available women in the neighbourhood plying a charitable needle in the Vicarage drawing-room. It was a magnificent opportunity for the exchange of news and views, and every woman nourished the hope that to her, and to her alone, there would some day be imparted the secret of the really delicious cake which always made its appearance at half-past nine. The hope was a vain one. Unassuming and obliging as Mrs. Ball had proved herself, neither hints, compliments, nor the offer of a fair exchange had achieved anything but a smiling shake of the head and a perfectly amiable, "Oh, I wish I could, but it is a family secret, and I had to promise not to tell before my Aunt Annabel would let me have it." Mrs. Pomfret, whose husband farmed his own land to the east of Greenings, had offered the real eighteenth-century recipe for frumenty, Miss Sims had tried to drive a bargain against an infallible way of keeping potatoes new until Christmas time, Miss Blake had put forward her great-grandmother's *crême brulée*, said to be superior to the famous Oxford variety, but without result. After each overture Mrs. Ball would at some time during the following evening heave a deep sigh and inform the Vicar that she really did feel terribly mean—"Only she did make me promise, John, and she said she would haunt me if I let it go out of the family." At which Mr. Ball had the barbarity to laugh and say from what he had heard about her aunt, he would prefer not to have her as a permanent guest.

Just before ten o'clock everyone was getting ready to go. Mrs. Alexander was heard to catch herself up in the middle of her good-nights and say,

"If I didn't nearly forget! That poor Annie Jackson was in early in the afternoon and she's wanting work, so I said I'd mention it. Seems her husband has lost his job, and there won't be anything coming in."

Miss Blake sniffed.

"Well, she *would* marry him, and look what has come of it! I said to her at the time, 'You'll only regret it once, Annie, and that will be for the rest of your life.' I'd known her all the years with Lucy Wayne, and I wasn't going to hold my tongue. And what do you think she said? 'We've all got our lives to lead, and this is mine.' And look where it's brought her! I never did like William Jackson—I don't

know anyone who does! And he's been going steadily
downhill ever since he got his hands on Annie's savings!"

Mrs. Ball said,

"It must be very hard for her."

Mildred Blake tossed her head.

"Oh, she's brought it on herself! If people won't be
warned they must put up with the consequences! Well,
good-night, Mrs. Ball. I can hear Arnold Random practising in the church, so I'll just step over and have a word
with him about Sunday week, because if I'm to play I must
have plenty of notice. He can't expect me just to sit down
and rattle off two chants, three hymns and a couple of
voluntaries as if I was in the way of doing it every day."

Mrs. Ball was glad to get away from the subject of poor
Mrs. Jackson. She said,

"Oh, yes, he was going up to London for the week-end—
wasn't he?"

The Vicarage stood next to the church. There was no
need for Miss Blake to go out on the road and in by the
lych gate. She took the short cut through the small side
gate into the churchyard and followed it to the door beneath that lighted window. It was, as she had known it
would be, ajar. Thirty years before, she had often slipped
in to listen to Arnold Random's playing and walked back
with him when he had finished. Those thirty years had
not softened her heart or sweetened her temper. They certainly had not left her with any indulgence for Arnold
Random.

As she skirted the church she became aware that he had
stopped playing. The sound of the organ had not, in fact,
been noticeable since she left the Vicarage, yet she had
certainly heard it whilst they were talking about Annie
Jackson. Arnold could not have gone, or he would have
locked the door behind him. He must be putting away
the music. Well, so much the better—she certainly didn't
want to have to sit and listen to his playing now. Music
was like a lot of other things, the interest went out of it.

Her fingers could still control the keys, but her mind had lost the overtones.

She pushed open the door and went in. The door led directly into the church. The organ, with a curtain to screen the organist, lay to the left. The light which had made that faint glow came from behind the curtain. Miss Mildred switched off the torch which she had used to guide herself through the churchyard, took a single step forward, and was aware of voices. Arnold Random's voice, high and cold, saying something about "nonsense". And someone answering him with a country accent which seemed to be a little slurred with drink. She came forward, moving without any sound, and heard William Jackson say,

"And suppose it isn't nonsense, Mr. Arnold? Suppose 'tis gospel truth as I'm telling you?"

Arnold Random said sharply,

"You're drunk!"

From where she stood she could see a part of William Jackson's arm from the shoulder to the elbow. The curtain had been drawn back, and he stood next to the gap with his rough coat-sleeve showing. Now he took a lurching step to the left, and she could see the back of his head with the reddish hair sticking up and catching the light. The head was being vigorously shaken.

"Not drunk. That's where you're wrong, sir. I didn't ought to have had that last pint, but I'm not drunk. Not so steady on my legs as I might be, but I'm clear enough in my head. And yesterday was a twelvemonth Mr. James Random called me into the study—me and Billy Stokes— and told us we was wanted to witness his will. Yesterday was a twelvemonth."

Arnold Random said,

"And what if it was?"

"That's what I've come here to have a word about. Mr. Random he took a turn and was dead before the week was out. Supposed to be getting well he was, and the nurse going to leave and all, but he took a turn and he died. And

Billy he went in the Navy, and got washed overboard. And never come home. So that leaves only me as could swear to Mr. Random signing of that will."

"Jackson, you are drunk! Naturally Mr. Random made a will, and it has been proved and all the business finished with. Now clear out and go home! I'm locking up."

She could see William swaying a little from one foot to the other.

"Not so fast, sir," he said. "If I can't say what I want— to you—there's others that'll be glad enough to listen. There's Mr. Edward for one."

"What do you mean?"

"That's what I'm wanting to tell you. Mr. Edward— three years ago there wasn't anyone but believed he was dead. Mr. Random, he believed it. Lawyer came out from Embank, and he altered his will. Maybe I wasn't going past the study window when the signing was going on— maybe I haven't got eyes in my head. Maybe I couldn't look through the window and see what kind of a paper Mr. Random was putting his name to. A great big stiff white piece of foolscap with typing on it, and Mr. Random lean-ing over to sign his name, with the lawyer and his clerk, and the lady that was staying in the house—what was her name—Mrs. Peabody—a-watching of him. Witnesses, I reckon they was, her and lawyer's clerk. And she went away next day—back to Australia or something."

"Jackson, you are drunk." The tone was steady but without life.

William laughed. The sound shocked Mildred Blake.

"I'm drunk—because I could look in through the study window and see Mr. Random a-signing his will? And a twelvemonth ago yesterday I seen him sign another will— blue paper instead of white, and his own hand instead of all that typewriting stuff, and me and Billy Stokes for wit-nesses instead of lawyer's clerk and Mrs. Peabody. A pint too much at the Lamb don't make you as drunk as all that comes to, Mr. Arnold, and I'll say the same when I'm stone-

cold sober. And so be you don't believe me, there's others
as will. There's Mr. Edward for one. Suppose I was to go
to him and tell him what I seen and what I heard? Billy
he'd gone out by the window, and Mr. Random he was setting there with his head in his hand, staring down at that
blue paper in front of him. I said, 'Will I go now, sir?'
and he looks up at me and he says very solemn, 'You and
Mr. Edward was boys together. I saw him last night in a
dream as plain as what I see you now, and he said, 'I'm not
dead, you know, and I'll be coming back.' That's why
you've been asked to witness this new will. He mustn't
come home and find there's nothing left for him. I'd like
you to remember that, William,' he says. 'And I'd like
you to tell him when he comes home.'"

He stopped. A time went by. Arnold Random spoke
into the silence.

"And why didn't you tell him?"

William Jackson shuffled with his feet.

"I thought I'd wait—I thought he'd be coming. I heard
tell as he was coming. It wasn't a thing I wanted to put
on paper. I didn't want to make trouble for myself, but
seeing you've took and given me my notice——"

"You thought you'd trump up a story like this!"

Miss Blake saw William Jackson shake his head.

"There's no trumping, Mr. Arnold, nor no making up.
It's gospel truth Mr. Random made that will, and I'd take
my Bible oath I saw him put his name to it, and Billy and
me, we put ours, and he told me Mr. Edward had spoke to
him in a dream and told him he wasn't dead. Not that I'm
wishful to make trouble, Mr. Arnold, and if you was to take
back that notice and maybe give me a bit of a rise——"

Arnold Random had received a numbing shock. Under
its impact all he could do was to repeat that William Jackson was drunk. It was the only weapon to his hand, the
only measure of defence he had, and even as he used it he
felt it weaken. If William was drunk to-day, he would be
sober to-morrow. The drink had put words in his mouth,

or it had loosened his tongue until he could bring himself
to speak them aloud. But having said them, could he, or
would he, unsay them again when the drink was out of
him? He might. For a consideration he would. If he was
given his job again and a rise, he would hold his tongue—
for this time. Until he was short of cash—until the appetite
for blackmail grew in him.

In the silence that was between them now the thought
came clear—he was being blackmailed. Give way once,
make one payment, and the chain is on your limbs for life.
Whose life? The chain will not loosen till one of you is
dead—and William was by more than thirty years the
younger man. Rage flooded up in him, sweeping everything before it. He broke into a fury of words:

"You damned blackmailer!"

That was only the beginning. Mildred Blake put her
hands to her ears, but the shouting voice came through.
Such language! And in church! Several of the words
were entirely new to her. How disgraceful! How un-
seemly! Quite sacrilegious!

She hurried out through the small side door and stood
on the gravel path, hearing the angry voices rise and fall.
She was shocked of course—really quite terribly shocked.
But her mind was working. She had not the slightest doubt
that William Jackson was speaking the truth. There had
been a later will than the one under which Arnold bene-
fited. In the last week of his life James Random had
received what he believed to be an intimation that his
nephew Edward was alive, and he had made another will.
There could be no doubt at all of what the terms of that
will must have been. If Arnold Random had destroyed it,
he faced disgrace and imprisonment. If he heard of it now
for the first time, he must submit to blackmail or lose his
inheritance.

Mildred Blake was one of the few people who guessed
what the possession of the Hall meant to him. Thirty years
ago they had come near enough to read each other's minds.

There had been a brief, a very brief, space when all was clear between them. What Arnold Random saw had startled him into retreat. What Mildred Blake saw she had not forgotten. It was with her now.

The voices were louder in the church. There was a sound of footsteps. Her eyes were accustomed to the darkness now. Without waiting to put on her torch she turned and ran down the yew tunnel to the lych gate.

Chapter 10

IT WAS SEVEN O'CLOCK NEXT MORNING WHEN JIMMY HEARD ran up to the front door of the Vicarage and beat upon it with all his might. He was twelve years old and a widow's son, so he helped by doing a paper round, and that meant bicycling into Embank for the papers which came in on the seven-twenty. His father had been cow-man on one of Lord Burlingham's farms, and the family had been allowed to stay on in a rather tumbledown cottage up the track on the far side of the stream. He beat on the Vicarage door, and when Mrs. Ball opened it in a dressing-gown he was choking and sobbing.

"Oh, Mrs. Ball, ma'am, he's dead! He's drownded! He's there in the water, and I can't move him! Oh, ma'am!"

She put a kind arm about the shaking shoulders. He was too thin—of course growing boys—there was somebody drowned. She said quickly,

"Who is it?"

He was shaking all over.

"It's—William Jackson! Oh, ma'am, he's drownded— down there in the splash! Oh, ma'am!"

Mrs. Ball called the Vicar, and the Vicar called the sexton. They went down to the splash together, and found William Jackson lying face downwards in no more than a couple of feet of water. It was plain enough what had happened. The big flat stepping-stone in the middle was practically awash after the heavy rain of Thursday night, and as the sexton put it bluntly, "If William was coming home sober it would be a bit of a wonder. Slipped on that there stone, he did, and come down, and too fuddled to get up again, though you would ha' thought the cold water would ha' brought him round. Must ha' been pretty far gone to drown in that there little pool. Well, I reckon you'd better ring up the police, sir, and I'll see no one comes along and meddles with him."

Jimmy was late for his papers. Mrs. Ball gave him hot cocoa and a couple of left-over scones, after which he was sufficiently fortified to go off on his bicycle, stopping to tell everyone he met that he had just found William Jackson drowned in the splash. If there had been more people abroad, he would have been later. But he told Mrs. Alexander who was watching for him out of her window to ask him to leave a message with her sister-in-law who lived next door to his paper shop, and Mrs. Deacon who was cleaning her front-door step, and Joe Caddle going off to his job on Mr. Pomfret's farm.

Mrs. Deacon and Mrs. Alexander wanted to know a lot more than he could tell them, but Joe, whose temper was bad in the mornings, only grunted and said some people had all the luck. Mrs. Deacon hurried up and got to the Miss Blakes' a good quarter of an hour before her time, which was eight o'clock. Rare put about, Miss Ora would be to think how she was in her back bedroom and out of the way of seeing Jimmy herself. She wouldn't lose a minute once she was told the news—trust Miss Ora for that. Not that there would be anything to see when she got to her sofa in the front room—Vicarage gate, and the church beyond, and the road going down to the splash. But you couldn't see the water, not if it was ever so. She almost ran down the village street and up into Miss Ora's bedroom with her news.

"Oh, miss—that there William Jackson—the one that married Annie Parker, pore thing!"

Miss Ora sat up straight in her bed, her hair in curling-pins and a shawl about her shoulders.

"I always said he was a bad lot. What has he done?"

"Oh, miss, he's drowned!"

"What!"

"Jimmy Heard found him and came over so funny he don't know how he got up to the Vicarage! And Vicar calls Mr. Williams, and they goes down and finds him just like Jimmy says, and Vicar comes back and rings up the police!"

Miss Ora was taking the pins out of her hair.

"Then they will be sending out the ambulance from Embank. I must get up at once! My comb and hand-glass, Mrs. Deacon! I don't see how anyone could drown in the splash. Unless he was drunk, which I suppose he was."

"Pore Annie!" said Mrs. Deacon.

Miss Mildred Blake said, "Nonsense!"

They had neither of them noticed the opening of the door. It startled them now to see her standing there, very grim and sallow in the old black coat which she wore in place of a dressing-gown. She went on harshly,

"There's no poor Annie about it, Mrs. Deacon. He's been a bad husband, and it was a bad day for her when she married him."

It was the general verdict.

Miss Ora got to her sofa in time to see the ambulance go by and presently come back again. She pulled a second shawl about her and had all the windows in the bay set wide so that she might miss nothing that was said by the passers by. She sent Clarice Dean on three separate errands to Mrs. Alexander's shop in order that she might be kept

abreast of local opinion. The women at least would be in
and out with their tongues going like so many mill-clappers,
but it irked her to the very marrow of her bones that there
was no one she could send into the Lamb when the men
began to assemble there. They would be careful of course,
because of the landlord. It was against the law to let a man
get drunk on your premises, and drunk William Jackson
must have been, or he wouldn't have drowned himself in
that little bit of water. Of course Mr. Parsons would swear
William had had no more than a couple of pints, and there
wasn't a man who wouldn't back him up. There was talk
of the licence not being renewed as it was, and they wouldn't
want to go to Embank for their beer. She said all this as
many times as it came up in her mind—to Mrs. Deacon, to
Clarice, to Mildred. None of them had much to say in
return.

Mildred sat down to her writing-table and went through
the housekeeping books. Terribly particular she was about
them. And presently she had out her Post Office Savings
book and went through that, and her bank book. Though
Miss Ora was the elder, she had nothing to do with the
accounts. Mildred was always saying how little they had
to live on, and how terribly careful they must be. She
certainly never spent anything on herself. Why, that old
coat she wore instead of a dressing-gown had been got more
than thirty years ago as mourning for poor Papa. And,
look at her now, in a darned flannel blouse and the dreadful
coat and skirt which had come to them with their old
cousin Lettice Halliday's things. She had wanted to send
it to a jumble sale, but Mildred had worn it ever since.

Miss Ora looked complacently from her sister's dingy
grey to her own pretty blue shawl. Figures made her head
ache, and she was more than willing to leave the accounts
to Mildred provided she could have her scented soap, her
bath salts, her blue ribbons, her pretty shawls, and her
library subscription. She read one sentimental novel after
another with the pleasure which comes from a comfortable

familiarity. She liked to know exactly what was going to happen. There must be no unpleasant surprises, no unforeseen developments. The lovely ward must marry her disagreeable guardian who is not really disagreeable at all but merely hiding a romantic passion under the cloak of austerity. The unjustly accused hero must be vindicated. Cinderella must have her Prince, and wedding bells must ring with a deafening persistence. In fact,

> Jack shall have Jill,
> Nought shall go ill,
> The man shall have his mare again,
> And all shall go well.

The ambulance came, and went. Knots of people gathered in the street to watch it go. William Jackson had had a glass too much and fallen into the stream and been drowned. The ambulance had taken him away, and Mrs. Ball had gone to tell his wife. There would have to be an inquest.

The morning passed.

Chapter II

WHEN LUNCH WAS OVER MILDRED BLAKE PUT ON HER HAT AND went out. Miss Ora watched her go, and felt herself aggrieved. Why couldn't Mildred come in and say where she was going? She watched her turn to the left, so she wasn't going to the Vicarage, or to see Annie Jackson. Miss Ora's blue eyes, which saw everything, watched her go by old Mrs. Palmer's—ninety-three and bedridden, and Mrs. Wood's—Johnny was the naughtiest child in Greenings and the subject of just suspicion if anyone missed their apples.

Mildred went past both cottages without so much as a turn of the head, right on and out of sight. Well, that could only mean one thing—she was going to see Emmeline Random. And without so much as changing out of that old coat and skirt! Miss Ora clicked with her tongue: Really Mildred was quite hopeless!

Mildred Blake did not turn in at the south lodge. She walked past Emmeline's bright, untidy garden without giving it a glance and went on up the long drive to the Hall, where she rang the bell and asked for Arnold Random. She had a little black book in her hand with a pencil hanging from it by a piece of string. Everyone in Greenings knew that book. Miss Mildred was a rigorous collector. When it wasn't the Sunday School Outing it was the Children's Christmas Treat, or the Mothers' Outing, or an Institute Tea. Doris Deacon who opened the door wondered which of them it was this time. A bit early for Christmas, and the mothers had had their treat in August. She was hesitating in her own mind, when Miss Blake said abruptly, "Mr. Random is in the study? Then I will just go in," and went past her without waiting for an answer.

"And I was going to put her in the morning-room and go and let Mr. Arnold know," she told Mrs. Deacon afterwards. "Gentlemen don't like people walking in on them that way, but I couldn't stop her."

"Nobody can't stop Miss Mildred, not when she takes it into her head she's going to do something," said Mrs. Deacon.

Arnold Random looked up, and wasn't pleased. He had had an excellent lunch and a particularly good cup of coffee. An intolerable pressure had been lifted. He could sit back and be at peace. William Jackson had been a menace. He was a bad husband, an unsatisfactory employé, and a blackmailer. He was most satisfactorily dead. There was nothing to worry about.

And then the door opened and Mildred Blake came in in her shabby old clothes, her head poking out in front of her

and her eyes fixed on his face. She had her black collecting-book in her hand, and he supposed he would have to
give her a subscription. It went through his mind to
wonder whether all those pennies and sixpences and half-
crowns, to say nothing of larger donations, did really reach
the objects for which they were subscribed. It was a quite
involuntary thought. Since all these sums were written
down, they would have to be accounted for, but if there
had been any way of getting round that accounting—well,
he wouldn't trust Mildred Blake not to avail herself of it.
Hard as nails and too fond of money by half. Predatory—
yes, that was the word—a predatory female.

She refused the seat he offered her, drew a chair up to
the table, and sat down, laying the black collecting-book
on the corner between them. There was a hole in one of
her cotton gloves. A bony finger poked through. With
her eyes still on his face she said,

"I have come to talk to you about William Jackson."

A faint uneasiness touched him. Ridiculous of course,
because she couldn't know anything. It lay between him
and a man who was dead. Two men who were dead. Billy
Stokes lost at sea, and William Jackson drowned in the
splash within a bare half mile of his home. Mildred Blake
would be getting up a collection for the widow. She certainly wasn't losing any time about it.

He had got as far as that in his thoughts, when she
said,

"I was in the church last night."

It hit him like a blow. He saw her sitting there, leaning
forward over a corner of the table, her hand on the black
collecting-book. The torn bit of the glove stuck up with
a ragged edge. The bare forefinger seemed to point at him.
Her eyes had a dark fire. He saw them recede into a mist.
They burned there. She spoke, but he couldn't see her
any more. The words meant nothing.

And then the first shock passed. The mist began to clear.
Mildred Blake came back into focus again, sitting there

with her hand on her collecting-book. He found himself saying,

"I don't know what you mean."

In her deep, resonant voice she said,

"You know perfectly well. I thought you were going to faint just now. You don't do that for nothing. Would you like a glass of water?"

"No, thank you."

"Very well, then. I was in the church last night. I came on from the Vicarage work-party. I was going to speak to you about the hymns and chants for Sunday week. I came in through the side door, and you were talking to William Jackson. I heard everything that was said."

He sat and looked at her. Her face showed a kind of fierce pleasure. He couldn't think of anything to say. There wasn't anything to say.

After what seemed like a very long time he said,

"He was drunk."

She nodded.

"A little. Enough to put the words into his mouth, but not enough to make him invent them. He said your brother James made a later will than the one under which you inherit, and that he made it because he had become convinced that Edward was still alive. James said he had had a dream. Well, people had dreams in the Bible, didn't they? Anyhow he made another will, and he called Billy Stokes and William Jackson in from the garden to witness it. Very inconvenient for you of course.. What did you do with that will?"

He put up a hand.

"Mildred, I give you my word——"

Her long nose twitched in a silent sniff.

"You may not have known about it at first. Perhaps it wasn't found until after the first will had been proved. It must have been a very nasty shock. Perhaps it wasn't found until after Edward came back, and you thought you would just wait and see what happened. Billy Stokes was dead, and William might not think anything but that the will he witnessed was the one that had been proved. You didn't know that he had been passing the window and had seen your brother James actually signing quite a different looking will from the one he was asked to witness a week before James died. And you didn't know that James had told him about having dreamed that Edward was alive. And not knowing those things, you might think it would be quite safe just to wait and see what happened. If the worst came to the worst and William put two and two together, you could have a search made and find the will."

Her eyes had never moved from his face. He had the horrified feeling that they could read his most secret thought. She went on.

"When nothing happened, you began to feel safe, but you couldn't have felt very happy when you heard that Edward was coming back as Lord Burlingham's agent. And then that business in the church last night. It was a great pity you should have lost your temper. It showed William that you were afraid of him. And really, Arnold, you shocked me. Such language—and in church! I hurried away as fast as I could."

He made an impatient gesture.

"It was enough to make anyone lose his temper. He was trying to blackmail me."

"Very foolish of him!" There was a mocking spark in her eyes. It came, and went again. "Very foolish indeed!"

He said in a controlled voice,

"What are you going to do?"

"My dear Arnold, what can I do? I shall have to tell my story at the inquest."

He stared.

"At the inquest?"

"Naturally. I overhear a serious accusation concerning the suppression of a will, followed by an attempt at blackmail and a violent quarrel. I hurry from the spot. Early next morning the blackmailer is discovered drowned in a shallow pool quite close to the scene of the quarrel. Naturally it is my duty to inform the police. I suppose there is no need for me to tell you what conclusions they are bound to draw."

He sat there paralysed with horror. When you can see a danger approaching, something can be devised to meet it. There is thought, contrivance, a means of defence, a way out. But this had come upon him suddenly when his mind was relaxed, taking its ease after strain. It would not move to serve him.

Mildred Blake nodded.

"It is a pity I came into the church last night, isn't it? I wanted to speak to you about the music. If I had gone straight home from the Vicarage, no one would ever have known that you murdered William Jackson."

The word was out. However many times it is spoken, it is always a dreadful word. It shocked Arnold Random into speech.

"My God, no! I never touched him! Mildred, I swear to you I never touched him!"

Her fingers tapped on the black account-book.

"He fell of himself? And couldn't get up again? In that shallow water? My dear Arnold!"

His usual pallor was suffused by a terrible flush. The blood throbbed in his veins and beat against his ears.

"Mildred, I *swear*——"

"And if I believe you, do you think that anyone else will? If you suppress a will and take what is meant for somebody else you go to prison. William Jackson could have sent you to prison. That is what he was telling you there in the church. You knew it, and so did I. He was blackmailing you—his job back and a rise! And that was only the beginning of it—it wouldn't stop there. And whatever he asked, you would have to pay—we both knew that. There was just nothing you could do about it except the one thing which you did. He had to go over the splash, and the stones were slippery after the rain. He had had too much to drink and he was unsteady on his feet. I could see him swaying there in the church when you were swearing at him. Really a most disgraceful scene—quite a smell of beer—and such language! A sober man wouldn't have drowned in the splash, but if somebody pushed a drunken man and held him down when he tried to get up again he could very easily be drowned, couldn't he, Arnold?"

He drew a long breath and sat back in his chair. The flush drained from his face, the drumming in his ears died away. His thoughts fell into place. He said,

"You are wrong—I didn't kill him."

"How many people, do you suppose, are going to believe that?"

"I don't know."

Her black eyebrows rose.

"Twelve men on a jury? Do you know, I doubt it."

He doubted it too. Accusation—threat—blackmail—the fury of the scene in the church—and William Jackson face down in a shallow pool, so very conveniently dead. He stared at her and said,

"It's not true."

She had been leaning towards him across the corner of the table. She straightened herself now, sitting back in the upright chair and folding her hands upon her knee.

"If I believed you——" she said.

He repeated what he had said before.

"It's not true."

She began to take off the torn right-hand glove in a slow, deliberate manner, looking away from him now, looking down at her own hand as it emerged. An ugly bony hand, not too well kept, the nails cut flat across the top—yellowish and bloodless nails. When the glove was off she put it carefully on the top of the collecting-book and said,

"We have known each other a long time. One has a duty to the public, but one has a duty to one's friends. If

I could believe that William Jackson's death was an accident——" She spoke slowly, dragging the words.

"How can I make you believe me? I never touched him!"

"If I could believe that, I might not think it was my duty to go to the police. I say I *might* not."

"Mildred!"

"You did not kill him?"

"No—no!"

"You didn't follow him down to the splash and push him in?"

Almost past speech, he shook his head, struggling for words which would convince her, move her. Only the simplest came.

"I never touched him. He went—I put the music away —then I went too. I never touched him."

After an agonizing pause she said,

"Well, I believe you. I don't suppose anyone else would, but on the whole I think I do. But if I hold my tongue I'll be taking a considerable risk. I suppose you know that."

"No one will—know."

"I hope not, but there is always the chance. I mentioned at the work-party that I intended to go over to the church to see you about the music. It is just possible that someone may have seen William Jackson either going up to the church or coming away from it."

He said,

"It was dark."

"Yes, it was dark. But there is that risk. I am not inclined to make too light of it. If I do this for you, I think there is something which you might do for me."

In his relief he could only stammer,

"Yes—yes—anything."

Her tone was precise and businesslike as she replied.

"At the time of his death your brother Jonathan owed us quite a large sum of money."

"Jonathan!"

"It can hardly be news to you that he was in the habit of running up debts."

"But James paid them—settled everything."

"He did not settle this one. You see, he had warned me against lending money to Jonathan. I had not taken his advice."

Arnold sat up straight. Two facts dominated his mind.

James had certainly paid all Jonathan's debts. To the last farthing.

He had no choice but to accept this suppositious debt of Mildred Blake's and discharge it. If he wanted to stop her mouth.

He had, in fact, exchanged one blackmailer for another, and a more formidable one.

Chapter 12

THE INQUEST WAS SHORT AND FORMAL, AND THE VERDICT "Death by misadventure". Mr. Ball read the funeral service, and the widow wept at the graveside in the old black coat and skirt which had been Miss Lucy Wayne's second-best. Next week she would be going into service again, at the Vicarage. There was Joe Hodges and his wife wanting the cottage, and even if she felt as if she could stay there by herself, there were nearly all her savings spent, and better to work while she could and have the rent coming in to put by for a rainy day. Mrs. Ball might be a newcomer, but she was a real lady. Annie knew a real lady when she saw one, and if she had to go into service again she would rather it was up at the Vicarage than anywhere else. Only when you've had a home of your own—— The

tears ran down her ravaged face. She knew in her heart
that she might not have had one for long. William had
been a bad husband. He drank, he had begun to knock
her about, and there was that girl in Embank. The cottage
had been bought with her money, but it was in his name.
She stood by the open grave and wept, and how many of
her tears were for William, and how many were for her
lost savings, and her lost hope, and her lost pride, she probably did not know herself.

The inquest and the funeral were still to come when
Clarice Dean rang up the south lodge just after lunch on
Saturday. The telephone was in Miss Ora's room, so she
waited till she had seen Miss Mildred go down the street,
and then slipped out to the telephone-box by Mrs. Alexander's shop. It was soundproof if you were careful to see
that the door had really caught, only of course you had to
remember that you were on a party line, and that anyone
might be listening in. Not that it mattered in this case.
She didn't mind who heard her talking in an intimate and
affectionate manner to Edward Random.

But it wasn't Edward who answered from the south lodge,
it was Susan Wayne. Clarice made a lively grimace. Was
Edward never at home? She had tried for him last night,
and as late as she dared. Of course Susan might be just
officious, butting in and taking the call, when she was only
a visitor in the house and it wasn't any of her business.
She said in her high, sweet voice,

"Oh, Susan, is that you? How nice! Have you started
up at the Hall yet?"

"No—not till Monday. Did you want to speak to
Emmeline?"

Clarice allowed herself a little silvery laugh.

"Well, no, darling. As a matter of fact Edward and I are
fixing up a cinema, and I find I can get off to-night. Is he
there?"

"No, he isn't. He's frightfully busy, you know, taking
over from Mr. Barr."

"But not on a Saturday afternoon! He simply can't be —it isn't civilized! When will he be back?"

"I haven't the slightest idea."

"Darling, you're not being a bit helpful! I suppose I couldn't ring him up at Mr. Barr's?"

"I shouldn't think so."

"Susan, you really aren't being any help at all! We do want this evening together so much, and it's so frustrating not being able to get hold of him just when I've found I can have the time off!"

"I'm sorry, Clarice, but I don't see what I can do. He wasn't back last night until a quarter-past ten. He might be earlier to-night, or he might not—he just didn't say. I can tell him you rang up."

Clarice gave that pretty, silly laugh again.

"Well, it won't be much good if he isn't going to be in till midnight, will it? Look here, I'll call up again after tea. We could still go over to Embank and see the big picture and have supper afterwards. What a nuisance it is having to work! It spoils all one's best dates, doesn't it?"

Edward came home at half-past four. Susan said,

"Clarice Dean rang up."

"What about?"

"You and a cinema. She says she can get the evening off."

"It's more than I can."

"She'll be ringing again after tea."

"Well, you'd better tell her——"

Susan shook her head.

"She'll want to speak to you."

"Say I haven't come in."

"Miss Ora probably saw you go by. Besides——"

"You cannot tell a lie? I remember you were really quite mentally deficient in that direction!"

Nobody likes to be accused of a virtue. Susan's fair skin showed a decided flush.

"If people want to have lies told, I think they ought to do it themselves!"

"Well, I should do it much better than you. I've had more practice."

She gave him her straight, candid look.

"Have you?"

His face darkened.

"Oh, yes—a great deal—in the best of all possible schools. Oh, what a tangled web we weave when first we practise to deceive, as the poet says! And I assure you it puts a fine edge on the practice when you know that if you do let the web get tangled it's going to cost you your life. Atropos with the shears—and a fine clean cut across your weaving!"

She said, "Don't!" and could have bitten her tongue out. He was talking to her, really talking, and she must needs cry out because it hurt.

And then all of a sudden he smiled that rather twisted smile and said,

"All right, you shan't tell lies for me, and I won't tell them to you. I don't know whether it's a compliment or not, but for what it's worth, I think it would probably always be easier to tell you the truth."

Clarice rang up at five o'clock, and this time she rang from the Miss Blakes' sitting-room with Miss Ora and Miss Mildred lingering out the last cup of tea and stretching their ears to hear what was said. It was, of course, quite easy to hear what Clarice was saying. They were neither of them at all deaf. But to catch what was being said at the other end of the line in Emmeline's little back room was another matter. An exasperating murmur in the throat of the instrument was all that they could distinguish. They would not even have known that the murmur was being contributed by Edward Random if it had not been for Clarice's repeated use of his name.

"Edward! At last! Darling, where have you been all day? I was to ring you up, and I simply couldn't get you!

Susan kept on saying you were out and she didn't know when you would be coming in! Quite maddening! Do you know, I began to have just a very, very faint suspicion that she didn't really want us to fix up that cinema."

As soon as he could stem this persistent ripple Edward said,

"It's no good nourishing that sort of suspicion about Susan. She has never learnt how to tell a lie, and no one will ever be able to teach her. Very reposeful."

"Edward—*darling*—it just couldn't sound duller! But then she is a bit on the dull side, isn't she? She always was. Worthy of course, but definitely boring. Now about this cinema. You told me to let you know, and I've got the evening off. So kind of Miss Ora! What about the six o'clock bus into Embank?"

At the other end of the line Edward said,

"Nothing doing, I'm afraid. I'm too busy, and I'm going to go on being busy for quite a long time."

"Darling, that's awfully sweet of you—to put it that way, I mean. But we've simply got to meet—haven't we? I mean, Lord Burlingham can't expect you to work all day and all night, can he? Would you like me to tell him so? He used to be rather sweet to me, you know."

No one had ever called Edward Random dull. He could see as far through a brick wall as anybody else, and through this particular wall he became vividly aware that Clarice was ringing up on the Miss Blakes' telephone, and that Miss Ora and Miss Mildred were almost certainly listening with all their ears and being suitably impressed with the idea that she was on the most affectionate terms with him. He became first angry, and then maliciously amused. All right, if she asked for it she could have it. He had meant to put in a good three hours' work on the estate accounts, but they could wait, and, as Clarice had just remarked, you can't work all day and all night. He said,

"Not on your life! But hold on—wait a minute, will you? I'll just see what can be done."

The pleased flush on Clarice's face was noted by the Miss Blakes. She had not the least objection to their noticing it. She even added to the effect by smiling to herself.

Edward left the receiver dangling. He encountered Susan coming down the stairs and reached up over the banisters to catch her by the wrist.

"We're all going to the cinema to-night."

She shook her head.

"Emmeline won't."

"Then the Croft boy—what's his name—Cyril. I want a chaperon. In fact I want two—one to talk to Clarice, and one to talk to me."

He was still holding her wrist as she looked down, his face more alive than she had seen it yet. Quite suddenly she began to feel happy. She laughed a little and said,

"I'm no good at being a chaperon. Besides they're all extinct, like the dodo."

His grip tightened.

"You're coming if I have to drag you by the hair—you've got a nice lot of it to take hold of. But I expect there's enough local scandal about me already, so you'd better come quiet. *Susan*——"

She looked down at him, smiling.

"I'm to cling to you?"

"Like cobbler's wax." He let go of her wrist. "I must now go back and tell Clarice what a nice party I've arranged."

Clarice had to make a very determined effort to maintain the sweetness of her voice.

"But, Edward darling—they really can't push in like that! It's just not done!"

In Emmeline's back room Edward said cheerfully,

"Well, I couldn't leave Susan out. And a party is always better fun, don't you think? I'll just ring Cyril, and we can all catch the six o'clock bus."

Clarice restrained an impulse to bang down the receiver, but since Edward had already hung up, there could be no possible object in doing so. She replaced it gently and said in a plaintive voice,

"Really, some people never know when they are not wanted. Poor Edward, he is so vexed—that tiresome Susan Wayne insists on coming too."

Miss Mildred opined that Susan was headstrong, and they had a very cosy little talk about some other defects in her character.

When Clarice went to her own room to dress she could at least feel that the Miss Blakes had been impressed with the idea that if she and Edward were not actually engaged they were pretty far gone in that direction. And what the Miss Blakes knew to-day Greenings would certainly know to-morrow.

Chapter 13

MISS SILVER COMES INTO THE GREENINGS AFFAIR IN THE MOST casual manner. Nothing could have seemed less important than the fact that having undertaken to match some wool for her niece Ethel Burkett, she should, after a long and un-availing search, have turned in to the tea-shop so conveniently situated just across the road from the scene of her last failure. Ethel would be disappointed. She had come across some good pre-war wool in a box which had been in store, and there was just not enough of it to make a dress for little Josephine. Such a good quality and such a pretty colour. It really did seem a pity. It was one of those grey London days when everything looks cold and drab. A cup of tea would be most refreshing. Scone and butter too perhaps. She really was quite hungry.

The tea-shop was full, but just as she came in, two people

got up from a table in the corner, and she thankfully took one of the chairs. She had just placed her handbag and umbrella on the other and was giving her order, when a girl came in and stood looking about for a vacant place. Quite a pretty girl with dark curly hair and a bright colour.

Very little ever escaped Miss Silver, and she was at once aware that the girl was dressed a little too smartly. Neither the cut nor the material was good enough to produce the effect which had obviously been aimed at. The fact that her own garments were both shabby and in a remote tradition in no way detracted from her ability to form a perfectly just estimate of another woman's clothes. The girl, as she saw at a glance, belonged to the class, so numerous in any large town, who endeavour to satisfy their social ambitions by wearing a cheap copy of the latest mode. As she reflected upon how much nicer the young woman would have looked in a plain, durable coat and skirt, her table was approached and a rather high, pretty voice enquired,

"Please, may I sit here—or are you expecting anyone?"

Miss Silver gathered up her bag and her umbrella and said pleasantly,

"Oh, no, I am quite alone. A cup of tea is so agreeable when one has been shopping, is it not?"

The girl said yes it was. She had a little puzzled frown. She opened her handbag, extracted a powder-compact, and began to do things to her face. The frown persisted. She put away her powderpuff, gave an order to the waitress, and listened with only the most surface attention to some amiable remarks about the weather. It was not until her tea and a plate of fancy cakes had been set down and the waitress had hurried away that she leaned forward rather with the effect of a jerk and said,

"You don't know me, but you are Miss Silver, aren't you —Miss Maud Silver?"

Miss Silver looked faintly surprised. If she had ever seen this girl she would have remembered her—the curly dark hair, the bright colour, the hazel eyes set a little too near together. She said,

"I do not think that we have met before, have we?"

The girl shook her head.

"No, we haven't met. But I was nursing a case in the house opposite the block of flats where Mirabel Montague had that fake robbery. The dancer, you know. I heard all about you then, because one of the police officers—well, he was rather a friend of mine. A nice boy, just out of the Police College, and quite well connected. And he told me it was you who put them on to its being a fake. He said they all swore by you at Scotland Yard, and he pointed you out to me. It was about a year ago, but I knew you at once as soon as I looked into the tea-shop!"

A year ago—a week or two after James Random's death —a month before she was offered the Canadian job—Dick Winnington laughing and saying, "If you want to see something out of the family album, just take a look at her! Miss Maud Silver—Maudie the Mascot, pride of the Yard!" She had liked Dick a lot, but he had faded—boys did. . . . She bit her lip and said,

"You were wearing that coat and hat."

The coat was the one which had reappeared every autumn for years. The black cloth of which it was made was still perfectly good, but there was that indefinable look of having been worn a good deal. The hat, a black felt with a kind of purple starfish on one side and some loops of mauve and black ribbon at the back, had been Miss Silver's second-best for a good many years. It would continue to do its faithful duty for at least two more winters.

She smiled and said,

"I am Miss Maud Silver. But I am afraid Mr. Winnington must have talked very foolishly about me. I happened to know something which was of some use to the police, and it is every citizen's duty to do what he can to promote the cause of justice."

Clarice Dean was a little taken aback. She had to collect

herself for a moment before she could get going again.
Then she said in a hurry,

"Yes, of course! I mean, that is really what I want to
talk to someone about! I was just thinking I would like a
cup of tea, and when I looked in and saw you sitting by
yourself in this corner I thought, 'Well, she'd be the one
to ask.' I mean, no one wants to get mixed up with the
police if they can help it, but I've been getting that worried
feeling, and instead of going off it seems to get worse. And
when it comes to not getting one's sleep—well, you do feel
as if you wanted to talk to someone!"

Miss Silver said gravely,

"What is worrying you?"

As so often happens, the mere fact of having spoken of
what was weighing on her had already brought relief.
Clarice said,

"Oh, it's nothing really. It's just that I haven't had anyone to talk to. But if you are mixed up with the police——"

Miss Silver coughed.

"I have no official connection with them."

Clarice gave her a shrewd glance.

"Well, I don't know about that. Not, of course, that
there is anything for the police to worry about. It's just I
don't know such a lot about the law, and the way I am
placed it seems as if I might find myself in trouble if I
talked, and I might find myself in trouble if I held my
tongue. I mean, I've got my living to earn, and it doesn't
do for a nurse to get a name for repeating things, if you
see what I mean."

"Do you want to tell me about it?"

Clarice helped herself to one of the fancy cakes.

"Yes—I think I do. But you're not to go to the police.
You see, it might be a good thing if someone else knew,
and as far as I can see, I'm the only one——" She paused
for quite a long time, and then said "now. You think of
awfully silly things when you wake up suddenly in the
night, don't you? And that's when it comes over me that

I'm the only one left. I've thought about telling Edward, but I just can't get hold of him. He's up to his neck in this new job, and when he isn't, that girl Susan just sticks to him like a leech."

Miss Silver poured herself out another cup of tea. The girl was in a state of nervous tension. She was crumbling her cake, lifting a piece of sugar icing half way to her mouth and dropping it, pulling her cup towards her and pushing it away again. It was a pity to let a good cup of tea grow cold. When she had sipped from her own she said,

"And who is Edward?"

Clarice began to tell her all about Edward Random and Greenings, and Mr. Random's two wills, and going down to nurse Miss Ora Blake. Only she changed some of the names. Greenings became Greenways, and Random—Rivers, but for the rest she used only Christian names and let the surnames go.

"And you see, I was there when he made that will the week before he died. I don't mean I was in the room, because I wasn't. But the night before, he called out, and when I went in, there he was, sitting up in bed and saying he had seen Edward in a dream—that was the nephew who was supposed to be dead. He said he had seen him, and Edward had told him he wasn't dead. 'So I'll have to do something about my will,' he said. 'As it is, it all goes to my brother Arnold, and if Edward is alive, that isn't right.' Well, I told him he had been dreaming, and he said there were true dreams, and this was one of them. Next day he was pretty well able to be up and dressed and down in his study. I had the afternoon off, and when I came back he told me he had made this will and called in two of the gardeners to witness it. 'So that's done,' he said, 'and I can die happy.' He didn't tell me where he had put the will, and a week later he was dead."

"And the nephew came home?"

"Six months afterwards. I had gone to Canada with a patient, and I was there for the best part of a year. That

was just after I saw you. I didn't hear anything about
what had happened until I got back again. Then I met a
friend of Edward's, and he said he had turned up all right
and was doing some kind of a land agent's course—said
he'd changed a lot, and no one knew what had happened,
or where he had been. And he said Edward was awfully
hard up because his uncle Arnold Ran—Rivers had come
in for all the money and everything. So I thought I'd go
down to Greenings and find out what about it, and I wrote
to the doctor there to see if he could get me a case."

The change from Greenways to Greenings did not escape
Miss Silver. The name had slipped out so easily as to convince her that it was the real one. Since it was a name with
which she was familiar, her attention was naturally arrested.
The daughter and son-in-law of an old friend had recently
gone to live at Greenings, and she herself had been most
kindly pressed to visit them.

"Yes?"

Clarice had warmed to her story. This dowdy little
person in her family album clothes was surprisingly easy
to talk to. She poured it all out—getting to Greenways—
she had very nearly said Greenings—and finding that
Edward was just coming down to take up a job he had been
offered. "And of course I want to talk to him—after all,
it is in his own interest. But I simply never see him alone.
That girl Susan I told you about, she just clings! She is in
love with him of course—it simply sticks out all over her!
But men never see that sort of thing. Edward doesn't think
about anyone but me—at least he wouldn't if I ever got a
chance."

Miss Silver gave a slight hortatory cough.

"You are not asking my advice on how to secure this
young man's affections?"

Clarice's colour brightened.

"Oh, no—no—of course not! There isn't any need for
that!" She gave her pretty, silly laugh. "It's just Susan
being so aggravating! Why, the other evening when

Edward and I were going to the cinema she positively insisted on coming too! Do you know, she simply never let us have a word together, and I had to talk to that awful gawky boy of the doctor's! And you see, I've simply got to have it all out with·Edward, only I'd like to know a little more about how I stand before I tell him his·uncle made another will."

"He does not know?"

"He hasn't an idea." She paused and looked about her. It was not very early, and the tea-shop was emptying. They were in one of the far corners, Miss Silver facing the room, and she with her back to it. The tables on either side of them had been cleared, and for all practical purposes they were as much alone as if they had been in a private room. She looked at Miss Silver.

"That's where I don't know how I stand. He'll be very grateful and all that—bound to be, don't you think? It's an old place, and there's a lot of money. I mean, I would be practically giving them to him, wouldn't I? But I would rather want to know where I was before I did anything about it. A girl has to think of herself, hasn't she? Of course it mightn't be such a bad thing anyhow, with this new job of his. There's quite a good house—only the old agent wants to stay on in it, so I really don't know."

Miss Silver looked at her across the table. She was accustomed to confidences, and she had listened to some strange ones. A pretty girl—without family or backing—brought up to think that she must fight for her own hand—self-centred and more than a little ill-bred—anxious to marry and be settled, anxious to secure her future—ready to use the knowledge she had acquired in any way which would contribute to this end. She said gravely,

"You say that the uncle did make a second will?"

"Oh, yes—he told me he had."

"And that it was not proved?"

"Oh, no—his brother Arnold came in for everything."

"And he has done nothing for his nephew?"

"Nothing at all. Everyone says what a shame it is."

"Then I think you have a plain duty. You should see the family solicitor, tell him what you know, and furnish him with the names of the witnesses. I think you mentioned that they were gardeners on the estate."

Clarice's colour changed.

"That's just it! That's why I wanted to talk to someone! Billy Stokes—he was one of them. Well, he went to sea and was drowned—washed overboard in a storm."

"And the other?"

She had not eaten more than half of her sugar cake. She looked down at it now. Crumbling the pink and white icing. Frowning.

"William—he was still there. I spoke to him about the will. He remembered signing it. I said not to talk to anyone until I had made up my mind what was the best thing to do. He wasn't drunk but he had been drinking—he does—I mean, he did. He said there might be money in it—for both of us. And I said, 'Now don't you do anything silly!' That was last Thursday, and on Saturday morning the daily woman where I am came running in and said he had been found drowned in the watersplash just beyond the village."

Miss Silver said,

"A watersplash would not be deep enough to drown a man unless he fell or was pushed. Even then he should be able to get up again."

"He was probably drunk—he very often was." Her voice was casual to the point of indifference, but her hand shook.

"There was an inquest of course. What was the verdict?"

"Death by misadventure."

"There was no suspicion of foul play?"

Clarice shook her head.

"Even my old ladies never thought of it, and they are the worst gossips in the place."

But she did not look at Miss Silver. After a moment she said,

"You see what I mean—the witnesses are both dead. I never saw the will—I only know he said that he had made one. I don't see it would be much good my going to the lawyer and saying that. I mean, would it? And a nurse has to be careful. If she gets a name for making mischief she's finished. I can't afford to run the risk of that."

Miss Silver said, "No——" in a meditative voice.

Hearsay word of a dying man, a hypothetical will, a pretty girl who couldn't even say that she had seen it, and who was doing her best to marry the beneficiary—the story was thin to vanishing point.

Clarice pushed back her chair.

"I thought you would say that. I suppose anyone would." She dusted the cake crumbs from her fingers and stood up. "I'll just have to do the best I can for myself."

Miss Silver was in two minds whether to answer that or not. She was always to be very glad that she had done so. She put out a detaining hand.

"You must not try to make a profit for yourself out of what you know. In certain circumstances that might be blackmail, which is a very heavily punishable offence. It is also extremely dangerous—for the blackmailer."

Clarice's laugh came a little too quickly.

"Who said anything about blackmail?"

"I did. It is not only a criminal practice, but an extremely dangerous one. I think there is something you are afraid of. If you know anything that you have not told me—anything which you ought to tell the police—pray make no delay in doing so. It is not only your duty, but it will be your protection. Let me urge you to think of what I have said, and to dismiss any idea of making a profit out of someone else's wrongdoing."

All the colour had drained out of Clarice's face. Her mouth opened, but the only sound that came from it was a little gasp. Then quite suddenly her face was red with anger. The brightly lipsticked mouth closed with a snap before opening again to say in a voice which had no sweetness left,

"Mind your own business, can't you!" She snatched at her gloves, her handbag, and was gone.

Miss Silver did not attempt to follow her. She sat where she was until she had watched the girl pay her bill and leave the shop. Then, with a little shake of the head, she took up her bag and umbrella and made her own way into the busy street and back to 15 Montague Mansions.

Clarice went back to Greenings in rather a disturbed state of mind. She had come up to collect a few more of her things, since she had now decided that it was probably going to be worth her while to go on putting up with the Miss Blakes for a bit. Now she sat in a third-class carriage and was not so sure. She had shaken the dust of the teashop floor from her feet in a hurry, but some of the things Miss Silver had said were not so easily left behind. Blackmail! What a thing to say! "Not only a criminal practice but an extremely dangerous one. . . . There is something you are afraid of. . . ." She tried to switch her thoughts to something—anything else. What a pity her brown coat and skirt was still at the cleaners. It would be just the thing for Greenings. The red was much smarter, and it was very becoming, but people in the country were so stuffy about what you wore. Any old rag of a tweed and you were all right, but the minute you put on something a little more up-to-date they looked down their noses and said you were overdressed. Edward at eighteen had been illuminatingly frank on the subject. "My dear girl, you can't wear that sort of thing down here. It simply isn't done." Clarice had remembered, and the red remained in the box Maisie Long was keeping for her. Her thoughts lingered upon it regretfully.

She was just beginning to plan a new high-necked woollen dress like the one she had seen in that very exclusive Bond Street shop—only of course she would have to make it herself, and it didn't look difficult, but there was always something that didn't come out quite right—and there was Miss Maud Silver's voice coming through like one of those foreign stations on the radio. "Not only a criminal practice but an extremely dangerous one." What rubbish! And who cared what a stupid old governess said anyhow?

And then Dick Winnington coming in quite strong and clear, as if he had been there in the carriage with her—"They think no end of her at the Yard." And Miss Silver again—"Not only criminal but *dangerous*." The word fell in with the clanging rhythm of the train—dangerous—dangerous—dangerous—dangerous——

She dragged her thoughts back to the stuff for the new dress. Emerald green—a good dark emerald green—those bright emeralds looked common. And a clip at the neck with green stones in it to bring up the colour. There were quite good shops in Embank. She could get the material there and a *Vogue* pattern to make it up by as soon as Miss Blake paid her at the end of the week. She meant to make quite sure about getting her money paid down on the nail. Miss Mildred held the purse-strings, and everyone knew how she hated to part with a penny. "But I'm not putting up with any of that sort of thing, and Dr. Croft will back me up if it comes to a show-down."

A show-down. The word jutted out from the rest of her thoughts and deflected them. Edward—she would have to have a show-down with Edward. He was dodging—making excuses—deliberately getting out of seeing her alone. Well, that meant he was afraid of her—afraid of what she might do to him—afraid of his own feelings. Some men were like that—shy—nervous—wary. Quite impossible to picture Edward as nervous or shy. Well then, he was wary—didn't want to get involved. She mustn't frighten him. The thing to do was to hint at something vague and say that she didn't quite know what to do about it. It could be something that she had got on her mind—something that his Uncle James had said to her before he died. Yes, that was the way to go about it—"And, Edward, I thought you ought to know, because, you see, I've been away, and it's been quite a shock to come down here and find that it is your Uncle Arnold who has come in for everything." Yes, that would be the way to do it, only she must lead up to it gradually, so as to make sure of their having to go on meeting and talking about it. She mustn't say too much at once —just be upset and having something on her conscience, so as to spin it out and keep him guessing. There wasn't anything wrong about that, was there? Too silly for words to mind what a stupid old maid like Miss Silver said——

The iron clang of the train came jangling through:

"Dangerous——dangerous——dangerous——"

Chapter 14

EDWARD WENT ON BEING EXTREMELY BUSY. TAKING OVER from old Barr was a leisurely process. Right in the middle of going through the books he would come upon an item for the repair of a roof and sit there wagging a finger and meandering through four or five generations of the family which had lived in the cottage for the past two hundred years. If Edward thought that he knew this corner of the country pretty well he was being obliged to eat humble pie. Mr. Barr's father and his grandfathers up to a great-great-great had lived and carried on an avocation of some sort or another upon the estate acquired in more recent times by Lord Burlingham, and what he did not know about the families rich, poor and middling within a radius of twenty miles was not worth knowing.

"Littleton Grange," he would say—"that was a place we took over. Now my great-grandfather had a story about one of the daughters there. Round about seventeen-forty-seven it would be. The young man she was to have married had got himself mixed up with the Jacobite rebellion, and she ran off to France and married him. That was the truth of it, but the family gave out she died of smallpox. It was an empty coffin they buried. My father remembered his grandfather saying so, and when they opened the vault to put away the last of the family a matter of seventy years ago, he was there, and he said it was true enough, for he saw the coffin himself, with the side fallen in and as empty as your hand."

Then when they had been going on for a bit he would come out with a yarn about Betsey Fulgrove who was ducked for a witch on Burlingham Green—"The same his Lordship picked to take his title from. And you can say what you like, but all I know is that when my grandfather had to see about the dry rot in the floor of what used to be her cottage they came on the bones of an infant wrapped in a fine linen sheet, so when Betsey died of her ducking— and die she did—it's likely enough she got no more than her deserts."

Edward found it extraordinarily soothing. Old Barr, with his ruddy, wrinkled face and the tang of the country on his tongue. Rural England, and the slow procession of the individual lives which go to make its history. The rise and fall of a family. The coming in of a new fashion of farming or a new breed of cattle, accepted sometimes after long doubt and debate, more often rejected and remembered as somebody's "Folly". There was a fellow who said he had got a new way of brewing—that was in Barr's great-grandfather's time. There were fads, fancies and follies enough. There was sin, failure, and reviving. There was crime, and murder, and sudden death. There was the year when the Plague came to Embank. There was the year of the great storm that sent the spire of St. Luke's in Littleton crashing right through the roof into the middle aisle. There were endless stories about an innumerable variety of people.

After a time it began to come slowly into Edward's mind
that whatever had happened to him, he did not stand alone.
He was one of a company, even here in this small corner
of England, who through the centuries had struggled,
suffered, failed, sinned and repented, or sinned and sinned
again—some leaving the world better for the struggle, and
some leaving it worse. As the days went by, things in him
which had been dead began to quicken—not all at once and
not all the time, but now and again. For an hour—or two
—for the part of a day or a night, there was a warming
and a waking—a time when the currents of thought ran
normally—hours of the night when he slept and did not
dream.

On the day after Clarice had been up to London he sat
in what Mr. Barr called the front parlour of the agent's
house. It had a bow window looking on to a neat garden,
and a double set of curtains, lace ones next to the glass, and
very old plush ones drawn across the bay. It was seven
o'clock in the evening and they were drawn now, making
the room a good deal smaller than it was by day. It was
full of tobacco-smoke and rather hot. Impervious to the
weather out of doors, when he was at home Mr. Barr preferred shut windows and a nice bright fire. He was a short
man, broad in the shoulder and broad in the beam. His
strong white hair curled all over his head, and it was his
boast that he could still keep his books without a pair of
spectacles to help him. If the parish register had not been
there to give away his age, no one could have guessed him
to be eighty-five. He might be going to retire, but Edward
was under no illusions as to its being a very genuine retirement. As long as old Barr had a finger to poke into a
Burlingham pie, that finger would not only be poked
but it would be in it right up to the hilt and stirring
vigorously.

The books had been closed. Old Barr was filling himself
another pipe.

"And you needn't think I'll be interfering with you

once I've handed over, because that's the last thing I'll do."

Edward was on his feet and ready to go. He laughed and said,

"I certainly expect you'll be doing it right up to the last, if that's what you mean. And I'm not expecting anything else, so don't worry about it."

Old Barr chuckled.

"I'm not worrying. Never made a habit of it, and what you don't make a habit of don't have a chance of getting hold of you. Men don't worry a lot, I find—not nearly so much as the women. Real bad worriers women are, and wives are the worst of the lot. One of the things that put me off marrying was hearing the way they go on. If it isn't their husbands it's their children, and if it isn't their children it's their clothes, or their hens, or their cats, or their dogs, or what their neighbours think. No woman's going to put her worrying on me—that's what I made up my mind to more than sixty years ago, and none of them has ever got me from it!" He chuckled and drew at his pipe. "I won't say some of 'em didn't have a pretty good try, but I held my own with 'em—I held my own. A respectable person to come in for the cooking and cleaning—that's all I want, and that's all I'll have, and Mrs. Stokes, she does what I want. You can't expect a woman not to talk, but she keeps it within bounds, and that's as much as anyone can look for." He dived into a baggy pocket and came out with a screw of paper. "Here's that chap's name—the one I was telling you about, Christopher Hale. Came to me in the night, and I got up and wrote it down and put it in my pocket. Must be getting old, or I wouldn't have to wait for a name to come back to me. But here it is for you— Christopher Hale—drowned in the splash eighteen-thirty-nine. I was round by the churchyard this morning and I went and had a look. The stone was put up by Kezia, his wife, with a lot of fancy verses. And my grandfather always did say she believed her husband was murdered. Maybe

he wasn't, and maybe he was. Come to think of it, it
wouldn't be so easy to drown natural in the splash—would
it now?"

The small, very bright eyes of old Barr looked sharply
at Edward from under a thatch of white woolly eyebrow.

Edward said,

"Oh, I don't know—a chap might if he'd had one or two
over the eight—just as William Jackson did the other day."

The sharp gaze persisted for a moment. Then Mr. Barr
swung round and kicked at a log in the fire. It broke in a
shower of sparks. He came about again and said, bluff and
casual,

"Oh, well, that's as may be, but Kezia always thought
her husband had been murdered."

Edward went out into a dark cloudy evening. The air
was cold and fresh after Barr's fuggy room. There was a
good driving road to Embank, and a lane about a mile away
which connected it with Greenings, but he took the bridle-
path through Lord Burlingham's woods and came out upon
the rough track which led down to the splash, a saving
of nearly half a mile and pleasanter walking at that. He
liked the crack of a stick under foot, the stir in the undergrowth which told of other creatures abroad on their no
doubt unlawful occasions. Only who was man that he
should say to fox or rabbit, badger, stoat or cat, "Only I
have the right to hunt"?

He walked on, not hurrying. The nights were getting
colder. These woods were very old. There were oaks that
must have stood five hundred years, yews that were older
still. He had seen a map of the county dated 1469, and it
showed forest right across this corner, and since then
owner after owner had come and gone. Norman names,
English names—tombs in the churchyard, brasses in the
church. And in the end Lord Burlingham taking his
name, as they all had done, from Burlingham village three
miles away. He had been Tom Thomson and had run
barefoot and sold papers in the streets when he was a boy,

and now he was Lord of the Manor like all the rest of them
had been. The new trees grew up amongst the old, and
they were strong and lusty.

He came out from among the trees into the track where it
sloped towards the splash. The sound of the running water
came to him. The stream was swollen still, but the stepping-stones should be clear of it if not too dry. He put on
his torch, came over easily, and had before him the slope
on the other side, with the church to the right, its shape
just distinguishable against the sky, and the black smear
running down from it which was the old yew way. He put
out his torch as soon as he was over the splash, and where
his eyes did not serve him memory did.

He was passing the lych gate, when something moved
there. A voice said,

"Edward, is that you?" The words came on a hurried
breath. The voice shook a little.

It was Clarice Dean's voice, and it annoyed him sharply.
What did she think she was doing, waiting about for him
like this? Because waiting for him she undoubtedly was.
She could have no possible business up at the church, and
since it was all of twenty past seven, the Vicarage would be
hotting its soup or doing whatever you did do to fish or eggs
preparatory to producing them at the evening meal. He
spoke her name with an involuntary sharpness.

"Clarice!"

She came running over the grass verge to link her arm
with his.

"Edward, you don't know how glad I am to see you!
Not that one can see anything in this horrid dark, but I
saw your torch, and I didn't think it could be anyone else,
because Mrs. Deacon says you always come this way and
hardly anyone else does—not now poor William Jackson——" She broke off, catching her breath. "Do you
know, I thought of the horridest things waiting there in
the dark! Your boots squelched when you came up from
the splash!"

"I got them wet. There's quite a lot of water in the stream."

She dug her fingers into his arm.

"I know! But I thought how awful it would be if it wasn't you at all—if it was—William Jackson—coming up all wet—out of the splash!"

Edward's voice was quite odiously practical.

"I never heard of a ghost with a torch."

She shivered up against him.

"Well, you don't think of those sort of things when you are frightened, and I'm not used to the dark like all you country people."

He laughed without amusement.

"Well, there's an easy answer to that—you have only to stay at home."

They had been walking, not because Clarice wanted to, but because Edward was being determined about it and Clarice had either to keep pace with him or let go of his arm.

"Edward, for goodness' sake don't go tearing along like this! Why do you suppose I came down that horrid place in the dark if it wasn't the only way I could get hold of you? Either you are never in, or Susan is there, and—there's something I want to talk to you about!"

"Well, let go of my arm, and you can talk as you go along. I suppose you know you've been pinching me black and blue?"

If anything, her clasp tightened.

"Edward, it's important—it really is! I mean, it's important for you—it's something I think I ought to tell you!"

They were past the churchyard now, and the Vicarage gate. The cottage where old Mrs. Stone lived with her bedridden daughter was in sight. The light in Betsey Stone's room shone cheerfully through the bright red curtains which had been a Christmas present from Emmeline. Other lights twinkled in the houses beyond. Edward con-

sidered that even Clarice could hardly do much confiding
in the village street. The Miss Blakes' house was in sight.
He said,

"Well, do you know, I think it had better be some other
time. We ought both to be getting along. I'm going to be
late for supper as it is, and I should think you would have
to watch your step with Miss Mildred, so if you don't
mind——"

He had quickened his pace. They were almost level with
the cottage now. Clarice felt her chance slipping away.
And she had planned to be so careful. She hadn't meant
to hurry him. Why couldn't he stand still for a bit, flirt
with her a little, give her a chance of leading up to what she
had to say? He wasn't giving her any help at all. She
had a feeling of urgency—as if this was to be her only
chance, and if she let it go it wouldn't come again. She
said,

"You don't understand! It isn't about myself, it's about
you! It's about your uncle's will!"

She could not have said anything more fatal. The old
defensive anger flared.

"I haven't the slightest intention of discussing my uncle's
will! You will please leave the subject alone!"

"But, Edward—you don't let me explain——"

"Haven't I made myself clear? I don't want any explanation, or any interference in my affairs! You will be good
enough to mind your own business, and to leave mine
alone! Is that sufficiently plain?"

They were level with the cottage now. The door was
opening. Old Mrs. Stone stood there, bent and shapeless,
with a candle in her hand showing a visitor out. The
candlelight flickered on Susan Wayne.

Clarice must have seen them before he did. She was
looking that way, whilst he was looking at her. Why
hadn't she stopped him? They must have heard the anger
in his voice, if not his actual words. The thought sprang
up in the dismay that filled his mind.

Then, before he could stop her, Clarice was clinging to him and sobbing.

"Edward—*darling*—don't be so angry! I can't bear it! It frightens me! Oh, *Edward*!"

Susan's voice came clearly across the short, the very short, distance which separated them from the cottage door.

"Good night, Mrs. Stone—and don't stand here in the cold."

She came to them, running.

"What is it? I can't see. . . . Oh, Clarice. . . . What is it—have you sprained your ankle or something? How stupid! Here, I'll come round on your other side, and you can lean on me as well. Hold up—we'll get you home." She raised her voice and called back over her shoulder, "It's all right, Mrs. Stone. She's only turned her ankle. You go back to Betsey."

Mrs. Stone went in with slow reluctance and shut the door.

"There wasn't nothing about her spraining her ankle, not before Miss Susan said it for them. You mark my words, Betsey, there's been something going on between her and Mr. Edward, and seems like he hasn't been treating her too well. Crying, that's what she was, and saying he frightened her."

Betsey Stone turned a sharp fretful look on her mother.

"And I don't wonder!" she said. "Why, I could hear him right in here, as angry as anything!"

Mrs. Stone shook her head.

"Mr. Edward always did have a temper."

When the cottage door had shut Susan said, ·

"Well, we had better be getting along, don't you think?"

If Edward was angry, she was angry too, with the cold anger which hurts. She couldn't think of anything more to say, and beyond giving a small choked gasp or two Clarice appeared to have nothing to say either. She might be crying, or she might be putting on an act. Susan was angry enough to believe that she was putting on an act.

Edward simply didn't utter. They had had enough publicity, and to stand and swear in the village street wasn't going to explain any of it away.

The three of them walked on together without a spoken word. When they came to the Miss Blakes' house Susan ended a silence which had come to breaking-point.

"You'll be pretty late for supper, I expect, and neither of them like being kept waiting, so you'd better hurry. But you'd better remember to limp, because it will be all over the village to-morrow that you sprained your ankle and were crying on Edward's shoulder."

Clarice gave a much louder gasp.

"Susan—you wouldn't!"

"I wouldn't, but Mrs. Stone certainly will. I only hope she remembers the bit about the ankle. Good night!"

Edward had not waited. She had to run to catch him up. And then for all the notice he took of her, she might not have been there at all. It was only when they had turned in at the entrance to the Hall and his hand was already on the latch of Emmeline's gate that he spoke.

"One of these days I shall probably murder that girl!" he said.

Susan felt a rush of warm agreement, very heartening and comfortable.

"What on earth was it all about?"

He gave an angry laugh.

"I've no idea! She seems to think she has a mission to interfere in my affairs, and I'm afraid I lost my temper."

"It certainly sounded as if you had."

He frowned there in the dark.

"How much do you suppose she heard—that old woman?"

"I don't know. She isn't deaf, so I suppose about the same as I did."

"And that was?"

"Well, I opened the door, and there you were, being angry. I didn't get any of the words—just that it was you, and that you weren't—exactly pleased. And then Clarice bursting into tears and saying you frightened her."

Edward's voice came short and grim.

"She said a good bit more than that. I suppose you heard it all, and I suppose Mrs. Stone did too."

"That's why I made up the thing about her ankle. She is just the sort of girl who would cry if she hurt herself—at least I think she is. Anyhow lots of girls do, and I hoped Mrs. Stone would think that was why you were angry."

Edward pushed open the gate and they went up the flagged path together. A pair of lambent green eyes watched them from under a rose bush. There was a plaintive mew and something warm and furry rubbed itself against one of Susan's ankles. Edward said,

"The place is alive with cats. How many do you suppose Emmeline would have accumulated by now if it hadn't been for the war?"

He stepped up into the porch, reached for the door knob, and said,

"For a first effort, and on the spur of the moment, you didn't produce at all a bad lie, Susan."

Chapter 15

CLARICE REMEMBERED TO LIMP. SHE WAS PUT TO IT TO FIND a story that would account for being so far along the street as Mrs. Stone's cottage, until it occurred to her how perfectly simple it would be to tell the truth and say that she had walked down as far as the splash to meet Edward Random.

"I turned my ankle. I'm not much good in the dark, I'm afraid. And we picked Susan up at old Mrs. Stone's and all came along together. I was really quite glad of her arm as well as Edward's."

Miss Mildred sniffed.

"Emmeline spoils that old woman! Always sending her eggs, or apples, or something for her tiresome Betsey! And if you are not good in the dark, Miss Dean, you would do better not to go wandering about in it. At least that is my opinion."

"I was hurrying because I was afraid I would be late."

"Which you are! "

Miss Ora produced a handkerchief and a waft of eau-de-Cologne. Mildred was going to be disagreeable. So unnecessary, so unpleasant. She attempted to create a diversion.

"Did Susan say that Betsey was any better? Dr. Croft was really anxious about her a couple of days ago."

Miss Mildred sniffed again.

"Betsey Stone will outlive us all. Her mother waits on her hand and foot, and everyone spoils them. I don't suppose Susan mentioned her. And if we're to have any supper to-night, I think we had better get on with it. I have had to turn the gas out under the soup twice already."

When supper was over Miss Mildred washed up and Clarice put Miss Ora to bed. There really was not the slightest reason why she should not take off her clothes and perform her ablutions without a nurse to help her, but she preferred to be helped, and when Miss Ora wanted something it was extremely difficult to prevent her from having her own way. Miss Mildred had given up the struggle many years ago. If Ora wanted to have a nurse she would go on producing one symptom after another until a nurse had been provided. It was a sinful waste of money, but it just had to be endured. When it came to Ora saying that half the income was hers, Mildred was obliged to admit defeat. It rankled, but at the price of taking over Ora's bank-book and Ora's accounts she constrained herself to put up with the nurses who followed one another in an endless

procession. None of them stayed for long, and only one
had allowed herself to be bullied or cajoled into helping
with the washing-up. A half-witted girl who had left after
three days.

When Miss Ora was safely in bed Clarice came down
holding an envelope in her hand.

"I just want to put this in the post. It won't take me
long."

It is a time-honoured excuse. Miss Mildred took one
glance at the envelope and decided that it was empty. If
she had wanted to make someone believe that she was going
to the post, she herself would have taken the trouble to
fold a sheet of paper and put it inside. She gave her silent
sniff and went on up to the sitting-room.

Clarice ran down the street to Mrs. Alexander's. The
letter-box was in the front wall of the shop, and the
telephone-box beside it. She had quite forgotten that she
was supposed to have a twisted ankle. She put the empty
envelope into her pocket, slipped into the telephone-box,
and rang up the south lodge. She must, she really must,
see Edward and make him listen. If it were not for the
fact that everyone in the village who had a telephone was
on the same party line, she could have talked to him now.
But you never knew who might be listening. Miss Sims,
Dr. Croft's housekeeper, was known to regard the telephone
as offering an alternative programme to the radio, and so
was Miss Ora—only of course she was in bed.

Clarice stood in the dimly lighted box and wondered
whether she could not at least drop Edward a pretty strong
hint. Only the worst of planning beforehand what you were
going to say was that it hardly ever came off. Either you
didn't get it said at all, or you said too little, or too much.

At the south lodge Susan was talking about her work up
at the Hall.

"Books can really get dustier than anything else in the
world. I shall have to go into Embank and buy an overall.
It's the filthiest job. I should think most of those books

haven't been out of their shelves for the last fifty years. I've
started at the window end with all the Victorian three-
volume novels."

Emmeline looked up from putting one of Amina's kittens
back into her basket.

"Jonathan always said the Victorians would come into
their own again some day—he used to read them, you
know. And he was right—look at Trollope on the wireless.
Susan dear, are you quite sure it didn't tire you going round
to the Stones? When there were five eggs today, it did
seem as if they were meant to have two of them. Unless—
Edward, I didn't think of it at the time, but could you have
managed another?"

Her tone had not varied at all. Jonathan's taste in fiction
and Edward's taste in food received the same sweet, half-
inconsequent attention. It was one of the things that he
found reposeful. Past or present, eggs or novels, people or
hens or cats, Emmeline just took them as they came, with
food for the hungry, kindness for the hurt, tolerance for all.

At the moment the kitten was trying to get out of the
basket again, and her attention had strayed to it before
Edward could protest his lack of interest in a second egg.
He was about to remark that old Mrs. Stone was a born
sponger but if Emmeline liked to spoil her it was her own
affair, when the telephone-bell rang from the back room
and he got up, observed that Barr had said he would ring
him up about an entry he hadn't been able to trace, and
went to take the call.

In the box outside Mrs. Alexander's shop Clarice heard
the click as he lifted the receiver, and his voice saying,

"Hullo—is that you, Mr. Barr?"

"No, it's me."

Clarice was not very often nervous, but she was nervous
now. She didn't know why, and it frightened her—it did
really frighten her. Her voice tripped and stumbled as it
hurried on.

"Edward—*darling*—I must see you—I really must!

There's something you ought to know—about your uncle——"

"And there's someone else on the line! Didn't you hear the click? I'm ringing off! And I'm not discussing my affairs on the telephone either now or at any other. time!" He hung up, and the line was dead.

If someone else had really cut in, he must have put back. his receiver at exactly the same moment that Edward did, because there was no second click. Perhaps there had never been a first one. Edward said he had heard it, but she hadn't heard it herself. She mightn't have heard it the way her heart was beating. Or it might have been just an excuse to get rid of her. And now the line was dead.

She hung up at her end and went back to the Miss Blakes. As she came into the dark hall, Miss Mildred. opened the kitchen door.

"You've been a long time posting a letter."

Clarice remembered that she was supposed to have a limp.

"My—my foot——" she said.

"I thought it was your ankle. There didn't seem to be anything. wrong with it when you came in. One of those quick recoveries! Well, now that you are here, perhaps you will go up to my sister. She has been ringing her.bell."

Chapter 16

IT WAS A COUPLE OF DAYS LATER THAT MISS SILVER RECEIVED a letter from the daughter of an old school friend. She had been out all day, and coming in from one of the heavy showers which were so greatly disturbing the weather, she took. the time to change her dress and her shoes and stock-

ings before sitting down beside the fire and looking at what
the second post had brought. It was pleasant to come in
from the wet street to this cheerful room. The carpet and
curtains which had replaced the well-worn servants of so
many years were very bright, very cosy. She had been
fortunate in being able to repeat the colour to which she
was so much attached, a lively shade of peacock-blue, the
carpet embellished by wreaths of roses in a number of
pleasing shades. This background set off the contours of
her Victorian chairs with their spreading laps, their bow
legs, their yellow walnut arms, their acanthus-leaf carving.
From the walls engravings of some of her favourite pictures
gazed down upon the congenial scene—*Hope*, by G. F.
Watts, Sir John Millais' *Black Brunswicker*, Landseer's *Stag
at Bay*.

To a stranger the only jarring note would have been the
large modern writing-table in front of the farther window.
To Miss Silver it was so necessary and useful an adjunct to
her professional life that it merely enhanced the pleasure
with which she regarded her flat and everything in it, for
was it not a visible symbol of her emancipation from what
she always alluded to as her scholastic career? For many
years she had had no other prospect than to spend her life
in other people's houses teaching their children, and in the
end to face retirement upon a pittance. It was her work
as a private detective which had made her independent,
and in a modest way prosperous. She herself conveyed an
impression of belonging to the same period as her pictures
and her walnut chairs. The hair with very little grey in
it coiled trimly at the back and arranged in a deep curled
fringe in front, the whole strictly controlled by a net; the
neat ladylike features; the dress of olive-green cashmere
with that air of never having been in fashion which per-
vades the garments considered suitable to the refined de-
pendant—all contributed to this effect. The neck of the
green dress was fastened by a formidable brooch upon
which the entwined initials of Miss Silver's parents were

raised in high relief upon a solid ground of eighteen-carat gold. It contained locks of their hair, and was a treasured relic. The furniture had been inherited from a great-aunt, and as she looked about her with appreciation and gratitude, she could feel that she was, as it were, in the bosom of her family.

So much for the remoter past. The photographs, framed in silver, in plush, in filigree upon velvet, which thronged the mantelpiece, the bookshelves, and every other available place except the writing-table, formed a record of more recent achievement. They were the gifts of people whom she had assisted in perplexity, freed from unjust suspicion, rescued from some unendurable predicament, and even saved from death. There were young men and girls, and babies who might never have been born if Miss Silver had not intervened to protect or exonerate their parents.

As she picked up her letter, her mind was pleasurably occupied with anticipation of the nice hot cup of tea which her faithful Emma Meadows was preparing. It would come in at any moment now, and whilst she drank it and ate one of Emma's excellent scones she would enjoy reading what her friend's daughter had to say. Mary Meredith had really been her dearest friend when they were at school together, but she had married before she was nineteen and become absorbed into the cares and duties of a busy parish. Letters became few and far between, but there was always one at Christmas—until a year ago when Mary's daughter had written the sad news of her mother's death. Attending the funeral, Miss Silver had found in Ruth a very strong resemblance to her friend, the likeness extending to their circumstances, since she also had married a clergyman. He had just been offered a country living—"A dear little place, and such a nice vicarage. And it's really nothing of a journey from town, so you will come down and see us, won't you, Miss Silver?" The invitation was warmly given, but press of work during the summer months prevented Miss Silver from availing herself of it.

She opened the envelope and unfolded the sheet which it contained. The heading was, "The Vicarage, Greenings, near Embank", and the date the previous day. Turning her chair so as to bring her chilled feet nearer to the fire, she read what Ruth Ball had written:

"DEAR MISS SILVER,

How nice to have news of you. I was so hoping that you would have come down to us during the summer, but I know how busy you are. Only you do sometimes take a holiday, do you not? When this happens, do please think of us. This is a small place, but John has a busy time, for the church here serves three parishes and there is a lot of very scattered visiting to do. In some ways we are very primitive here, but in others quite up to date. For instance, though the road beyond the village is interrupted by a watersplash—a poor man was actually drowned in it the other day—yet we have the telephone, though it is a party line and so not really at all private. The church is old and considered very interesting—there is a Crusader's tomb and some good carving and brasses. We inherited the late Vicar's housekeeper—rather old, but such a good cook. And you will think I am in the lap of luxury when I tell you that I have just engaged a house-parlourmaid! She is the widow of the poor man who was drowned in the splash. You know, John had no private means when we were married, but an old cousin of his who died two years ago left him enough to make us very well off. If only we had children to share it with! But John is the best husband in the world, and we have so much to be grateful for.

Yes, I think I do know the girl you were asking about. If she spoke of a Miss Ora she could hardly be anyone except Clarice Dean who is nursing an elderly lady in the village, Miss Ora Blake. The name is such an uncommon one, and your description of the girl fits Miss Dean very well. She has been down here before. She nursed Mr.

Random of the Hall—he died just before we came—so
she knows most of the people here. There is some idea
that she is having a romance with Mr. Random's nephew.
But that is gossip, and perhaps I ought to cross it out,
only if I do it will make my letter so untidy, and I haven't
got time to write it again. Don't you think it is very
difficult to be sure whether one is gossiping or not? In a
village you know everybody so well, and naturally you
take an interest in what is going on. John is rather strict
about it, but one can't be stiff and unfriendly, can one?
And do you think it matters, so long as you only have
kind feelings about the people? Dear Miss Silver, it was
so nice to hear from you.

> Yours affectionately,
> RUTH BALL."

Miss Silver laid the letter down on her lap. She thought,
"Ruth would never be unkind."

And then the door opened and Emma came in with the
tea-tray. A calm, ample person with a rosy country face
and grey hair neatly brushed back from an open brow.

"Now here's your tea, and you'll drink it up whilst it's
hot. I don't suppose you had any lunch to speak of, so I've
cut you a sandwich or two, and there's honey to go with
the scones. And here's the evening paper. I'm in a couple
of minds whether to let you have it, because you want to
get that tea down inside you whilst it's hot, but I suppose
you'd be asking for it if I didn't bring it along."

Miss Silver put out her hand for the paper. She began
to say, "Emma, you spoil me", but her eye was caught
by a headline and the last word was never said. She
straightened the paper out and read:

GIRL DROWNED IN WATERSPLASH—STRANGE COINCIDENCE

Chapter 17

THE BODY OF CLARICE DEAN WAS DISCOVERED BY EDWARD
Random. It was striking ten by the church clock when he
came down to the watersplash and turned the ray of his
torch upon the nearest of the stepping-stones. It showed
more than he had bargained for—a woman's hand lying
palm downwards on the dark glistening stone. Just a hand,
in the circle of the ray. That at the first glance. Then as
he slanted the torch, the light picked up the line of the
wrist, the drenched sleeve of a coat, the vague darkness of
a body half covered by the water. She lay in the pool
which had drowned William Jackson. The flow of the
water had drifted her hand on to the sloped edge of the
stone and kept it there, moving it a little, so that it looked
as if it still had some feeble life in it. There was a moment
when Edward had no certainty as to who the woman might
be. She lay face downward in the water, and it covered
her. She lay still, but the hand moved slowly.

He set his torch on the bank and went down into the
pool. She was in the deepest part of it, but the deepest part
did not reach his knee. It was a mere narrow pot-hole. If
she had put her foot in it and fallen she would have come
down in the shallows. She would hardly have drowned.

She *had* drowned.

He got her out—no such easy matter, with the bank
slimy under foot—and when she was clear of the water he
turned the torch upon her. He saw that it was Clarice
Dean. He also saw that there really was no chance that she
wasn't dead. He felt her wrist, but there was no pulse. He
had known that there would be none, but he had to make
sure.

In all the talk that followed, it was not to be denied that

99

having got her out of the water, Edward could have done no more than he did, which was to lay the body face downwards on the slope so that the water might drain out of it, and then run to the Vicarage for help.

But Clarice Dean was dead. Dr. Croft found Edward and the Vicar doing the best they knew with artificial respiration, but it was all to no end. The ambulance from Embank made its sinister journey once again, and before the village knew that there had been a second death Clarice Dean was gone from Greenings.

Dr. Croft had to break the news to the Miss Blakes. At his knock on the door Miss Mildred came down to him in her old coat over a cheap flannelette night-dress with a candle in her hand.

"What has happened, Dr. Croft? Why have you come?"

The candlelight flickered between them. She peered at him through it.

"Did you know that Miss Dean was out?"

"No, of course not. She went to bed early—she said she had a headache. What makes you think she would be out? She never goes out so late as this—why should she? It is eleven o'clock!"

"Very nearly. But that is beside the point. She did go out—I'm afraid there is no doubt about that."

"You are afraid? What do you mean? Has anything happened?"

He said, almost with impatience,

"Yes, it has. It will be a shock to you, and you had better keep it from your sister until the morning. Miss Dean has met with an accident."

"An accident? What sort of an accident? What has happened?"

"She has been drowned in the splash."

Miss Mildred set down the candlestick upon the newel-post of the stair and said,

"Impossible!"

"I'm afraid not."

The old coat had fallen open, showing how scanty was the garment she wore beneath it. It had been white once but was now a dingy grey. A woman would have wondered how old it might be. Dr. Croft, being a man, only thought with distaste that she looked as if she had come out of a slum, and wished his errand done. He said briskly.

"Well, there's nothing to be done about it to-night. The police will be round in the morning. They will want to know whether there were any signs of depression. Don't touch anything in her room. They will have to go through her things. I'll look in and see Miss Ora to-morrow. Good night!"

Miss Mildred sniffed.

"I don't know where we'll get another nurse," she said in an acid tone.

Dr. Croft shut the door with rather more force than it really required.

Chapter 18

BY NINE O'CLOCK NEXT MORNING EVERYBODY IN GREENINGS knew that Clarice Dean had been drowned in the splash. After Dr. Croft's housekeeper had walked along the street and spent twenty minutes in Mrs. Alexander's shop a good many people had made up their minds that she had drowned herself for love of Edward Random. Miss Sims, it appeared, had thought she heard the telephone-bell ring last night in the doctor's surgery.

"It would be about a quarter-past eight, and the Doctor still out, so I went down to answer it. But when I took up

the receiver all I got was that Miss Dean on the line, talking
to Mr. Edward Random. Ever so upset she sounded. I
don't know that I ever heard anyone worse, and her voice
not a bit like her usual. . . . Oh, yes, it was *her*. The
telephone is right by the surgery window, and I'd only to
push the edge of the curtain to see who it was in the call-
box. The light isn't good there—we all know that—but the
surgery was all in the dark, for I'd just run in like I was,
and I could see that it was her. There was no mistake
about that. And it was her voice too if it comes to it, only
all upset the same as I said. 'Edward,' she says, 'I must
see you—I rëally must!' And something about nursing
his uncle, only I didn't rightly get that bit, because I heard
the doctor's key in the door. And just as I was putting the
receiver back, there was Mr. Edward on the line, and speaking that sharp you wouldn't believe it. 'Edward,' she says,
'I *must* see you!' And him shutting her up and as angry
as you please. Well, it's my belief the pore girl just took
and drowned herself. Stands to reason that's what she must
have done. You couldn't drown in the splash unless you
wanted to, not without you were drunk like William Jackson was."

But an hour later after old Mrs. Stone had been up to the
shop a more sinister rumour began to spread.

"Heard it with my own ears. Very good hearing I've
got, I'm thankful to say. Miss Susan had been in with an
egg or two for Betsey after the bad turn she had Tuesday.
Up all night I was, and never thought she'd live to see the
morning. Well, Miss Susan was there, as I was saying, and
I'd just got the door open showing her out, when along
come Mr. Edward and that Miss Dean. Acourse I didn't
know it was them, not at the first of it—only a man and a
girl quarrelling, and her crying. And then there she was,
calling out his name for everyone to hear. 'Edward,' she
says, and calls him 'darling'. Holding on to him too.
'Don't be so angry!' she says, 'I can't bear it!' And, 'Oh,
you do frighten me!' she says."

Mrs. Alexander frowned.

"She hadn't got any call to be frightened of Mr. Edward."

Mrs. Stone gave her a sideways look.

"Well then, it seems she thought different, because that's what I heard with my own ears. 'You frighten me when you're like that!' she says, and he tells her to leave him alone. Well, maybe if he'd ha' left her alone, it'd ha' been better for her, pore thing. Frightened was what she was, and there's no smoke without any fire."

"Mr. Edward wouldn't hurt a fly," said Mrs. Alexander.

Mrs. Stone was large and shapeless. Winter and summer she wore a raincoat and a man's cloth cap. She leaned on the counter and said,

"Maybe he would, and maybe he wouldn't. And I wasn't talking about flies neither. That girl was frightened, and if a man had spoke to me the way Mr. Edward spoke to her— well, I'm not saying I wouldn't have been frightened too. And 'Darling!' was what she said, and begging of him not to be so angry, and you won't get me from it."

She went back to Betsey—a slow progress, because she met three or four people on the way, and every time she told her tale Clarice became in retrospect more frightened and Edward Random harsher. The currents of village thought and feeling began to change. Girls have drowned themselves before now when a man has treated them badly. Clarice Dean might have drowned herself if Edward Random had treated her badly. The word "frightened" began to crop up whenever two people stopped to talk to one another about Clarice Dean.

She was frightened.

Mrs. Stone said she was frightened.

Miss Sims said she was frightened.

They had both heard her talking to Edward Random, and she was frightened.

She was frightened of Edward Random.

And she had been drowned in the splash.

They began to say to one another that she wasn't the sort to be frightened for nothing. And if she was frightened, what was she frightened about? And, at the tail end of it, "There are other ways of getting drowned than by drowning yourself."

The police, in the person of Inspector Bury, came out from Embank to interview the Miss Blakes—Miss Ora in her best shawl, eyes bright with interest and quite becomingly flushed; Miss Mildred at her grimmest and most detached. They united in assuring him that Clarice Dean had seemed rather—"well, excited, Inspector, if you know what I mean." This was Miss Ora, the more forthcoming of the two.

The Inspector turned a shrewd grey eye upon her.

"And when did you first notice this excitement?"

"Oh, it was after lunch—wasn't it, Mildred? Yes, definitely after lunch. I know it was then, because I had just seen Mr. Edward Random go by, and I was rather wondering about that, because as a rule he goes by in the morning and doesn't come back until late. Not as late as he was last night of course. I hear it was he who found the poor girl's body, but that would be something quite unusual—I mean, his being so late. He is taking over from Lord Burlingham's agent, you know, and it must be very trying for Mrs. Random never knowing when he is going to be in for a meal. And not as if she was his own mother after all——"

"Now just a moment, Miss Blake. You say this excitement of Miss Dean's became noticeable soon after lunch?"

Miss Ora nodded.

"That was when I noticed it. She was helping my sister to carry some of the things downstairs—not very convenient being obliged to use an upstair room for meals, but I am a sad invalid and cannot attempt the stairs. And when she came back she was all flushed and smiling, as if something pleasant had happened."

"Did she say what it was?"

"Oh, no. I didn't ask her of course. It doesn't do to encourage too much in the way of confidence, does it?"

The Inspector turned to Miss Mildred, sitting there in her shabby old clothes darning a stocking which had left its better days a long way behind. The darn she was imposing upon it was of a rigid nature. He reflected that it would be most uncomfortable to wear. He said,

"You went downstairs with Miss Dean——"

"She went downstairs with me."

He accepted the correction.

"Whilst you were downstairs together did anything happen which would account for the excitement mentioned by your sister?"

Miss Mildred sniffed.

"Am I expected to account for every passing mood of a flighty girl?"

"You considered Miss Dean flighty?"

"Most young women are flighty. Their moods change from one moment to the next. One cannot be expected to account for them."

"Then whilst you were downstairs nothing happened which would account for a change in Miss Dean's mood?"

She sniffed again.

"I do not feel called upon to account for Miss Dean. As to anything happening, she went to the front door, and I thought she took something out of the letter-box."

"Took something out of the letter-box, did she? You only have the one post here, early in the morning, so if there was a letter for her after lunch, it could hardly have come by the post. Do you think she really did get a letter, Miss Blake? You can see that it might be important."

"I am quite unable to say. She went to the front door, and I thought she took something out of the letter-box, but I did not see her do so. I was on my way to the kitchen with a tray, and I was not sufficiently interested in Miss Dean's affairs to take any further notice."

He turned back to Miss Ora.

"Well, madam, I wonder if you can help me at all. With regard to this letter, whatever it was, that Miss Dean took out of the letter-box. You have your sofa close up to the window. Would you be able to see whether anyone came up and dropped a note into the letter-box?"

She shook her head regretfully.

"Well, no—I'm afraid not. You see, this bay is really built out over the footpath. The pillars which support it are right upon the edge of the street. It is considered very quaint and attractive. Strangers who are passing through always remark on it, and one of them told me that there is a house near Guildford which has the same peculiarity. He said the famous beauty Miss Linley climbed down one of the pillars when she eloped with Sheridan. Now if you will come over here, you will see for yourself that the curve of the bay just screens our front door."

He came to stand by the sofa, and when he bent his head to the level of hers he could see that what she said was true enough. The front door was out of sight. Anyone walking between those supporting pillars and the side of the house would be able to slip a note into the letter-box and Miss Ora be none the wiser.

As he went back to his seat, she said in a consolatory tone,

"I have a splendid view right up and down the street, you know. I really see everyone who comes and goes. It is only at just the one point that the view is interrupted."

He sat down, and engaged her in a long desultory review of all that she had seen and noticed during the course of the previous morning.

"You see, Miss Blake, we should very much like to know a little more about that note. The person who left it here must have walked along the street and passed this house. You may have noticed him—or her, even if you did not witness the actual delivery of the letter."

Miss Ora beamed, informed him that she always noticed

everything, and embarked upon a detailed description of all the comings and goings of the day before.

Mrs. Random—Mrs. Jonathan Random, that was—Edward Random's stepmother, had come down with a basket and gone into Mrs. Alexander's shop, where she had remained for twenty minutes. "She can always spare time for a talk there, but too busy to come in and see me of course. And it wasn't for what she bought either, for her bag was still quite flat when she came out."

Mrs. Stone had come up the street. "Likes a gossip too, and I'm sure I don't blame her, living with that dreadful invalid daughter. At least they all call her an invalid, and I dare say her mother has made her one, waiting on her hand and foot as she does, but if you ask me, I don't believe there's very much wrong with her, and I dare say she could get up and do an honest day's work if she wanted."

Mrs. Stone did not appear to be at all a likely person to have left the note. Difficult to imagine that she could have anything to communicate which would either raise or depress a young woman's spirits. When it appeared that she had not even passed the house, he was put to it to possess his soul in patience, but possess it he did. Sifting out all the odds and ends of what could hardly be called a statement, most of the people whose life histories Miss Ora touched upon and whose characters she dissected could be ruled out for the same reason as Mrs. Stone—they had not actually passed the house. It was therefore impossible that they should have delivered the note. Of those who had passed the house, there were three or four men on their bicycles who came home to their dinners and afterwards returned to their work. These also could be ruled out. There was Jimmy Stokes who had bowled an iron hoop from one end of the street to the other, with his mother calling out to him that he would be late for school—but he was never out of Miss Ora's sight.

And there were three members of the Random family. Mr. Arnold Random had passed the house whilst his sister-

in-law was in Mrs. Alexander's shop. After walking the
whole length of the street he had gone in at the lych gate
and disappeared in the tunnel of yew which led up to the
church. It was about half an hour before he returned.
The Inspector gathered that there was nothing very unusual
about this. He played the organ, and he had a key to the
church. Friday evening between nine and ten was his usual
time for practising, but of course there was nothing to
prevent him from going in at other times. Miss Ora
wondered whether Mrs. Ball didn't find it trying at the
Vicarage, the church being so near and an organ having
that booming kind of sound. She really wouldn't have
liked it herself, but if you married a clergyman, she supposed you had to get used to that kind of thing.

And then there was Edward Random. He had passed
the house on two occasions. During the morning, when he
joined his stepmother, accompanied her to the Vicarage,
and presently came back alone. And again in the afternoon when he passed by only just before the note—if there
really was a note—had been taken from the letter-box by
Clarice Dean.

Three members of the Random family, and so far nothing to connect any of them with the girl who had been
drowned.

Except that Edward Random had found the body.

He went presently to the room which had been occupied
by Clarice Dean. Rather dark, rather gloomy—much too
full of furniture. The dead girl's trunk under the window,
her clothes in a vast mahogany chest of drawers or small
and lost in the cavernous wardrobe. It did not take him
long to go through them—a couple of coats and skirts and
a woollen dress, a bright dressing-gown, a girl's flimsy
underclothes. The trunk was empty except for a suit-case,
also empty, which had been put inside it. In the left-hand
top drawer of the chest of drawers there was a writing-pad,
a packet of envelopes, and a fountain-pen. There were no
letters.

It was when he passed the fireplace for the second time that he noticed that there was something white under the bars of the old-fashioned grate. He knelt down and retrieved a screwed-up sheet of paper. Unfolding it with meticulous care, he discovered it to be not only crushed but torn. A slight fall of soot from the chimney had blackened it, but the few typed lines were fairly legible. They ran:

"All right, let's have it out. I'll be coming back late tonight. Meet me at the same place. Say half-past nine. I can't make it before that."

The signature had been torn right through. It had consisted of two initial letters. The first one was rather badly damaged, the torn edge rubbed and blackened by the soot. The letter might have been any one of several. There was a just discernible cross stroke half-way down which might have formed part of an A, an E, or an F. The second letter might, or might not, be an R.

Chapter 19

SUSAN SPENT A DUSTY MORNING FINISHING UP THE VICTORIAN novelists. There seemed to be an incredible number of them. An entire set of Mrs. Henry Wood, including no less than three copies of the famous *East Lynne*. A notorious tear-jerker—but three copies! There were also sets of Charlotte M. Yonge, an author beloved by Susan's Aunt Lucy, and whose descriptions of vast Victorian families she herself had always found enthralling. There they were, in their original editions, and obviously well read. She remembered to have heard that strong men in the Crimea with death and disease running riot all about them had

wept when the ill-fated Heir of Redclyffe died upon his
honeymoon.

There was something tranquilizing about the ebb and
flow of these family histories, even when they dealt with
such tragedies as this. The people who died in them would
all have been dead anyhow to-day. The people who lived
in them were really still very much alive. Susan found
herself dipping here and there, relieved to get away from
the thought of Clarice Dean drowned only last night in
the watersplash. She hadn't known her very well, and she
hadn't liked her very much. No, she hadn't really liked
her at all. But she was a girl, here in Greenings, and if she
hadn't drowned herself, then somebody had drowned her.
It gave you a horrid cold feeling. And then for it to be
Edward who found the body——

She went on dipping, and trying to forget about Clarice
Dean.

Edward was out all day. Susan and Emmeline had lunch
together. They discussed the now urgent problem of finding homes for Amina's kittens.

"And of course I would love to keep them, but if Arnold
is really going to turn us out——"

"Darling, you can't possibly keep them! You have
eleven cats already!"

Emmeline looked at her wistfully.

"Is it really eleven? I find them so difficult to count."

"It is. And there will be floods of more kittens before
you can turn round. I think they would take one up at the
Hall, and Mrs. Alexander says her sister-in-law in Embank
would have one if it is really pretty."

"They are all pretty," said Emmeline fondly. "Amina's
kittens always are. I don't think I can bear to part with
them. Arnold hasn't said anything more about my going,
so I think perhaps he didn't really mean it. Jonathan
always did say that he was like that—doing things in a
hurry, you know, just to bolster himself up and make himself believe he had one of those strong, ruthless characters.

But he isn't really like that at all. My dear Jonathan was a very good judge of character, and of course Arnold being his own brother, he did know him very well. So I think perhaps that was just a bit of make-believe—telling me I must go. I think he was put out about the garden being untidy—and the cats—and Edward coming here. Especially about Edward. You know, Susan, I quite thought there was something he was afraid of about Edward. Of course people have been saying that he ought at least to give him a share of what James left, and it might have been that. But he went away very quickly when I asked him why he was afraid of Edward coming back."

Susan was looking surprised. She said,

"Afraid——"

"Oh, yes, I think so. And perhaps my saying it showed him that it wouldn't do. People would blame him a good deal if he turned me out, and I expect he will have thought of that by now. So I really think I might keep the kittens. Don't you?"

Neither of them mentioned Clarice Dean.

At two o'clock Susan went back to the Hall, where she encountered a really horrifying book about a man who was transported to Australia in the old Botany Bay days. It was called *For the Term of His Natural Life*, and dipping into it felt exactly like opening the door upon a hurricane in which all the forces of evil were let loose. It was some time before she could get the door shut again.

That finished the Victorians as a body, though she was to discover stray volumes here and there all over the place. She now mounted a ladder, began to investigate the upper shelves, and found herself in the eighteenth century. Volumes of the *Spectator* and the *Rambler*. *Gulliver's Travels*, original and unexpurgated. *Johnson's Dictionary*, and the first edition of *Rasselas*. These would be valuable —but she wasn't sure of the values. She could write to a crony of the Professor's who had that kind of bookshop and find out, if Arnold Random liked.

She went on discovering treasures and making a list of them.

Round about four o'clock she got down from the ladder and proceeded in search of Arnold. She found him behind a newspaper in one of the big study chairs. In his stiff way he seemed quite pleased to see her—said he had no idea of selling the books, but if any of them were valuable, it would be just as well to know. The probate people had accepted the insurance figures, but he didn't suppose there had ever been any real valuation by an expert.

Susan was saying, "Well, I'm not an expert, but I can make a list and send it on to someone who is, if that is what you would like me to do," when the study door was thrown open and Doris Deacon announced,

"Miss Blake——"

She had managed to get to the door before her this time, but she had almost had to run to do it.

"Walking past anyone as if they wasn't there!" she told her mother that evening. "And with no more than a 'You needn't trouble—I know the way, Doris!' Well, I know my manners, if she doesn't know hers, and I got there first and showed her in. Mr. Arnold didn't look any too pleased to see her neither. And who would! He'd got Miss Susan there, talking about those old books she's sorting, and they didn't either of them look any too pleased."

"Miss Mildred wouldn't bother herself about that," said Mrs. Deacon with conviction.

Arnold Random was facing the door. He saw it open with a horrid sense of foreboding. Mildred! And what did she want this time? A blackness came up in his mind. He could neither see past it nor through it.

She came into the room with her head poking a little forward, her nose jutting from the long sallow face, her eyes set upon him in a bright unwinking stare. A vulture —that was what she looked like—a creature who would tear the very flesh from your bones. He remembered that he had come near to marrying her a long time ago, and it made him feel physically sick.

She had her black collecting-book in her hand, and she said,

"Perhaps I could just have a word with you, Arnold."

Susan's presence was being dispensed with. A light nod of the head intimated as much. She had always thought that Miss Mildred was probably the rudest woman in the world, and she was sorry for Arnold Random, but she did not see her way to remaining. She said, "Well, another time, Mr. Random," and withdrew.

Miss Mildred seated herself. Arnold remained standing. He said,

"What do you want, Mildred?"

Her smile horrified him.

"Can you not guess?"

"I certainly cannot."

She laid the collecting-book on her knee.

"You should be feeling very well pleased, I think."

It was true. But he was not prepared to hear it said. He had felt a relief of which he could not but be ashamed. He felt it no longer. A sense of dreadful strain began to impose itself. Mildred Blake's regard did nothing to avert it. He said in his coldest manner,

"I really have no idea what you mean."

"Have you not?" She tapped the black collecting-book with a gloved finger. The tear had been mended, but it showed, thick and ugly like some flat crawling insect. "Well, my dear Arnold, let me enlighten you. Miss Dean's death though extremely inconvenient to me—Ora is really quite intolerable when we are without a nurse—must have been a considerable relief to you."

"To me?"

"Naturally. Since there is always the possibility that your brother James might have told her he had made another will. As a matter of fact, from something I heard her say on the telephone to Edward, she stated plainly that she had something of importance to tell him, and that it concerned his uncle."

Arnold Random groped for his handkerchief and passed it across a sweating brow.

"What did she say?"

Mildred Blake fixed a look of malicious amusement upon him.

"Do you really need to ask me that? I have an idea that you must have been listening too. A party line is so very convenient when you want to know what is going on. But if you wish to pretend with me, of course you can. She didn't tell him anything, as I think you very well know. And she won't tell anyone anything now, will she? Of course I can't help feeling that you have been rather imprudent. I quite see that you couldn't afford to give her the time to overcome Edward's reluctance to be confided in. The idea was, of course, to restore the rightful heir and then marry him, and Edward was so much taken up with avoiding being married out of hand that he hadn't any attention to spare for her hints about James' will. But she was being very persistent, and I suppose you couldn't really afford to wait. Only I do think it was a pity to make it a Friday——" She paused, and added, "*again*."

He was staring at her, the handkerchief crumpled in his hand.

"I don't know what you mean."

She went on being amused.

"Everyone knows that you practise in the church from nine to ten on Friday nights. William Jackson drowns in the splash on one Friday night, and Clarice on the next. By the way, you must have known her quite well. Or didn't you? Did you ever make love to her?"

He flushed with anger.

"Of course not! I didn't even like her!"

She tapped the black collecting-book.

"Well, I don't think I should say too much about that if I were you. You know, Arnold, I am warning you seriously.

that the whole thing doesn't look too well. First you were going away for the week-end, and I was to play the organ. But that meant you would have no excuse for going up to the church to practise on Friday night, so as late as Friday morning you dropped a note in at our letter-box to say that you would not be going away after all. And that meant you had the excuse you needed if you were to meet Clarice Dean down by the splash."

"You're mad! What are you saying?"

"I am not mad at all—I am very sensible. And pray don't waste my time and your own by protesting that you had nothing to do with Miss Dean's death. I shouldn't believe you, and you might annoy me so much that I shouldn't bother about helping you any more."

He took a step towards her and said in a voice that shook with rage,

"I never saw her! I never touched her! I never thought of touching her!"

She gave a short staccato laugh.

"See if you can find anyone to believe it! William Jackson was the only surviving witness of a will which you suppressed. He drowned in the splash. Clarice Dean knew about the will—she was trying to tell Edward about it. She drowned in the splash. And both these drownings are on a Friday night—one last week, and one this week. And you up at the church, hardly a stone's throw away."

His face was grey. There were patches of livid pallor about his mouth. He could find no more to say than what had come to him with the first impulse of fear and shock.

"You are mad!"

She shook her head, and went on shaking it. The deliberate motion turned him giddy—her head in the battered hat —the predatory nose, like the beak of a carrion bird—the glitter of the eyes. Moving from side to side. Swinging like a pendulum. . . . Mist invaded the picture.

When it cleared he was leaning forward with both hands on the writing-table, and she was still again. Waiting.

Looking at him and waiting. He remembered that in the old days of the torture chamber a man who swooned upon the rack was given a space to recover in order that he might be tortured again.

When he had straightened himself he put out a hand behind him, groped for a chair, and sank back upon it. He hadn't anything to say. If she had, let her say it.

She broke the silence complacently.

"Now really, Arnold, there is no need for you to put yourself in such a state. I am sure that it must be very bad for you. You ought to know by now that I am willing to do anything I can to help you. After all, we are very old friends. It was naturally a shock to you to realize how strong the evidence against you might be if——" She paused, and repeated the word with a good deal of stress upon it. "I say *if* it were placed before the police. But you have to remember that this evidence doesn't make sense unless the facts with regard to James' second will are taken into consideration. Now both the witnesses are dead, and Clarice Dean is dead. Neither she nor William Jackson can supply the police with information about the will which you destroyed, or with the only credible motive for their deaths. I am the only one who can do either of these things. I heard William Jackson accuse you of suppressing the will, and I can bear witness to the fact that you did not deny it. And there is the danger point! Once you are suspected of destroying the will, all the rest follows—a motive for the drowning of William Jackson—a motive for the drowning of Clarice Dean. You are in my hands. I can destroy you, or I can save you. That sounds a little melodramatic, but it happens to be the bare truth. If I tell the police what I know about the will, I really do not see that they can do anything but conclude that you murdered William Jackson and Clarice Dean. If I hold my tongue, nobody will be in a position to tell them anything at all, and they will never know that your brother made a will which cut you out. I hope that is all quite

clear. I shall be taking a certain risk, and I shall expect
compensation. You can't expect me to do it for nothing,
you know. Now can you?"

He looked at her, and felt himself without power. If she
went to the police, it would be all over. He had the desper-
ate mental picture of a rock balanced on the brow of a hill.
It did not move yet, but at a touch it would move, and once
it moved there would be no stopping it. He could see how
it would stir, and start, and gather speed, until it went
bounding down the slope and out of sight.

Looking at Mildred Blake and hating her with the
strength of misery, he said,

"I think you are a devil!"

Chapter 20

IT WAS NOT UNTIL THE EVENING THAT THE FIRST TRICKLE FROM
the now rushing stream of Greenings gossip reached Inspector Bury. He had taken statements from Edward
Random and the Vicar, and from the Miss Blakes, but no
one had thought of telling him that a work-party met at the
Vicarage on Friday evenings, or that Miss Sims and Mrs.
Stone were sponsoring a highly sensational rumour involv-
ing Edward Random. Inspector Bury was not a local man,
and had only been a year or two at Embank, but his wife's
stepmother was a cousin of Miss Sims, and one of her
uncles had married a distant connection of the Stones. The
uncle had a flourishing confectionery business in Embank,
and old Mrs. Stone came over twice in the week to pick up
a good-sized basket of the left-overs. Saturday was one of
her days, and she hadn't kept her mouth shut. Mrs. Bury,
who had called after dropping in to see her father and step-

mother, was able to pass on what Miss Sims had said to them, and to garner what had been contributed by Mrs. Stone. She had both versions hot and spiced all ready for her husband when he came off duty. He received them first with a frown, and then with a burst of sarcastic laughter.

"Now, isn't that the public all over! There I was on the spot for the best part of the morning, and could anyone tell me that the girl and young Random were supposed to be sweethearting, or breathe a word about their being heard quarrelling on the road, or his telling her off on the telephone? Of course they couldn't—not one blessed word! But they could pay their bus fares into Embank and go whispering it round among their relations!"

Mrs. Bury tossed a pretty carroty head.

"Well, they're my relations too!" she said.

He gave her a rather absent-minded kiss.

"Now, Lil, I'm not saying anything against your relations."

There was a second and more vehement toss.

"And you'd better not!"

"Much as my place is worth," he said good-humouredly. "Now look here, Lil, you know these people, and I don't. How much of what they say is likely to be true, and how much is what you might call window-dressing put up to make you think there's something behind it?"

They hadn't been married very long, but she knew already when it wasn't any good trying to tease him. She dropped her flirting manner and said soberly,

"Miss Sims is a talker all right, but she doesn't make things up. If she says she heard that on the telephone, then she heard it. She'll take an age to tell you a thing, but it will be true all right. She's the kind that will keep you waiting till you've got the fidgets while she makes up her mind whether a thing happened at four o'clock or at five minutes past."

"And this Mrs. Stone?"

"Well, she's a perfectly horrid old woman," said Lil frankly. "And no relation of mine, thank goodness! And only a far-off cousin of Aunt Ivy's, if it comes to that. Some people wouldn't take any notice of a family that's gone down in the world like the Stones have, but Uncle Bert and Aunt Ivy are ever so good to her."

"You say she's a horrid old woman. The point is, does she tell the truth?"

"Well, I don't know. She can pitch a tale all right—always coming round and making out she and her daughter are next door to starving. Goodness knows what she doesn't get out of Uncle Bert and Aunt Ivy!"

With these sidelights on the characters of the prospective witnesses, he went over to Greenings bright and early on the Sunday morning. Both ladies stuck to their stories, and he certainly got the impression that they were telling the truth. For one thing, in neither case did the story differ from the version repeated to him by his wife. Miss Sims took a long time over hers. He had to hear exactly what she was doing when the telephone-bell rang, and all about the confinement case which had kept the doctor out and made him miss his surgery, together with her reasons for not taking a light into the study, and a good deal of corroborative detail as to how it was that she was able to see who was in the telephone-call-box, but in the end it came down to the words which Lil had repeated—"Edward—darling—I must see you—I really must! There's something you ought to know!"

So far Miss Sims was in no doubt at all. Then it appeared her attention had been distracted by the sound of the doctor's latch-key; and all she was sure of after that was that Mr. Edward was speaking to the poor girl very harsh indeed—"And the Doctor came in to his supper, so I couldn't wait any more. You wouldn't believe what it is with the meals in a doctor's house—never knowing when they'll be in, and everything to keep hot."

Upon this favourite theme she could have said a great

deal more, but she was not given the opportunity. She complained afterwards to Mrs. Alexander that people were always in a hurry these days—hardly gave you time to finish a sentence before they were off. "And I'm sure I'm sorry for poor Lil if he's like that at home. She's my Cousin Emily's daughter, you know, and I wonder at her marrying into the police."

The Inspector found Mrs. Stone in her garden. He had knocked twice on the front door, when she came shuffling round the corner of the house with the front of her skirt picked up to hold half a dozen apples which, she explained, had come down in the night—"And I have to wait to let them fall, for I can't shake the tree, nor I can't climb it, and no one to do it for me. My daughter's a shocking invalid. Chronic, that's what Dr. Croft calls her. And no appetite, but she fancies a bit of apple now and again."

The Inspector said he fancied a bit of apple himself. He found Mrs. Stone just as ready to talk as Miss Sims had been. She opened the cottage door and showed him just how she had stood with the candle in her hand showing Miss Susan out.

"And the two of them coming up the road quarrelling something dreadful."

"How do you mean, quarrelling? Could you hear what they said?"

"Not at the first of it I couldn't. But you don't need to have the words to know when people are quarrelling. Proper angry, that's what he was, and Mr. Edward isn't the one you'd like to get that way with you. I felt sorry for the pore girl even before I knowed who she was. And she was sorry for herself too, I can tell you that. Holding on to him with both her hands she was, and crying ever so. 'Oh, Edward!' she says, and calls him darling. And, 'Don't be so angry!' she says, and, 'I can't bear it!' And 'It frightens me!' she says. And no good Mrs. Alexander nor anyone else letting on that she hadn't any call to be frightened. 'That's as may be,' I told her, but she thought different. 'You frighten me when you're like that!' was what I heard the pore girl say with my own ears. And he tells her to leave him alone. And Miss Susan Wayne heard it all, same as what I did. She had to make up a story about Miss Dean turning her ankle, but it wasn't no ankle she was crying for, and you may take my word for that."

At the south lodge he found Miss Susan Wayne. From the fact that she was wearing a hat he deduced that she was thinking of going to church. Well, he wouldn't need to keep her long.

She took him into the drawing-room, which contained no more than a couple of the cats, and said she would tell Mrs. Random. "I think she is dressing for church."

"As a matter of fact, Miss Wayne, it was you whom I wanted to see."

"Yes?"

Stupid to feel nervous. Stupider still to show that she was nervous. And he had gone over to the window, so that she had to stand and face the light.

"Won't you sit down?"

He said, "Thank you," and chose the window-seat, which made things worse.

She took the arm of one of the big chairs. She had the light in her eyes. He could see their dark unusual grey and the fine grain of her skin. He could see whatever he wanted to see. She straightened her shoulders and folded her hands in her lap.

"What is it, Inspector?"

"Well, Miss Wayne, I have a statement here from Mrs. Stone who lives in the end cottage before you come to the Vicarage. She says you were visiting her on Thursday evening. Do you remember what time it was when you left?"

"Oh, about a quarter-past seven, I think. We have supper at half-past, but it is always difficult to get away from Mrs Stone. She likes to talk."

"Yes, I have noticed that." Bury's tone was dry. "She

has been talking to me. She says that when she was showing you out two people came up from the direction of the
watersplash—Mr. Edward Random and Miss Clarice Dean.
She says that they were quarrelling, and she has given me
her version of what they said. I have come here to ask you
for yours."

He saw her colour change. She looked down at her
hands. Her thoughts raced. If he had been talking to
Mrs. Stone, then he knew everything that Mrs. Stone knew.
It wouldn't do any good for her to contradict it. Lies
weren't any good, really. She had a deep, quick instinct
about that, and she was no good at them anyhow. She
lifted her eyes to his face and said,

"It wasn't exactly a quarrel."

"Will you tell me just what you heard?"

She frowned a little. He saw that she was trying to remember.

"The voices at first—his voice—Edward Random's——"

"You recognized it?"

"Oh, yes. I didn't hear any words—only his voice."

"Speaking loudly? Angrily?"

"Not loudly. He sounded—well, put out."

"Yes? Go on."

"The girl was Clarice Dean. You know that of course.
She was—behaving very stupidly—making a fuss."

"Will you explain what you mean by that?"

Susan's fair skin had flushed.

"It sounds so horrid to say it when she is dead, but she
was the sort of girl who likes to make everything into a
scene. She dramatized herself, and she did her best to
make other people play the kind of part she wanted them
to play. She was having a pretty dull time with the Miss
Blakes, and she was trying to get Edward Random to play
up to her."

"Is that what he told you, Miss Wayne?"

The flush deepened.

"It's what I could see for myself. She was always

ringing up—trying to fix dates with him—that kind of thing."

"Mr. Random told you that?"

He got an emphatic shake of the head.

"Of course not! He has been very busy taking over from Mr. Barr, and often very late coming home. If he was out, I had to answer the telephone. If he was in, Mrs. Random and I could hardly help hearing his side of the conversation. The telephone is in a little room at the back. He generally leaves the door open."

He went back to the Thursday evening, taking her over what she had heard, putting Mrs. Stone's statement to her for corroboration.

"Miss Dean was crying?"

"Oh, yes."

"And clinging to him?"

"She was holding on to his arm."

"Now, Miss Wayne, did you hear her use these words, 'Edward—*darling*—don't be so angry! I can't bear it when you are like that! It frightens me!'?"

"It was that kind of thing. She was putting on an act. That was why he was angry. It was done for Mrs. Stone to hear."

He went on with his questioning.

Chapter 21

AT TWO O'CLOCK THAT AFTERNOON INSPECTOR BURY WAS TALK-ing to his Superintendent, a big man with the air of being on very comfortable terms with his world. He had a pipe in his mouth, a glass of beer at his elbow, and a pair of easy slippers on his feet. He was hoping that Bury would get on with it and get it over and leave him to his Sunday afternoon nap, but with almost his very first words the prospect receded.

"Dr. Connolly dropped in and said he'd done the post-mortem, and there's no way out of it, it was murder. Bruise at the base of the skull. It wouldn't have killed her, but it would have knocked her out. Someone hit her good and hard, and she either fell into the water or was dragged there and left to drown. She was alive when the blow was struck."

Superintendent Nayler drew at his pipe.

"Nasty business," he said.

Bury didn't smoke, and he had refused a drink. He sat on an upright chair and leaned forward, full of what he had to say.

"It seems there was something going on between her and Mr. Edward Random. He found the body, you remember."

The Superintendent remembered a lot more about Edward Random than that. He had been born and bred in Embank and so had his wife, and between them there wasn't much they didn't know about most of the families in the county. He knew all about Edward being missing for the best part of five years, and about Mr. James Random giving him up for dead and leaving the property to his brother Arnold. He had heard most of the rumours that were going too, and that Lord Burlingham didn't believe them and had stuck up for Mr. Edward through thick and thin and given him the agency. Mrs. Nayler had actually been in the fish queue when he came over and told Mrs. Random all about it at the top of his voice for everyone to hear. He said in his placid way,

"Not much time for them to have been carrying on by all accounts. Mr. Edward Random has been off the map for the best part of five years. Thought to be dead. Turned up six months ago and been at Norbury brushing up this agency business. Well, the girl wasn't there, because according to Dr. Croft she had only just come back from Canada when she wrote and asked him to find her a job in Greenings."

"There was something between them all the same. They were heard quarrelling on the road coming up from the watersplash on the Thursday evening. Here's a statement from Mrs. Stone, and Miss Susan Wayne doesn't deny it. Later on that evening Miss Sims, who is Dr. Croft's housekeeper, heard them talking on the telephone."

The Superintendent nodded.

"Livens a village up having a party line," he said.

"Well, here's what she says. . . . Then after I'd seen Miss Susan Wayne I went back again to the Miss Blakes. Miss Mildred had gone to church, but the other one was full of information. Said the girl was setting her cap at Edward Random—always ringing him up and trying to make dates with him—talking in a very confidential kind of way and calling him darling every second word."

"That don't go for much these days."

"I said that too, but Miss Ora stuck to it the girl was very affectionate. And she said it wasn't a new thing— they had known each other before. Seems she had nursed his uncle, Mr. James Random."

The Superintendent took his pipe out of his mouth.

"That's nonsense. It's a year since Mr. Random died, and nobody knew that Mr. Edward was alive for another six months after that."

"But that's not what she meant. She says the girl came down to the Hall to nurse Mr. Random as long as seven years ago, and that she and Edward Random were very friendly then."

Superintendent Nayler made the sound which is generally written "Pooh!"

"Old maids' gossip!" he said. "Seven years ago! Why, he wouldn't have been twenty then!"

"There might have been something between them all the same, and she might have come down to Greenings to pick up with him again. Anyhow she did come down, and by all accounts she made a dead set at him, and he wasn't much for it. Suppose now there was a child and he was afraid of it coming out. Miss Sims states she heard her say, 'There's something you ought to know.'"

Nayler drew at his pipe.

"You've been reading fancy novels, my lad," he said.

Bury flushed.

"That's all very well, but look how it fits in. They were very friendly seven years ago. Then he's missing for five years, and there are some pretty queer stories going round as to why he let everyone think he was dead. Then he and Clarice Dean come back to Greenings within twenty-four hours of each other, and she keeps on telephoning and trying to see him. She says, 'There's something you ought to know.' Then they are heard quarrelling on the way up from the watersplash. He comes home that way, and it's plain enough she went to meet him. Mrs. Stone hears her asking him not to be angry and saying he frightens her. Next morning someone puts a note in through the Miss Blakes' letter-box. Well, you've seen it. It says, 'All right, let's have it out. I'll be coming back late to-night. Meet me at the same place. Say half-past nine. I can't make it before that.' It's only signed with initials, and I don't say anyone could swear to them, but they could be E.R."

The Superintendent leaned back in his chair with half-closed eyes. A deep and peaceful silence settled about him. When it had lasted as long as he wanted it to he said,

"Might be—or might not. Plenty of other letters in the alphabet, and pretty well all of them to choose from. Have you put any of this to Mr. Edward?"

"No—he was out. I thought I had better see you first."

There was a slow, comfortable nod.

"Quite right—quite right. No hurry that I can see. When it comes to a case like this, there's a lot to think about. Very tricky, it might be, and a matter of looking before you leap. It don't matter a lot to me—I'm due to retire in the spring—but you are an ambitious young fellow, and you've got your way to make. I'm not speaking officially. I'm here in my own house on a Sunday afternoon, and I'm off duty, and what I say is off the record. There's a lot of wheels within wheels, and you don't want to put a foot wrong. Randoms have been at Greenings a good many hundred years. Mr. James Random always very much respected. Chairman of the Bench, treasurer of the hospital before it got taken over—all that kind of thing. Then through his mother Mr. Edward is related to some very influential people in the county." He removed his pipe, blew out a mouthful of smoke, and repeated the words with a slow emphasis upon them, "Very—influential—people. And on the top of that—and I don't know that it's not the most important of the lot—there's Lord Burlingham that's been sticking up for him through thick and thin and has just put him in as his agent." He set his pipe back in his mouth and sucked at it meditatively. "You know, Jim, if I had to pick on someone in the county to get up against, it wouldn't be Lord Burlingham—that's all."

Bury stared indignantly.

"You don't mean to say we're to stand by when a girl has been murdered and do nothing because Lord Burlingham wouldn't like it if we arrested his agent!"

The Superintendent was quite unruffled.

"There you go—jumping to conclusions. Everyone in the wrong except yourself. Who said anything about standing by and letting girls be murdered? Too much imagination, that's what you've got, my lad, and you'd better watch it. And not miss what's under your nose. If I've got to dot my i's and cross my t's, I'll do it, and maybe next time you'll know for yourself. If Mr. Edward has been up to anything, then he'll be for it the same as any Tom, Dick or Harry. The law is no respecter of persons, and don't you forget it. If he was responsible for this young woman's death he'll be run in for it. What I've been getting at, and what you are too set in your own opinions to get hold of, is that there isn't any call for it to be us that run him in. I can go along to the Chief Constable, can't I, and put it to him the same as I've put it to you, only more delicate if you take me, and when he's got a hold of it I can come in quite easy and natural with a piece about all the young woman's friends and connections being in London, and what about asking Scotland Yard to take a hand."

Bury looked cross and dubious.

" Call in the Yard? "

Nayler gave a slow laugh.

"You heard me. And if they take over—well, that let's us out, don't it? Nobody's going to give us any black marks once the Yard has been called in."

" Or any good ones either," said Bury ruefully.

Nayler drew at his pipe.

"You won't find any good marks knocking about over this business, my lad. Get out of harm's way and stop there, same as I'm going to, and same as you'll find the Chief Constable will."

Chapter 22

THERE WAS STILL SOME COLD, SALLOW DAYLIGHT OUTSIDE, BUT Miss Silver's bright blue curtains were drawn and the electric light shone down upon a well-furnished tea-table. Emma Meadows had made some of her feather-light scones, there were two kinds of sandwiches, and a highly ornamental cake with almond icing. All this for the benefit of Detective Inspector Frank Abbott who had come to tea on this Sunday afternoon.

"Emma spoils you," said Miss Silver with an indulgent look.

Frank, long and lazy in one of the Victorian chairs, reached for another sandwich. The light shone upon mirror-smooth fair hair, a beautiful dark blue suit, the latest and most restrained of ties, handkerchiefs and socks, and upon shoes which did full justice to long, elegant feet. Nobody, in fact, would have taken him for a police inspector. He said in a languid tone,

"It does my Unconscious no end of good to be spoiled."

Miss Silver registered disapproval.

"My dear Frank!"

"It was thwarted when I was a child. You didn't know my grandmother, but you've seen her portrait. She was a good thwarter, and if your grandmother thwarts you when you are three, you get a complex, or an inhibition or something that sours you for life."

Miss Silver remembered the portrait very well. It hung in the house of his uncle, Colonel Abbott, at Abbotsleigh, and it depicted a very formidable woman. Old Lady Evelyn Abbott had tyrannized over three generations and spoiled the lives of a good many people. Frank, whom she had cut out of her will, had inherited the very fair hair, the cool pale eyes, the long narrow face, the definite touch of arrogance. Fortunately for himself, he possessed a much stronger sense of humour and a kinder heart, though this was sedulously concealed. She remarked that at the moment the trouble appeared to be that a good many people had not been thwarted enough.

He gazed at her between half-closed lids.

"How right you are! As always! Spare the rod and spoil the child!"

Miss Silver coughed.

"I do not approve of children being beaten. It is always a confession of failure. A person who does not know how to control them will not succeed by using force."

He sat up.

"Esteemed preceptress! If I eat any more sandwiches I shall not be able to cope with the cake. Will Emma be devastated if I plump for the sandwiches?"

Miss Silver was pouring herself out a second cup of tea.

"She will certainly be hurt if you do not have any of the cake."

"She seems to have surpassed herself all round. When the figure is irretrievably gone, she must be content to bear the blame. My tailor tells me I have put on half an inch round the waist. It is probably the beginning of the end. I shall have to spend my next leave at one of those horrible places where they give you nothing but orange juice for a week."

Miss Silver waited until he had finished his slice of cake. Then she said,

"I have something very much on my mind."

He leant across to put down his cup.

"What is it?"

"There was a case in the papers yesterday morning. I would have rung you up about it if you had not been coming to tea this afternoon. A young woman named Clarice Dean was found drowned in a watersplash at a place called Greenings."

"Yes."

"You read the account?"

"I saw it. Suicide or accident."

"Neither, I believe."

"You know something?"

"I know of a possible motive for her murder."

He whistled.

"Oh, you do, do you? Now what have you been up to?" She did not smile.

"Nothing so far. There has not been time. I am thinking of going to Greenings."

Those very light blue eyes were fixed upon her now. As always when his attention was engaged, they had rather a bleak expression.

"Oh——"

She smiled gravely.

"I think I had better tell you about it."

"I think you had."

She put down her cup upon the tray, reached for the knitting-bag which was never far away, and took out a ball of pink wool and four bone needles upon three of which there appeared the faint rosy outline of a baby's vest. Inserting the fourth needle, she began to knit with great rapidity in the continental fashion, her hands low in her lap. The vest, one of a set, was for Mrs. Charles Forrest who had been Stacy Mainwaring, and who was expecting a baby in the early spring. Since this kind of knitting did not require her attention, she looked across the tea-table and began to tell Frank Abbott about her interview with Clarice Dean.

"Quite a coincidence, but such things do happen, and I had been pointed out to her."

"By whom?"

"It was that young Winnington who was on the Mirabel Montague case. He seems to have been a friend of hers for a short time. He pointed me out, and I am afraid he told her some highly coloured tales about me."

Frank looked very bleak indeed.

"Oh, he did, did he? Well, you have produced the coincidence and the girl. What did the girl produce?"

She told him with the accuracy which he had learned to expect from her. When she had finished he said,

"She never actually saw this second will?"

"No. That was the weak part of the story."

He said dryly,

"It would certainly want some backing up, especially if she was aiming to marry the chap. After all, what does her story amount to? An old man makes a will cutting out the nephew whom he believes to be dead. He dies, the will is proved, and the estate passes to his brother. Six months later the nephew turns up. Six months after that this nurse

comes back from Canada, where she has been since the old
man died, and goes down to Greenings, where she finds the
nephew who has just gone back there to take up a job.
The rest depends solely upon her unsupported testimony.
She *says* the old man woke up in the night and told her
that he had seen his nephew in a dream, that he wasn't
dead after all, and that he proposed to make another will.
She went out on the following afternoon, and when she
came back she *says* he told her that he had actually made
this will and got two of the gardeners in to witness it. One
of them has since been lost at sea, and the other is the
subject of the coincidence featured in last night's headlines. He gets himself drowned in the watersplash at
Greenings just a week before Clarice does. And she told
you—but there again we have only her word for it—that
she had talked to him about the will, that he remembered
witnessing it, and that he was contemplating a spot of
blackmail. He seemed to think that Uncle Arnold would
probably ante up. She says she asked him to keep quiet
about it for a bit, and she gave you the impression that she
was considering just what kind of profit she could make
out of it all for Clarice Dean. Well, we don't know whether
she did anything about it or not, because she drowns in the
watersplash just a week after Jackson does——" He broke
off suddenly. "Do you know, I started out to debunk Miss
Clarice Dean and her story, and I have half talked myself
into thinking that there may be something in it. Candidly
now, how did it all strike you at the time? Intuition is your
long suit, isn't it? Well, how *did* it strike you? And how
did she strike you? Hoax? Hysterical girl telling the tale?
Exhibitionist with unique opportunity of showing off to the
famous Miss Maud Silver?"

"My dear Frank——" Her tone reproved this extrava-
gance, but in an abstracted manner, and she continued
immediately with a serious, "Oh, no, I do not think so.
She was in a state of considerable nervous tension. The
death of this man Jackson had alarmed her. She felt the

need to unburden herself to someone. I do not think that she could have had any ulterior motive in telling me what she did. She was driven to it by her uneasiness, but she had certainly no intention of taking my advice."

"Which was?"

"That she should not attempt to make any profit for herself out of what she knew, that to do so might amount to blackmail, and that blackmail was not only a punishable offence but an extremely dangerous one for the black-mailer. I urged her to think over what I had said, and if she knew anything which she thought she ought to tell the police, to make no delay in doing so."

"And what did she say to that?"

Miss Silver's needles clicked, the pink ball revolved.

"She turned extremely pale and told me to mind my own business. After which she ran away."

"Frightened?"

"I thought so."

He whistled.

"And on the strength of that you propose to go down to Greenings?"

She smiled.

"It is not quite so absurd as it may sound. The daughter of one of my oldest friends is married to the Vicar of Greenings-cum-Littleton. She has been urging me to visit her for some time. Miss Dean's story made so strong an impression on me that I wrote and asked Mrs. Ball for a little more information. Miss Dean did not intend that I should be able to identify the village of which she spoke. She had, as I told you, disguised it as Greenways, but she was careless enough to let the real name slip, and my attention was naturally arrested. I wrote to Ruth Ball saying that I had come across a girl who I thought was nursing a patient in Greenings—an elderly lady to whom she had alluded as Miss Ora. Perhaps you would care to see her reply."

She handed it to him and watched whilst he read it.

When he had finished he said,

"It was written before the girl was drowned, I see."

"Yes. But I had hardly read it, when Emma came in with the evening paper, and there was the headline, 'Girl drowned in watersplash. Strange coincidence.' You cannot be surprised that I have given the matter some thought."

He said in a meditative voice,

"No. A watersplash is not usually deep enough to drown anyone. If a man and a girl manage to bring it off on two successive Fridays, the long arm of coincidence would seem to be doing a record stretch, and when both the man and the girl are mixed up with a missing will—well, it does begin to look as if someone had been busy. If one was on the case, which one is not, and therefore as much entitled to an opinion as any other member of the intelligent public, one might feel inclined to ask, '*Cui bono?*' To whose advantage would it be to do away with the only two people who seemed to know anything about this inconvenient will?"

Miss Silver coughed and said primly,

"There can, of course, be only one answer to that."

"Uncle Arnold?"

"Mr. Arnold Random."

Chapter 23

"SO THEY'VE ASKED US TO TAKE OVER THE CASE."

Chief Detective Inspector Lamb sat back in the chair which he filled with so much solid worth and looked across the intervening writing-table at Inspector Abbott, who was at the moment engaged in expert ministrations to a sulky fire. He stood up now, dusting his hands with one of those handkerchiefs which his Chief derided as "posh".

"Yes, sir?"

Lamb frowned.

"I used to know Nayler pretty well. He's the Superintendent at Embank, and he's a bit of a Mr. Facing-both-ways. Not that you'll be any the wiser for that. Children aren't brought up on the *Pilgrim's Progress* these days like they used to be, and more's the pity."

"Well, sir, I was. Anyhow the name speaks for itself. Which two ways does Nayler face?"

"He don't want to upset the county people, and more especially he don't want to upset Lord Burlingham."

Frank allowed himself a disrespectful whistle.

"Oh, *he's* in it, is he? Rather the heavy armoured car type and all that."

"This young chap they suspect is his agent. Old county family, and relations all over the place. Just the kind of thing that Nayler wouldn't like. On the other hand he don't want the Labour people to have any handle for saying there's one law for the rich and another for the poor, and all that kind of thing. The Chief Constable is in pretty much the same mind—he don't want to offend anyone. So between them they're tumbling over each other to hand the bomb over to us before it goes off."

Frank put his handkerchief back into his breast pocket. Then he said in a meditative tone,

"The Greenings case—girl drowned in a watersplash. Sounds quite a feat, doesn't it? Name of Clarice Dean. Not an indigenous product. Down there nursing a Miss Ora Blake."

Lamb fixed him with a suspicious eye.

"Got it all pat, haven't you?"

"I read the papers, sir. The case made good headlines. Also"—his tone was negligent in the extreme—"I had tea with Maudie yesterday."

The November light striking through a tall window disclosed the thinning patch on the Chief Inspector's crown. Strong dark hair with a tendency to curl surrounded it, but just at the top there was a definite thinning. When his colour deepened as it did now from crimson to plum the patch glowed too. Frank Abbott from his standing position was able to observe this danger signal and to be inwardly amused by it. His Chief's rather protuberant eyes stared at him.

"Miss Silver? You're not going to tell me she's mixed up with this!"

"The girl met her in a tea-shop a couple of days before the drowning and told her a very odd story."

"In a tea-shop?" Lamb's tone was both angry and incredulous.

"Well, it appears she did know her by sight. Some ass had pointed her out as a famous detective, and the girl just sat down at her table and proceeded to spill the beans."

"What did she say?"

Frank repeated the outpourings of Miss Clarice Dean.

When he had finished, Lamb banged the table with the flat of his hand and said,

"It don't make sense!"

"In what way, sir?"

Lamb's eyes bulged.

"If that Miss Silver of yours was to tell you black was white, you'd believe it! And what's more, you'd come here and expect me to swallow it too! Here's Nayler putting up this Edward Random as his suspect, and then you come along with a story that gives Edward Random the best motive in the world for keeping the girl alive. He's been done out of his uncle's property, and she says there was a will made which would give it back to him. What possible motive can he have had for killing her? Seems to me you've got hold of the wrong end of the stick somewhere. You'd better give Miss Silver a ring and ask her to step round and see me. All this second and third-hand stuff— well, I ask you, what's the good of it? It's not evidence, and it can't be used as evidence!"

"It sometimes puts you in the way of something that is evidence."

"And I don't need you to tell me that, my lad! Put that call through and tell her to put her best foot forward!"

Mentally translating his Chief Inspector's message into something a good deal more deferential, Frank addressed himself to the telephone.

But it was Emma Meadows who lifted the receiver at the other end, and her voice which said,

"Oh, no, Mr. Frank—she's not in. Gone away down into the country—packed her things overnight and off this morning as soon as she'd finished her breakfast. Will you be wanting the address?"

He said, "Thank you, Emma, I think I know it—The Vicarage, Greenings, near Embank. That's right, isn't it?"

"Oh, yes, sir."

He turned from the surprise in her voice to meet Lamb's fixed and angry stare.

"Gone down there, has she?"

Frank found himself echoing Emma.

"Yes, sir."

"And what does she want to do that for?"

"I believe she has a most pressing invitation to stay with the Vicar's wife."

Chief Detective Inspector Lamb said, "Tchah!"

Chapter 24

MISS SILVER'S RECEPTION AT THE VICARAGE WAS IN EVERY sense of the word a warm one. She was given a room which looked south, her things were unpacked for her by the pale, middle-aged parlourmaid, and she was made to feel herself a valued and most welcome guest.

There was time for a little walk before lunch, and Mrs. Ball took her down to the watersplash and along the village street, pointing out such objects of interest as the yew tunnel leading up to the church—"It is said to be eight hundred years old"—and the Miss Blakes' house with its jutting bay and the pillars which supported it. They walked as far as the south lodge, and saw Susan Wayne coming down from the Hall. Mrs. Ball exclaiming that it must be later than she had thought, Susan explained that she had come away earlier than usual because Mr. Random's housekeeper was out of baking-powder and she had promised to get her some at Mrs. Alexander's and take it back with her when she went up in the afternoon.

Miss Silver considered this a pleasing instance of the give and take of country life. She regarded Susan with approbation. Such pretty hair, such a lovely skin, such agreeable manners. Susan walked back with them as far as the shop, and when they had left her there Miss Silver expressed herself with warmth.

"Really a very charming girl. Does she live here?"

"She was brought up here by an aunt, but she is only on a visit just now. She is making a catalogue of the books at the Hall and staying with Mrs. Random. Her aunt, Miss Lucy Wayne, was the daughter and grand-daughter of two former vicars, but she died before we came here. I have only met Susan quite lately. You know, Miss Silver, it may be wrong of me—John says it is—but I do feel that we shall have to be here till we are about a hundred before anyone stops thinking of us as strangers. By the way, my house-parlourmaid, Annie Jackson, was with Miss Lucy Wayne for twenty-four years, I believe." She turned round blue eyes upon Miss Silver. "You see what I mean—there —there is something dwarfing about it."

Miss Silver coughed.

"Did you not mention in your letter that your new house-parlourmaid was the widow of the unfortunate man who was drowned in the watersplash?"

"Oh, yes, I did. It was so foolish of her to marry him. She was much older than he was, and Miss Wayne had left her a little money. At least that is what everybody says——" She broke off, colouring deeply. "John is always telling me not to fall in with the uncharitable judgments of the crowd. He says villages are terribly censorious. But don't you think sometimes they *know*?"

Miss Silver agreed.

Ruth Ball went on talking about Annie Jackson.

"It seems so soon for her to be going out to work, but she said she would rather, and John thought it would be the best thing for her. Her cottage is a very lonely one on the other side of the splash. She said she didn't want to stay there, and she has got a good tenant, so we said she could move in as soon as she liked after the funeral."

Annie Jackson was certainly very good at her work. Lunch was deftly and efficiently served—the walnut table in a high state of polish, the glass shining, and the silver bright. But the poor woman herself looked like a burdened ghost. The word kept recurring to Miss Silver's mind. Annie Jackson looked like a woman who carried a heavy burden. Her shoulders sagged under it, and her strength was ready to fail.

When lunch was over Miss Silver sat with her old friend's daughter in the charming small sitting-room which was so much more easily heated than the rather too spacious drawing-room. Ruth Ball produced some domestic sewing, and Miss Silver the pale pink vest which she was knitting for Stacy Forrest's expected baby. The afternoon stretched cosily before them. Afterwards Ruth was to wonder how much of their conversation would have escaped John's strictures upon gossip. They had certainly talked about the village and its people—the Randoms up at the Hall, James and Jonathan who were dead, and Arnold who reigned in James' stead—Jonathan's widow, Emmeline,

who lived at the south lodge, and his son Edward, who had
been away for five years and was now taking up his duties
as Lord Burlingham's agent.

"He is living with his stepmother. They have always
been very fond of each other."

"What is he like, my dear Ruth?"

Mrs. Ball's needle remained poised above a hole in one
of the Vicar's socks.

"I really don't know. I have only just met him—I
haven't really even spoken to him. He came out of the
south lodge one day as I was going in. One of the kittens
ran up my skirt. He picked it off, and I said thank you.
Mrs. Random has dozens of kittens—no, of course I don't
mean that, and John says it is wrong to exaggerate, but she
does have a great many."

Miss Silver shepherded her gently.

"And you only met Mr. Edward Random on this
occasion? But sometimes a first impression——"

"Oh, yes—I do agree about that! And I did have an
impression—quite a strong one—about his being unhappy.
But when I passed him in the road the other day—I had to
go out early, and he was on his way to Mr. Barr's—I did
think he looked a good deal better. After all, nobody
knows what happened to him during the five years he was
away, and it must have been horrid for him to come home
and find his uncle gone and everything left away from
him."

"It must indeed."

They went on talking about Edward Random, about his
Uncle Arnold and his stepmother Emmeline, about Susan
Wayne, about the Miss Blakes, and Mrs. Stone, and Miss
Sims, and the various stories, rumours and conjectures
which were going round as to the deaths of William Jackson
and Clarice Dean.

Miss Silver had finished the vest she was knitting and had
begun another before it was time for tea. She had been
for the most part content to listen, merely prompting Ruth

with a question if the stream of information appeared to be running dry. She lingered a little on the subject of the watersplash.

"It is not at all deep, is it—just that one pool? Really quite a difficult place to drown in."

Ruth nodded.

"That is just what I said—only John says it would be better if I didn't—because odd things do happen, and the poor man was drunk."

Miss Silver pulled on her pale pink ball.

"But not Clarice Dean," she said.

"No, no, of course not—that must have been an accident. There has been quite a lot of rain, and the stones are slippery. She may have hit her head. You see, she must have been going to meet Edward Random—there really isn't anything else that could take her over the splash. And if she was in a hurry she could easily have slipped on the stones."

Miss Silver reflected on the improbability that an active young woman would drown in a pool which seemed to be no more than two feet deep. Unless somebody or something held her down. She coughed in an absent-minded manner and enquired,

"Has anyone ever been drowned in the splash before?"

Ruth became animated.

"Oh, yes! But it was a long time ago, right away back in the nineteenth century. His name was Christopher Hale, and you can see his tombstone in the churchyard with some very quaint verses on it. I can show it to you if you like."

Miss Silver said that she would like to see it very much, and the Vicar came home to tea.

As it turned out, Miss Silver found the grave of Christopher Hale for herself. Tea being at four o'clock, there was still a good deal of daylight left when they had finished. The evening was mild and fine, and after an afternoon spent indoors the thought of a stroll in the churchyard was agreeable. Since Ruth Ball had a visit to pay in connection with the Sunday School, she asked in what direction the grave was to be found, and made her way to it. An old country churchyard is always full of interest. With how much heavy marble had some of these previous centuries weighed down their dead. What human tragedies were recorded on some of the stones. What human grudges had been set forth for posterity to read, "Here lies Alice Jane Masters, wife of Thomas Henry Masters. She that would master as well as mistress be, let her to buriall come like thee." The date on this was 1665.

Christopher Hale was buried at the far end beyond the church. The spot was a sheltered one, which might account for the fact that the verses on the tall headstone were quite legible. Or perhaps, being something of a curiosity, they had been carefully preserved. In the quiet evening light the lettering stood out plainly.

To the Memory of
CHRISTOPHER HALE
Born March 10th, 1800. Drowned March 11th, 1839.
This stone is erected by Kezia his wife.

In dark of night and dreadful sin
The heart conceives its plan
And wickedness in secret plots
Against the righteous man.

There is a Judge whose awefull law
Shall all thy deeds require.
Better to drown in water now
Than burn in endless fire.

Miss Silver read the inscription through several times. She found it enigmatic. Was it the dead man under the stone who had conceived and plotted against the righteous man, or was he himself the person who had been plotted against "in dark of night and dreadful sin"?

She turned, not at a sound but with the instinctive feeling that she was no longer alone. It was just a little startling to find Annie Jackson so near. She was bareheaded in a black indoor dress, and she had come quite silently across the grass in her thin house shoes. She looked white and strange as she said,

"His wife put up that stone." She lifted a hand and pointed. "It's there for everyone to read—this stone was put up by Kezia his wife. It doesn't say she wrote the verses, but she did."

"Do you know what she meant by them, Mrs. Jackson?"

Annie Jackson was already so pale that it would not have seemed possible that she could lose colour, yet she did. It might have been an effect of the waning light, but Miss Silver did not think so.

Annie dropped her voice and said,

"Don't call me that. He's drowned, and I'm not married any more. I'm back in service like I was with Miss Wayne. I'm Annie Parker again, that's what I am."

She turned, walked a few steps, and came back again.

"I'll not be putting up a stone for William," she said. "He was a bad husband. He drank, and he went with other women. I didn't ought to have married him. They all said so, but I didn't take any notice."

The sun was almost gone, but not quite. Here from the churchyard, sloping to the west, they could see it lie like a golden ball between two clouds on the rim of the sky. The clouds were flushed and streaked with scarlet. Standing on the edge of the grass, Annie was full in the last level ray. It struck her forehead and the side of her head as she faced Miss Silver, and there, where the hair blew back in the lightly stirring air, was the mark of a livid bruise. It had not showed as she went about her work in the house, but it showed now.

Miss Silver regarded her with grave compassion. She came a step nearer.

"I'd no call to think well of him nor to speak well of

him. But murder—that's another thing! Christopher Hale, he was a loose liver like William, he was. And Kezia to her dying day she said he was murdered, and what's more she named the man. Wanted to put it on the stone, but the old Vicar wouldn't let her. He was Miss Wayne's grandfather, and he was Vicar here. And his son, Miss Lucy's father, after him. Miss Lucy had all the papers. And murder isn't right—it isn't *right*. You can't get from it." A shudder went over her. She said in a changed voice, "I'm sure I beg your pardon—talking like this. I heard Mrs. Ball say you were clever at finding out such things. She said you'd done it many's the time, and found out what was being kept secret. So it just come over me, and I'm sure I beg your pardon. You won't mention it, I hope—not to Mrs. Ball nor to anyone. It's easy to set people talking."

Miss Silver said,

"I shall not mention it to Mrs. Ball, Annie."

Annie Jackson turned and went away over the grass, making no sound at all. The light was failing now. The sun was gone. There was a greyness and a chill.

But it was some time before Miss Silver went back to the Vicarage.

Chapter 25

THE BALLS AND THEIR GUEST WERE STILL AT THE BREAKFAST table next morning when Annie Jackson came in to say that the Inspector from Embank was there and another gentleman, and could they see Miss Silver?

Standing there facing a window, no one could help noticing how pale and cold she looked. She kept her hand on the door as if she needed its support. Miss Silver folded her table-napkin neatly and followed her into the hall. Just before she closed the dining-room door behind her she heard the Vicar say, "Really, my dear, that poor woman looks dreadfully ill."

Coming out of the bright room, the hall seemed dark. Annie said,

"They're in the morning-room." Her voice shook.

She looked at Miss Silver and shivered. Then she went away down the passage which led to the back premises.

Miss Silver took her way to the morning-room.

It was Frank Abbott who came to meet her. Since he was expecting her, there was no surprise on his side. If there was any on hers, it was not allowed to be obtrusive. She smiled, expressed pleasure at seeing him, and shook hands with Inspector Bury. After which they all sat down, and she was invited to give the local Inspector an account of her interview with Miss Clarice Dean.

It was evident that it did not suit his book. He put a number of questions obviously intended to shake the accuracy of her recollection, and then said in rather an abrupt tone,

"Inspector Abbott tells me that you are to be relied upon not to repeat this story——" at which point he suddenly found himself floundering.

Without any real movement on her part she appeared to have withdrawn to a rather awful distance. Or perhaps it was he who had receded. His neck burned, and the colour mounted to his prominent ears. At Miss Silver's gentle yet remote, "I beg your pardon, Inspector," he found himself very earnestly begging hers, with the Inspector from Scotland Yard enjoying the scene.

But it was Frank who rescued him.

"That is all right, Bury. I have worked with Miss Silver before, and you haven't. You can say anything you like in front of her. I propose to show her all the statements we've got and ask her what she thinks of them."

Miss Silver accepted both the apology and the tribute with a faint but gracious smile.

Bury's ears resumed their natural colour.

"We've got to be careful, you know, and this story—well, if that is what Miss Dean was up to, it rather knocks Mr. Random's motive on the head, doesn't it? You say she told you she knew about a will in his favour. That being the case, he had a good deal to lose by her death."

Miss Silver coughed.

"She had not told him that she knew about the will. She was finding it difficult to see him alone. She had made the mistake of trying to combine her proffer of information with a very determined attempt at a flirtation for which Mr. Edward Random was not inclined."

"She was running after him?"

"Undoubtedly. She spoke quite frankly about it. She wished to be comfortably settled. She hoped to make some kind of a bargain from what she knew about the will. She hoped to secure Edward Random's gratitude. And she intended to marry him if she decided that it would be worth her while."

Bury looked at her with growing respect.

"A pretty cold-blooded business."

"And a dangerous one. I warned her about that."

He said quickly,

"What made you think it might be dangerous?"

"If her story was true, a will had been suppressed, and the surviving witness to that will had just been drowned in very suspicious circumstances. Miss Dean was, I believe, quite well aware that her position was not a very safe one. A person who has suppressed a will might kill to cover up his crime. A person who has killed once may do so again. I formed the opinion that Miss Dean was in a high state of tension. She unburdened herself to me because she felt that she would be safer if someone shared her secret."

Inspector Bury frowned.

"I don't see how all this is going to fit in. Inspector

Abbott wanted me to come along and hear what you had to say. Well, I've done so, and I don't see how it's going to fit in. We're handing the case over. He's at liberty to handle it the way he thinks best. I've got a job out at Littleton, and I'll be getting along."

When the door had shut behind him Frank Abbott permitted himself to smile.

"A good chap," he said, "and as keen as mustard. He would like to have finished the case himself, but the Superintendent and the Chief Constable have got the wind up—Random relations on one side all over the county, and the watchful eye of Labour on the other. Which is why I am here to pull the chestnuts out of the fire for them. After which lovely bag of mixed metaphors I think you had better read the statements and tell me how they strike you."

She took the typewritten sheets and gave them grave attention. When she had finished she lifted her eyes from the last page and said,

"Mr. Edward Random's statement merely describes the finding of Miss Dean's body."

"Yes, I was going to tell you about that. When Bury searched the girl's room he found a note crumpled up under the grate. Here is a copy. The original was typewritten too. The signature consists of two typed initials so badly defaced that it is practically impossible to say what they were, though the first one seems to have had a cross bar, which would make it A, E, or F."

She said,

"Defaced? In what manner?"

"A rubbed crease amounting to a tear—a fall of soot down the chimney. The typewriter has not been identified, and the only fingerprints are Clarice Dean's."

"My dear Frank!"

He nodded.

"Odd, isn't it? It didn't come by post, you know. Somebody typed it, put it in an envelope, stuck it down, and dropped it into the Miss Blakes' letter-box. Miss Mildred

Blake says Miss Dean went to the box when they were carrying the lunch things down, and she thinks took something out of it. Miss Ora Blake says that Edward Random went down the street and past their door at about two o'clock. Her sofa is drawn up to the window in that jutting bay, and she has an excellent view of the whole street, with the unfortunate exception of the stretch of footpath which runs under the bay and which includes her own front door. Edward Random could therefore have dropped the note into the letter-box without her seeing him, and so could two other members of the Random family—his stepmother, Mrs. Jonathan Random, and—Uncle Arnold. Miss Ora has an eye for detail, and I asked her whether any of these people were wearing gloves. Well, Edward Random wasn't, but Mrs. Jonathan and Uncle Arnold were. Uncle Arnold always does. He plays the organ, and is finicky about his hands. But gloves or no gloves, there should be more fingerprints than Miss Dean's on that note. Even the most finicky person doesn't sit down to type in gloves. Which means that the prints have been deliberately removed. And that looks like premeditation."

Miss Silver said,

"The initials were typed?"

"Yes."

"And are now defaced?"

"Practically. The second one could be an R."

"Has Mr. Edward Random been asked about this note?"

"Yes. He denies writing it. Look here, this is what I have got roughed out so far with regard to possible suspects. We'll take Edward Random first.

"*Motive.* In the light of your conversation with Clarice Dean, weak to the point of being non-existent. But there may be things in their relationship which we do not know about. She was obviously pestering him, and he was obviously angry about it, *vide* statements of Miss Sims and Mrs. Stone—'He spoke very harsh', and, 'She said he frightened her when he was like that, and I'd have been the same'. I suppose she could have exasperated him to the point at which he hit her over the head and left her to drown."

"She had been struck?"

He nodded.

"On the back of the head—and then drowned. As I was saying, I suppose a man might lose his temper to that extent, but—*there were no fingerprints on the note, except her own.* So whoever typed that note meant to murder her. And that does away with any theory of sudden provocation. You see, it isn't going to be easy to fit Edward out with a motive. But when you come to *Opportunity*, everything in the garden is lovely. It was ten o'clock when he ran up to the Vicarage and said there was a woman drowned in the splash. He was on his way home after spending the afternoon and evening with Mr. Barr, Lord Burlingham's old agent from whom he is taking over. The distance to the splash is about three-quarters of a mile—but he left Mr. Barr's house at a quarter-past nine. Bury and I saw him last night, and he says he took a bridle path through the woods and didn't hurry. Says he likes being in the woods at night. All very understandable and possible, but a bit unfortunate in view of the fact that the typewritten note makes an assignation with Clarice Dean at half-past nine. The meeting-place was obviously the watersplash, since the note says 'Same place', and that is where they were coming from when Mrs. Stone saw them the evening before. Well, he had time to keep that appointment, quarrel with her, knock her out, and make sure that she was dead before going up to the Vicarage for help. You see, it begins not to look so good for Edward Random."

Miss Silver gazed at him thoughtfully.

"Mrs. Ball informs me that though Mr. Edward Random habitually came and went by way of the watersplash, there is quite a good road from Mr. Barr's house which connects with Greenings by way of a lane which you may have

observed just on the Embank side of the village. If Mr.
Edward had killed Miss Dean, would he have gone to the
Vicarage for help? There was no need to attract attention
to himself by doing so. He could have made a point of
taking the other way home, or at least of saying that he
had done so."

Frank shrugged.

"A man doesn't commit murder in a perfectly reasonable frame of mind."

Miss Silver said,

"If Clarice Dean was murdered by the person who removed his fingerprints from that note, then the whole thing
was very carefully planned. If this person was Edward
Random, he would not have left his actions after the
murder to chance."

Frank nodded.

"I agree to that. But he might have thought that he
would divert suspicion by going off hot-foot to fetch help.
By the way, there is no typewriter in Mrs. Random's house.
Mr. Barr has two, but the note was not typed on either of
them. You don't happen to know if the Vicar has one, do
you?" He laughed as he spoke.

But Miss Silver answered seriously.

"There is one in the Church Room, I believe. It is used
for typing notices."

"By whom?"

"I really do not know. By the Vicar, I presume, and by
Mrs. Ball—perhaps by other church helpers."

"Is the room kept locked?"

"I think not—in the day-time. It is behind the Vicarage,
you know. There is a small lending library there, and
people come to borrow books."

"I see. We will go and have a look at it. But to return
to our suspects—what about Uncle Arnold? He has got a
whale of a motive, but what about opportunity?"

Miss Silver said with gravity,

"He plays the organ for the services. Mrs. Ball tells me

that he is in the habit of practising in the church between nine and ten o'clock on Friday evenings."

"And William Jackson gets himself drowned on a Friday evening, and so does Clarice Dean. Almost too convenient, isn't it? Of course we don't know exactly when William drowned, but pubs close at ten, and he is supposed to have left the Lamb a little before that. Since, I gather, he usually had to be more or less thrown out, his reason for going earlier and of his own accord could have been that he wanted to see Arnold Random and try out a spot of blackmail. He could have caught him nicely if he had hung about by the lych gate, and, as you are about to observe, it is only a step from there to the splash. Arnold would merely have to temporize, follow him down to the stepping-stones, and push him in. If he was fuddled, as seems likely, it would not be too difficult to hold him under until he drowned. As regards Clarice, it is easier still. With the party line at his disposal, Arnold could have heard her insisting to Edward that she knew something about his uncle's affairs. He could have typed the note which brought her down to the splash at half-past nine—something rather phoney about it being typed, don't you think—especially the initials. He was one of the people who could have dropped it in the Miss Blakes' letter-box, and he had a perfectly good excuse for being on the spot. He always practised in the church on Friday evenings. He had only to nip down the yew tunnel, knock the girl out from behind —remember it was almost certainly Edward whom she was expecting and she would be looking for him to come from the direction of the splash. Arnold could come up behind her and she would never know what happened. The whole thing need not have taken more than a few minutes. Would anyone in the Vicarage have noticed if the organ had stopped for those few minutes?"

Miss Silver said in a thoughtful voice, .

"I do not know. Mrs. Ball has a work-party here on Friday evenings from eight to ten."

"Oh, she does, does she? That's a bit of a complication. Or is it? If there were a lot of women here all talking nineteen to the dozen, I don't suppose any of them would notice whether the organ was off or on. They'll have to be asked of course. But as regards William Jackson—let's see —he's got to have time to come down the road from the Lamb, meet Arnold Random, and get himself bumped off. Well, suppose Arnold is still playing the organ when he comes along. He could go up to the church and see him there all nice and private. Even if the Vicarage party is breaking up, there wouldn't be anything to attract attention. The organ would stop, but what about it—Mr. Arnold had finished his practising. William comes and goes by the yew tunnel, and the ladies all go the other way home. Yes, it fits in. And I'd better have a word with Mrs. Ball. Do you think you could get hold of her?"

Chapter 26

INSPECTOR ABBOTT WAS NOT IN THE LEAST WHAT RUTH BALL expected.. She found it difficult to believe that he was a police officer. Solid worth was what one associated with the Police Force. A slim, elegant young man in a beautifully cut suit was disturbing. She would have been more comfortable if he had worn large clumping boots and talked with a country accent. But she was most anxious to be helpful.

"Now let me see—which Friday is it that you want to know about? . . . Oh, both? Well, on that first Friday— I know Mrs. Pomfret was there—and Miss Sims—and of course Miss Mildred Blake—and—yes, Mrs. Alexander. But not Mrs. Jonathan Random or Susan Wayne."

"And when did they go away?"

"Well, the party is supposed to be over by ten, but you know how it is—there are the good nights. I know Miss Blake went away early. She wanted to have a word with Mr. Random, who was practising in the church. She was going to play on one of the Sundays. We are very fortunate in having two good amateurs actually in Greenings, because the parish could not really afford a professional organist."

"At what time did Miss Blake leave?"

"It must have been just before ten—not so early after all. But the others were a little later."

"And you could hear the organ then?"

"Oh, yes. Miss Blake remarked on it. She said she would just go over to the church and see him about the music."

When she had left them Frank said,

"Well, there goes a very promising case against Mr. Arnold Random. If he and Miss Blake were talking about music in the church round about ten o'clock, then he wasn't murdering William Jackson. I must go and see her on my way back. I'll ask her how long she was there, and whether she and Arnold walked home together. If they did, he's got a nice water-tight alibi, and we have lost our chief suspect. You haven't got another one up your sleeve by any chance, have you?"

He was taken aback when she said very soberly indeed,

"I do not know, Frank."

One of his very fair eyebrows lifted.

"And what do you mean by that?"

She fixed her eyes upon his face.

"I believe that I should tell you, but I am reluctant to do so. The person whom I have in mind has had a severe shock and is an object of compassion. There is, I believe, some want of balance: It is because this might prove a danger either to herself or others that I do feel I have a duty in the matter. I had a very curious interview in the churchyard last night."

"An interview? With whom?"

"With William Jackson's widow. I had gone to see rather a curious old tomb, and she came up behind me whilst I was looking at it."

"Is she the woman who let us in? Bury told me she was working here. She looks very ill." -

"She has had a severe shock, Frank. Her state of mind is a disturbed one. She said some strange things to me whilst I was looking at the tomb. It is that of a man who was drowned in the splash more than a hundred years ago."

"What did she say to you?"

She told him in her own quiet, accurate way. When she had finished he said,

"It certainly sounds odd. But what are you suggesting —that she drowned him?"

She shook her head.

"Frank, I do not know. He was a bad husband—he took her money and spent it on other women. She has a bruise on the side of her head. It is not noticeable in the house, but in the churchyard when the wind blew her hair back it was distinctly visible. It has occurred to me that those verses on the tombstone might have suggested a method of murder to someone in a not very balanced state of mind." She quoted them slowly and with emphasis:

> "In dark of night and dreadful sin
> The heart conceives its plan.

"And again:

> "There is a judge whose awefull law
> Doth all our deeds require.
> Better to drown in water now
> Than burn in endless fire.

"It is those last two lines which I find particularly suggestive. To an unbalanced mind it might appear that to drown William Jackson would be the means of saving him from further sin."

He was frowning.

" And Clarice Dean? "

Miss Silver shook her head again.

"I can only repeat that I do not know. Once a lack of balance has led a person to kill, I suppose the act might be repeated, and with a lesser motive. Or the second murder may merely have been suggested by the first, and carried out by a different hand. No—perhaps that is going too far. Let us return to the safer realm of facts. I have thought it my duty to tell you that Annie Jackson's state of mind is not altogether normal. I have given you an account of her words and behaviour at the tomb of Christopher Hale. I do not wish to go any farther than that, and I beg that you will not ask me to do so."

A subsequent interview with Annie did not add very much to this. She was pale and quiet. She answered what was asked of her in a manner so devoid of emotion that she might have been repeating a lesson. She had been married nearly three years. The cottage had been bought with her money. William was not a good husband—everybody knew that. He wasn't doing himself any good, and Mr. Random had given him his notice. No, he didn't seem upset about it. He said Mr. Arnold would be sorry, and maybe he'd get his job back, and a rise. But she didn't take any notice of that—she thought he was just boasting. She knew he was getting careless over his work, and Mr. Arnold was particular, he wouldn't put up with it.

All this while her hands were strained together in her lap. There was no other sign that she was exercising a rigid control until Frank Abbott said,

"Mrs. Jackson, did your husband ever talk to you about a will that he had witnessed? "

She gave a kind of gasp at that and said,

"No."

"Are you quite sure about that? "

"Quite—sure——" Each of the words seemed to use up all the breath she had.

"He never spoke as if he knew something which could be turned to his advantage?"

This time she did not attempt to speak, only shook her head. Frank Abbott leaned forward, his light eyes intent. "Your husband didn't usually come home till after closing time, did he?"

This was a relief. She managed a fluttering "No——"

"He was sometimes the worse for drink?"

She nodded.

"Did you ever come and meet him? As far as the splash—to see him over the stepping-stones?"

Her eyes widened until iris and pupil seemed to merge and show like a dark O against the white.

He said,

"Did you come to meet him on that Friday night—the night that he was drowned?"

She had taken a quick breath. Now it went out of her in a sigh. Her straining hands relaxed and she slipped sideways to the floor in a faint.

Chapter 27

INSPECTOR ABBOTT WENT OVER TO THE CHURCH ROOM WITH the Vicar, who would have preferred to show him the church.

"Perhaps some other time when you are not on duty," he said in a regretful voice. "We have a list of the incumbents from 1250 onwards, and there are a good many points of interest besides the Crusader's tomb, which is in an unusual state of preservation. The Church Room, which was very kindly given by the late Mr. James Random, has, I fear, a strictly utilitarian appeal. Fortunately, the Vicarage screens it from the road, and these poplars from the church-yard."

It proved to be one of those large plain structures, admir-ably adapted to its purpose but devoid of charm. The door was locked, but as the Reverend John Ball explained, the key was not far to seek, since it hung on a nail at the side of the shallow porch—"Out of reach of the children, but convenient for any of the church helpers."

As they entered upon a big bare room which smelled powerfully of varnish, Frank made discreet enquiries with regard to these helpers. It appeared that Mrs. Jonathan Random came in and out to do the flowers.

"There is a most convenient little room through there with running water and a sink, and of course it saves a great deal of mess in the church. The Sunday School meets here, and we have a small lending library supervised by Mrs. Pomfret and Miss Blake. One of them, or of their helpers, makes a point of being on duty from six to half-past on Wednesdays and Fridays, and for half an hour after the Sunday morning service. Now let me see who the helpers are. Miss Sims of course—she is Dr. Croft's housekeeper. And I believe Mr. Random's housekeeper from the Hall occasionally takes a hand."

Frank looked about him. A row of uncurtained windows broke the varnished wall on either side. There were a number of rush-seated chairs, a singularly hideous yellow harmonium, and, at the far end, the shelves which housed the library. In the opposite corner to the harmonium there was a writing-table, and upon the writing-table a rather elderly-looking typewriter.

"The gift of Mr. Arnold Random. It was his brother's, and he very kindly presented it to the Room after Mr. James Random's death."

"And who uses it, sir?"

Mr. Ball gave his genial smile.

"Oh, most of our helpers can type a little, I think. Not in a very professional manner, but sufficiently well to produce a legible notice, or texts for the children to learn at home—that kind of thing, you know."

"Do you mind if I try my hand at it?"

"No, no—of course not."

Frank sat down at the table, found a sheet of paper, slipped it into the machine, and began to type in a style which no doubt compared favourably with that of the helpers. What he typed was a copy of the note which had brought Clarice Dean to her death:

"All right, let's have it out. I'll be coming back late tonight. Meet me at the same place. Say half-past nine. I can't make it before that."

He left it without signature, folded the sheet, and put it away in his pocket-book. After which he allowed the Vicar to show him round the church, where he duly admired the Crusader, one Hugo de la Tour, and some fine brasses. At his own request he was conducted to the grave of Christopher Hale—dismissed rather contemptuously by Mr. Ball as "really comparatively modern, but of some topical interest".

When he had read Kezia's verses and admired the accuracy with which Miss Silver had rendered them, he took his way back to the house and asked if he might have a word with her before leaving.

It was characteristic of her kind heart that she should reassure him as to Annie Jackson before making enquiries as to whether he had met with any success.

"She has had a nice cup of tea, and is now really quite recovered. It is always distressing to have to question someone who is in trouble, and I am sure you will be glad to know that she is not any the worse for the experience——" She paused, and then added, "physically."

"And just what do you mean by that?"

"That she has something on her mind. She fainted because she was frightened. You asked her whether she had gone to meet her husband at the watersplash, and she was suddenly very much afraid—so much afraid that she fainted."

"You think she did go to meet him?"

"I think she may have done so."

"Do you think she pushed him in?"

"I think she may have seen the person who pushed him in. And if she did——"

"If she did?"

"She may be in danger herself, and she may know it."

After a pause he said,

"Keep an eye on her. Don't let her go out alone after dark. Don't let her go down to the splash. If she were found drowned there, it would be quite a plausible suicide. And now here's one of the facts you were talking about. The note that brought Clarice Dean to meet the person who murdered her was typed on the machine in the Church Room."

Miss Silver said,

"Dear me!" And then, "The Church Room?"

He nodded.

"In the odour of varnish and sanctity. Perhaps by one of the church helpers, or by anybody else in the parish capable of reaching the door key which hangs conveniently from a nail in the porch at about the height of the top of my ear. Everybody just helps himself and goes in and out upon his, or more probably her, parochial occasions. It might be Mrs. Pomfret, who is a well-to-do farmer's wife, or Miss Sims, or Miss Blake, or Mrs. Jonathan Random who does the flowers, or the Vicar, or the Vicaress, or any other of the adult inhabitants of Greenings. Arnold Random may have slipped across to the Church Room and done it. Edward Random could have had the same bright idea. The only certainty is that the note was typed on that machine. The 'e' is worn in exactly the same way as in the note, and the 'm' is defective—looks as if someone had taken a chip out of it—possibly one of the Sunday

School children. Well, there you are—we have achieved one fact at last, and it leaves the case as open as the sky."

Chapter 28

"I REALLY DO NOT SEE WHY I SHOULD HAVE TO ANSWER ANY more questions, Inspector Abbott."

Miss Mildred Blake sat stiffly upright on an old-fashioned chair with a long straight back and a small unyielding seat. She was engaged in darning the right elbow of a very old black cardigan already converted into a kind of patchwork by a series of previous repairs. She held her needle poised as she spoke, and looked at Frank with severity.

Miss Ora was regarding him in quite a different manner. Personable young men were an agreeable change. There had been a time when she had attracted them, and though of course it would have been very inconvenient to have to keep house and look after children, she did sometimes regret that she had never been able to make up her mind between Cyril Jones and George Norton. She had liked Cyril the best, but he had got tired of waiting and married a horrid dark girl who played badminton. She frowned at the recollection, but she smiled upon Frank Abbott.

"It must be very tiresome for you having to go round asking a lot of questions which people don't want to answer."

Miss Mildred stabbed her darn with an angry needle.

"*Really*, Ora—I haven't the slightest objection to answering any necessary question. But since Inspector Bury has already been here twice, once by himself, and once with this other Inspector, I fail to see——"

Frank's cool gaze rested upon her. Now why all this

heat? If she could have run the needle into him, it would have given her a good deal of pleasure. He said,

"I won't keep you any longer than I can help. There is just a small matter which I hope you may be able to clear up."

"I have already told you that I know very little about Miss Dean."

"I realize that. But this has nothing to do with her. Mrs. Ball tells me that you were at a sewing-party in the Vicarage on Friday week."

"Certainly. I am most regular in my attendance."

"Mrs. Ball says that the party broke up soon after ten o'clock, but that you had left rather earlier as you wanted to have a word with Mr. Arnold Random, who was in the church playing the organ."

"Yes. He always practises on Friday evenings."

"You went over to the church to speak to him. I suppose you took the direct path from the Vicarage?"

"Of course."

"When you reached the church, was he still playing?"

"No. He was beginning to put the music away."

"He was alone?"

"Naturally. The organ has been supplied with electricity from the Hall—there is no need for a blower now. It used to be most inconvenient. Fanny Stubbs was the last one we had, and she was most unreliable."

"I see. Then you are quite sure that Mr. Random was alone in the church?"

She gave him her hard black stare.

"Of course I am sure!"

"How long did you stay, Miss Blake?"

"A few minutes. Mr. Random was putting things away. Then he locked up and we went home."

"Together?"

"As far as this house—yes."

"Did you fall in with any of the ladies who were coming away from the work-party?"

"No—it was too early."

He said, "Past ten o'clock?"

She had a grim smile for that.

"You have never watched a church work-party break up. Mrs. Ball provides tea and cake, and there is a lot of chatter. As far as I am concerned, I pack up my work and·go, but she is lucky if she gets rid of most of them by a quarter-past ten, and I have seen Miss Sims come home after the half-hour. The smaller the village, the more there is to say, you know."

Miss Ora fingered the pink edge of her shawl.

"Very interesting things can happen in a village," she said. "And you get to know about them, which of course is what makes them so interesting. Now, in a big town you can live next door·to someone and never know a thing about them. I remember poor Papa used to say that if you could take the roof off every house in Embank, a lot of people would have to leave the place and change their names. You know, Inspector, even when someone is living in the same house like Clarice Dean you don't really know what is going on—do you? Why, we didn't even know she was out of the house the night she was drowned—but girls always do slip out. It wasn't the first time, I suppose, and of course she didn't know it was going to be the last."

"You think she had been slipping out at night?"

Miss Ora's blue eyes widened.

"Oh, I expect so. She was crazy about Edward Random, you know."

Miss Mildred said, "*Ora——*" in a repressive tone. A frown drew her brows together until they made a straight black line above the jutting nose. She looked Frank Abbott in the face and said,

"Since you insist on asking all these questions, you may as well have the truth. What my sister says is true—Miss Dean was making a dead set at Edward Random. I do not pretend to know when the affair began, or how far it had gone, but I believe he was already sick of it, and it would have been better if she had been warned in time. But that sort of girl never is, and they haven't the sense to see that it really isn't safe to go on. I have known Edward Random since he was a child. His temper has always been a difficult one, and since his mysterious and unexplained absence, which I suppose you have heard about, he has really been what I can only call morose. In fact the last man to play tricks with. But her pursuit of him was shameless. And now, Inspector Abbott, I must really ask you to go."

Frank went.

As soon as he had left the house Miss Mildred rang up Mr. Arnold Random. To his rather weary "Hullo?" she responded briskly.

"It is I, Arnold. The Inspector from Scotland Yard has just been here to ask about my coming over to speak to you in the church on Friday week. He wanted to know whether you were alone there. Such an extraordinary idea! I can't think what can have put it into his head. Of course I told him just what happened—that you had finished playing and were putting away the music—that we talked for a minute or two and then locked up and came away together. You remember the work-party at the Vicarage had not broken up, so we did not see anyone as we came along the street. You are, of course, in a position to confirm all this. Really, police officers are most intrusive, but I suppose they have their duty to do, and of course we all wish the whole matter to be satisfactorily cleared up."

At the other end of the line Arnold Random stared blankly at the opposite wall and said,

"Of course."

Chapter 29

MRS. BALL AND MISS SILVER TOOK TEA WITH THE MISS BLAKES, following a most pressing invitation from Miss Ora.

"I hope you don't mind," Ruth said in an apologetic voice, "but she rings up and makes it practically impossible to say no. If we hadn't been able to go to-day, it would have been the next day, or the next, or the next, so I thought it would be better to get it over. Once she knows anyone has a visitor she can't rest until she has had them to tea—and she really does have a very dull life, poor thing."

Miss Silver said she would be delighted to have tea with the Miss Blakes.

"An invalid is deprived of so much."

They found Miss Ora in her best shawl—quite a new one of a delicate shade of pink, the price of which had filled Miss Mildred with gloom. Her hair was disposed in very becoming curls, and she was wearing her mother's rings, a diamond half-hoop and a diamond and sapphire cluster on one hand, and a pearl and turquoise on the other. She received her guests with smiling amiability.

"My sister will not be long. She is just making the tea. Mrs. Deacon goes away after lunch, you know, and my health quite prevents me doing anything. I am really helpless without a nurse. Miss Dean's death has been a sad deprivation. Such a shocking affair! You will have heard of it of course from Mrs. Ball. Even the Vicar, who is so strict about gossip, would hardly expect her not to talk about a murder which took place, as you may say, at his own doorstep."

Miss Silver agreed that it was all very shocking, adding that they must hope that it would prove to be an accident.

It needed no more than this to set Miss Ora off. Edward

Random and his strange disappearance—"For disappear he did, and everyone thought he was dead. And no explanation—not even to his stepmother or his uncle, for I asked Emmeline Random myself, and all she did was to look vague—really sometimes one would think she wasn't quite all there—and to say she wouldn't dream of asking. A girl is very foolish to embark on a flirtation with a young man who has a background like that. I am sure you will agree? And his temper—simply shocking! You know, I called to him out of this window on the very first day he was back. There he was, striding down the street as if the whole place belonged to him and looking—well, arrogant is the only word I can find to describe it. And when I called out to him and said how glad he must be to be back, and when was he going to come up to see me and tell us all about where he had been and what he had been doing, what do you think he said?"

"Young men can be very impatient," said Miss Silver.

Miss Ora fluttered the white curls with a very decided toss of the head.

"Impatient? He looked as if he would like to murder me! And he said, 'I'm afraid you wouldn't be interested'—just like that, and he walked on. I could believe anything of him after that!"

Ruth Ball felt her colour rising. John would certainly disapprove of this conversation, and Miss Silver was encouraging it—it was no good pretending that she wasn't. And how was it to be checked? John always said, "Your presence should be enough, my dear," and in his case, of course, it was. But she wasn't nearly so good—all she could do was to be uncomfortable and feel herself getting red.

Miss Silver was not unaware of this discomfort. She regretted it. But Miss Ora must not only be allowed to talk, she must be encouraged to do so. In the ten minutes or so which went by before the arrival of the tea she heard all about Jonathan Random's debts and Emmeline's cats.

"Really quite a mania, and most insanitary! Kittens all

over the place! As my sister told Arnold Random—she has a great deal of influence with him, you know—they are friends of very long standing—in fact they might easily have been something more, only it didn't come to anything—— Dear me, where was I? . . . Oh, yes, she told him quite plainly—Mildred is always frank—that he had much better give her notice to quit and get the place cleaned up."

It was at this point that Ruth Ball found herself unable to keep silence.

"Oh, Miss Blake, he couldn't! Not his own brother's widow!"

Miss Ora turned placid blue eyes in her direction. So long as she was comfortable, what did it matter if another woman was turned out of her home? She said in her amiable-sounding voice,

"Well, I believe he has done so."

A fierce little verse from the Psalms about people who were enclosed in their own fat came up in Ruth's mind. David said it, and it was in the Bible, and whether John would approve of it being applied to one of his parishioners or not, that was how she felt about Miss Ora Blake. She gave her really quite an indignant glance. But Miss Ora slid away from it.

"It is really very good of you both to come out to tea with me. I have been an invalid for so long that I feel it is very brave of anyone to be out in the dark—and I am afraid it will be very dark indeed by the time you leave. Such a dull evening. And of course no street lighting— one of the drawbacks of living in a village."

Miss Silver smiled.

"I really do not mind the dark at all. I have an excellent torch."

Miss Ora nodded.

"We have one too, but of course I do not use it myself."

Miss Mildred came into the room as she spoke, carrying a small and rather dirty japanned tray with a teapot and hot water-jug of heavy Victorian pattern. When she had set it down and shaken hands with Mrs. Ball and Miss Silver, her sister pursued the theme.

"Miss Silver has a very good torch, Mildred. I was telling her that we have one too."

"I suppose everyone in Greenings has one," said Miss Mildred in her deep voice.

Miss Silver coughed in an interrogative manner.

"You go out a good deal in the evenings?"

The remark was addressed to Miss Mildred, but it was Miss Ora who answered it.

"Oh, no—not at all. Just church, and the Vicarage work-party on Fridays. There is really no entertaining at all since the war—people have not the staff. But Mrs. Ball's parties are so very pleasant, everyone says. I only wish I could go to them. She beamed upon Ruth. "Mildred is most regular—in fact I don't know when she missed. Except, of course, last Friday, when we all thought we would go early to bed. Miss Dean had a headache—at least she said she had, but we found out afterwards that it was just an excuse to run out and meet whoever it was that murdered her—and I suppose most of us can make a guess as to who that was!"

Miss Silver said,

"Poor thing! And you did not hear her go out?"

"Oh, no—we had no idea. Mildred had a headache too. Of course I always go to bed early myself—Dr. Croft says it is most important. So we were going to have an early night, only of course in the end we were up till all hours. Such a terrible shock, the Doctor coming round and telling us Miss Dean was dead, when we had no idea that she was even out of the house. And you know how it is, if you are waked out of your first sleep, it is most difficult to go off again."

Whilst this narrative proceeded Miss Mildred had been putting about three drops of milk into each of the cups and pouring out a faint straw-coloured brew, all in a grim silence. For which it was perhaps hard to judge her. Her manner was certainly not pleasant, but her sister must be trying to live with.

Reflecting on this, and looking at Miss Ora in her shell-tinted shawl, Ruth Ball could not help feeling irresistibly reminded of a pink blancmange—the sort you have at children's parties, all shapeless and wobbly. As for Miss Mildred, she thought that she had never seen her look more dingy. She had not troubled to change out of her shabby clerical grey, and it seemed to have entered upon a new phase of deterioration. The sagging skirt was crumpled at the hem, and either there were new stains upon it and upon the cuffs, or else the overhead light showed them up more plainly. It shone down upon the greyness of her skin, and on the hands which looked as if they had not been washed for quite a long time. She poured out the tea in a manner which did very little to suggest hospitality, and broke in upon her sister's remarks as to the courage required to go out in the dark with a sharp,

"It would be a great deal better if more people stayed at home. All these girls slipping out to go walking in dark lanes with their young men—well, it isn't surprising if they get into trouble. And if one of them gets herself murdered, it's no more than is to be expected."

Miss Silver gazed at her innocently.

"You mean that poor Miss Dean. Do. you think that she was meeting someone?"

Miss Mildred thrust a plate of bread and butter at her and said in her harshest voice,

"I think she was meeting Edward Random. She had been running after him ever since she came here. Nobody could help noticing it."

Miss Ora heaved a sigh.

"Of course we don't know that he murdered her."

Mildred Blake turned a frowning gaze.

"I didn't say that he had, Ora. Perhaps we had better talk about something else. Will you have some bread and

butter, Mrs. Ball? I hear Annie Jackson has moved in at
the Vicarage. How do you find her? I thought she looked
very strange at the funeral."

Ruth Ball pressed her lips together and was thankful that
Miss Silver absolved her from the necessity of answering.

"A very trying experience, poor thing. She is sadly
shaken."

Miss Mildred drank from a scalding cup to which she
had added neither milk nor sugar.

"I have known her for years," she said "—all the time she
was with Lucy Wayne. I never thought it would take very
much to send her off her balance. Her father was a cow-
man on the Burlingham estate. He drank and beat his
wife. None of the children were very strong in the head.
Annie certainly couldn't have been, or she wouldn't have
married that good-for-nothing William Jackson. Lucy left
her five hundred pounds, and of course that was all he was
after."

If the tea was a meagre one—a plate of bread and butter
that was really margarine, and a plate of home-made
biscuits, with a slab of fruit cake which Miss Mildred made
no attempt to cut; if the milk ran short and there were only
half a dozen lumps of sugar in the Victorian basin which
could easily have accommodated a pound—there was at
least no stint about the gossip which flowed in rich
profusion.

As they walked home, Ruth Ball said with vexation in
her voice,

"Every time I go there I make up my mind never to do
it again. But what is one to do? It's go, or start a quarrel
—and you simply can't do that in a village."

Chapter 30

ARNOLD RANDOM WALKED DOWN TO THE SOUTH LODGE THAT
afternoon. The burden upon him was now so great that he
no longer noticed the untidiness of Emmeline's garden.
Even the fact that three of Scheherazade's kittens were
playing at being tigers in the jungle, and that Lucifer
actually darted across his path and nearly tripped him up,
made very little impression upon the unhappiness of his
mood. What had happened had happened—you could
never go back. But he need not turn Emmeline out. Sitting in the least uncomfortable of her chairs, he told her
so, his manner very stiff, his face lined and grey.

"I came to say that I—in fact my plans have undergone
an alteration."

Emmeline gazed at him. It was impossible for her to
look unkindly at anyone, and she felt a real concern.

"Yes, Arnold?"

"I hope I did not cause you any distress. My plans are
changed. I felt that I should set your mind at rest. About
the house."

The tears came into her eyes.

"Dear Arnold—how kind——"

He stared past her at his brother's portrait on the wall.
How comfortable to be dead and buried, with your virtues
proclaimed upon the headstone of a nicely tended grave and
all your faults forgotten. Jonathan had had faults enough,
but he had been loved, and Emmeline always spoke of him
as if he were a saint. His thoughts pressed as heavily upon
him as if they had indeed been churchyard clay. He said,

"I wanted to set your mind at rest. I was afraid you
might have been upset."

"But I never thought you really meant it. I thought it

was just the cats—and Edward. Susan says I must find homes for Amina's kittens. And please don't go on minding about Edward. It is such a pity to have quarrels in a family, instead of all being happy together."

He got up with a jerk and reached for his hat. One of his gloves fell and he bent to pick it up again, his sight blurred by a sudden moisture. Emmeline made everything sound so easy. But it was too late—too late. He found himself saying the words aloud as he went past her and out through the porch with its shallow step. The kittens were still at their game, but he didn't see them. He said, "It's too late, my dear," and went away up the avenue to the Hall.

Edward came home early. When they had finished tea, during which he listened in silence to Emmeline's recital of his Uncle Arnold's kindness, he announced that he and Susan would wash up, and carried out the tray.

The sink was in the kitchen. When he had set the tray down upon the draining-board he shut the door, leaned against it, and said,

"If they don't arrest me to-night, they will to-morrow. I thought you had better know."

Susan stood in a white mist that smelled of fish and said to herself, "This is the sort of thing that can't possibly be true—it just can't."

The smell of fish was because of the cats, who had cods' heads and other horrible remnants boiled down for them. The kitchen was always full of it, but it had never been full of tragedy before. The two things made a horrid clash in her mind, like a collision in a nightmare. She did not know that all her rosy colour had drained away, but she heard herself say, "No——" in what she thought was a whisper.

The next thing she knew was that Edward had both his hands on her shoulders and was shaking her.

"Hold up, can't you! Good God, Susan, you can't faint here!"

She stared at him and said,

"I can if I want to."

"Then come off wanting to! Here, put your head down! I've got to talk to you!"

He sounded so angry, and was so entirely Edward in a temper, that the nightmare feeling receded. She said,

"I'm sorry. It—it was the fish. I'm all right now. Let's go into the back room and talk there."

"No—we're going to wash up. You can dry. You don't expect me to believe you are such a ninny as to faint because there's a smell of fish."

Susan took a tea-cloth and leaned against the drip-board.

"It just didn't mix—with what you said."

He gave a sudden short laugh.

"About my being arrested? No, I suppose it didn't. Anyhow I think we had better talk about it. I don't want Emmeline to get any more hurt than she must."

She said in rather a surprised voice,

"Emmeline doesn't get hurt. She gets away from things."

"Yes, I know. But this——"

"She will be quite sure you are all right, because she will be quite sure you haven't done anything to be arrested for."

He handed her a hot, dripping plate.

"And you?"

She hadn't got anything to say. If Edward was arrested, she couldn't get away from it. It would hurt too much. All she could manage was,

"I'm not like Emmeline."

He gave her two more plates and a saucer.

"Don't let them get cold, or they'll dry with smears on them. Do you mind telling me why you are not like Emmeline? Do you really think I knocked two people on the head and drowned them in the splash?"

"No, of course I don't. Why should the police—why should anyone?"

He was swishing out the teapot.

"Because someone wrote Clarice just the sort of note I might have written her. It was dropped in at the Miss Blakes' letter-box some time before two o'clock on Friday. I walked past at two, and I could have dropped it in. It was typed, and it said, 'All right, let's have it out. I'll be coming back late to-night. Meet me at the same place. Say half-past nine. I can't make it before that.'"

"You didn't write it!"

"No, but I might have done. Don't you see, she was bothering my head off to go into a huddle and talk about Uncle James' will. I hadn't the slightest intention of doing it, but suppose she had worn me down to the point where I felt it would be better to see her and get it over, that is exactly the kind of letter I might have written."

"When did you see the police?"

"They came out to old Barr's this afternoon—the Embank man and a chap called Abbott from Scotland Yard. One of the cool, polished Police College kind—very much on the spot. He had found out that the note was typed on that old machine up at the Church Room which used to belong to Uncle James. Of course I knew that as soon as Bury showed it to me. Why, I learned to type on it—but I didn't tell them that."

"But anyone, absolutely anyone, could get in and use that typewriter."

"As you say—and me amongst them. Very especially and particularly me. You see, I was there on Friday morning."

"Oh——"

He nodded.

"Emmeline went up to do the flowers, and I went with her. Miss Sims was there. Perhaps she had just been typing the note. After she went away I looked up a point about the Old Close at Littleton. Barr and I were having an argument, and I knew there was something about it in your grandfather's history of the county. It's still there, at the end of the bottom shelf, just as it used to be when we went to Sunday School. By the time I'd finished with it the Vicar dropped in. He didn't stay, but he'll remember that he saw me there. It wouldn't have taken me more than three minutes to type that note, and I could have done it either before he came or after he went. Emmeline was over at the church, and Miss Sims had departed. I went on dipping into your grandfather's book, but I could just as easily have been typing that note. I went away in the end because Miss Mildred came along to collect some of the hymn books that wanted mending. And I could very easily have dropped the note in her letter-box on the way back, or after lunch on my way to Mr. Barr's."

Susan bit her lip.

"How was it signed—or wasn't it?"

"Two typed initials. And here's something that's odd— the note has been creased right across them and partly torn. It was found crumpled up and dirty with soot under the grate in Clarice's room. The letters might be an E or an R, but nobody is very dogmatic about it. You know, I can't see why Clarice should have thrown the note away under the grate. It seems to me she would either have destroyed it or taken it with her."

Susan said,

"I don't know—people do all sorts of things. She was the careless sort, and she wouldn't know that someone was going to—murder her."

"No—she wouldn't know." His tone was dark. "If she thought the note was from me—well, I simply hadn't got a motive. You don't kill a girl because she bothers you." He gave a mirthless laugh. "Do you remember, when we were coming home on Thursday night after the scene outside Mrs. Stone's, I said I should probably murder her some day. We were just coming through the gate. I hope nobody heard me."

Susan hoped not too. It wasn't only the words, it was the way he had said it, with a kind of savage exasperation.

She had finished drying the tea things now. She turned and hung up the damp cloth, and was glad that Edward could not see her face when he said,

"Even without that, I think they are pretty well bound to arrest me. It's only the lack of motive that sticks in their throats—in her case, and in the other. Nobody has even begun to suggest a motive for my bumping Willy Jackson off. Everything else is just too easy—opportunities of typing the note and dropping it in—a nice story from Mrs. Stone who heard me giving Clarice the rough side of my tongue and heard her say I frightened her—and a piece from our Miss Sims, who listened in on Thursday night when Clarice rang up and said she had simply got to see me. She reports that I 'spoke very harsh'. I know I meant to."

Susan said without turning round,

"They don't know that you were up at the Church Room on Friday morning."

"Oh, I gave them that one. I thought it would look better if it came from me. No, the really damning part is that the note made an appointment for half-past nine, and that I left old Barr's at a quarter-past but I didn't report finding the body until it was striking ten. They naturally want to know why it took me three-quarters of an hour to get as far as the splash."

She turned round then and leaned back, gripping the edge of the draining-board.

"Why did it?"

He laughed.

"One of those things which are so simple that no one believes them. I like the woods at night—I always have. There was a moon, rather fitful between the clouds, and there was a fox—quite a young one—he was amusing to watch. But you can't expect the police to lap up that sort of thing. Or a jury. More especially if it's a jury of townsmen. Can't you hear counsel for the prosecution? 'Gentlemen, you are asked to believe that the prisoner spent this time, during which the unfortunate Clarice Dean was murdered, in the woods watching a fox!'"

She said,

"Edward, *please*—I can't bear it!"

He had his darkest look.

"You can bear a lot more than you think you can."

He went over to the door again and stood with his back against it.

"I haven't told them yet where I was for the four and a half years I was away, but I shall have to now. They'll find out, so I had better make a virtue of necessity. I don't suppose it's going to do me any good."

"Are you going to tell me?"

"Oh, yes. I was in prison."

She heard herself say "Nonsense!" and was glad that her voice sounded quite firm.

"Well, it was a labour camp. I went into Russia to look for a friend who had gone there to look for his wife—after my historic row with Uncle James. It seemed quite a reasonable thing to do at the time. The girl was Russian, and they wouldn't let her out, so Mark went in to get her."

"He must have cared for her—very much."

He laughed.

"Sentimental, aren't you!"

A hot anger came up in her. She stamped her foot on the hard stone floor.

"I'm not! People do care like that—sometimes."

"And it's love, it's love, it's love that makes the world go round! As a matter of hard fact, Mark didn't get on with his wife, but she *was* his wife, and he was hanged if he was going to have her dictated to by a bunch of Bolsheviks. Well, he wasn't hanged, he was shot. After four years in a labour camp."

"How do you know?"

"I told you. I was there. We escaped together. He was shot. It took me four months to get out of Russia. It was like some filthy nightmare, and I didn't want to talk about it. Now I shall have to."

"You can't just keep everything bottled up—it does things to you."

He put out a hand.

"Come here, Susan."

"Why?"

"I'll tell you. Just come."

She came over to him. He linked his hands lightly behind her shoulders.

"You're a nice child."

"I'm not a child!"

"'A nice woman' sounds a bit stodgy, don't you think? Shall we just say you are nice and leave it at that?"

Her eyes were on his face. What they saw there hurt. She said quite gravely,

"'Nice' is a bit stodgy too. It sounds like bread and butter."

"Well, there isn't anything wrong about bread and butter. A very clean, pleasant, wholesome, and nourishing comestible."

Her colour rose brightly.

"And I suppose you think anyone is going to like being called wholesome and nourishing!"

"There are worse things. What are your views about kissing? Any conscientious objections?"

"Not when people are fond of each other."

"Am I fond of you?"

For a moment her heart had beat so hard that she was afraid he would feel it. She went on looking at him because she wouldn't let him see her look away, and said,

"I think so——"

He nodded.

"Nice to have about the place. I expect quite a lot of people have told you that. Well, what about you? Are you fond of me?"

It was unutterably soft and silly, but the tears came into her eyes with a rush. She lifted her face to him and he kissed her. He had been holding her lightly, but with that first kiss everything was changed. She was caught against him roughly, her heart thudding—or was it his heart that beat so hard against her breast? And his kisses were rough too—vehement and snatched at, as if there was only this one short time for them. The extraordinary thing was that they did not frighten her. Her arms went round his neck and held him close. It was as if they stood in a storm together, but that somewhere in the centre of it there was security. Only she must not let him go. She must never let him go.

In the end it was he who put her away as suddenly as he had caught at her.

"Stupid business," he said. "I hadn't any right to do that. I now beg your pardon, and we forget it ever happened."

She thought the first words shook, but it might only have been that she was shaking so terribly herself. His voice was hard and steady enough at the end. But this couldn't be the end—not after they had been so close. She tried desperately hard to pull herself together. This was the sort of situation where you must, you simply *must*, pull something out of the wreck—courage—dignity—self-control. And all at once she didn't have to try. She saw the bleak pain in his eyes and forgot all about Susan Wayne.

"Yes, we're stupid," she said, and her voice sounded all right. "You frightened us both. I don't believe they are going to arrest you. You didn't murder those people, and somebody else did. What is the good of the police if they can't find out who it was?"

"Rhetorical question? Or am I supposed to provide an answer?"

She said,

"I hope *they* will."

"Pious child! Let us go on hoping—it will help to pass

the time. And now we had better put these tea things away and go back to Emmeline, or she'll think there is something up."

Chapter 31

SUSAN DID NOT GO BACK INTO THE SITTING-ROOM. SHE SLIPPED on a coat and went out. At first there was just the need to get away, to be out in the dark, and to be alone. If she went to her room she would be almost certain to cry until her face was a mess, and then Edward would know. And it was beyond her to go in and sit there with him and with Emmeline and wonder how soon the police would come.

She turned out of the drive and stood there, undecided whether to go to the right or to the left. After a moment she turned in the direction of the village. She wanted to be alone, but not too much alone. This way there would be a glow behind a curtain, the sound of a wireless programme, the opening and closing of a door, the passing of someone who might be anyone, in the dark.

She tried to think steadily of what had happened between her and Edward. He wasn't in love with her—why should he be? He was fond of her in the same sort of way that you are fond of your relations, or even of a dog, or of a cat. He found her pleasant, and he liked having her about. And he was all starved inside. Loneliness and unhappiness, and all the things that had come and gone in those last years. He had just grabbed at her the way people do grab when they are starving. It wasn't anything more than that, and as far as she was concerned, better face it and have done. If there was anything that was the slightest use or help to him—well, all she wanted was to let him have it. She wouldn't have come to Greenings if she had not thought that she had got over loving him, but she had only to see him again, and there it was, just as bad as ever. If everything had been going all right for him, she might just have had enough decency to keep it down. But what can you do when you see someone starving? You don't say, "I don't care if you do", and go decently and self-respectingly by on the other side—not if you care so much that the thing which is hurting them is like a twisting knife in your own heart. This horrid simile, which presented itself a good deal too vividly for comfort, caused Susan to rebuke herself for indulging in melodrama. She had always been considered sensible, and she wasn't behaving sensibly.

She had by this time arrived at Mrs. Alexander's shop. It was still open. Mrs. Alexander kept easy hours and liked to chat with people whose work was done for the day. Seeing the lighted window, Susan had the prosaic thought that it was touch and go if there would be enough marmalade for breakfast. Emmeline would certainly be grateful if she brought a pot back with her. She lifted the latch and walked in.

The shop was empty except for Mrs. Alexander herself, who beamed on her and stretched out the buying of the marmalade to a good ten minutes.

"And how do you like sorting all those old books, Miss Susan? Doris was in last night, and she says no one wouldn't believe what the dust is like. No one being allowed to touch the shelves except just with a feather brush, not even at spring-cleaning, when we all know what bookshelves want is everything taken out and the books clapped and dusted thorough. With a nice bit of beeswax and turpentine on the shelves before they go back. Not that anyone makes the real old beeswax and turps like my mother and my old Granny before her. It's all Mansion and suchlike nowadays, and not for me to grumble about it, because that's what I'm here to sell, and very good polish too. But it's messy work for you, cleaning up after nobody's done it all these years."

Susan said,

"Oh, I don't mind. And it's interesting too. You never know what you're going to find. Some of those old books are valuable, you know."

Mrs. Alexander looked surprised.

"You don't say! Sounded more like mucky old rubbish, from what Doris had to say, and most of them never taken off their shelves from one year's end to another."

As Susan turned to go, Mrs. Alexander said,

"You wouldn't be dropping in at the Vicarage by any chance, would you now?"

"Well, I could quite easily. What was it?"

Mrs. Alexander pulled out a drawer and took out an envelope.

"That little lady that's staying with Mrs. Ball, she dropped this when she was in this morning. Must have come out of her bag when she was getting out her handkerchief. And I don't like having other folk's letters lying about—it might be private—especially when it's a lady that's visiting at the Vicarage. Very pleasant she was, and told me she and Mrs. Ball's mother was old friends and at school together. Well, my dear, if you really don't mind. I was going to take it up myself when I'd shut the shop, but I've been on my feet all day."

The envelope had been through the post, and had been opened. It was obvious that it contained a letter. As Susan took it, her eye was caught by the address,

Miss Maud Silver,
15 Montague Mansions.

And then the London address crossed out and,

The Vicarage,
Greenings,
near Embank,

in a clear sensible writing.

A little shutter clicked open in her mind. She stared rather hard at the envelope before she slipped it into the pocket of her coat with the jar of marmalade.

Out in the dark street again, she walked slowly in the direction of the Vicarage. Miss Maud Silver—it was the Maud which had caught her attention. And the address, 15 Montague Mansions. Ray Fortescue telling her about the Ivory Dagger and—Miss Maud Silver. "I just can't tell you how wonderful she was. I don't see how anyone could have thought Bill didn't do it—I mean people who didn't know him, like the police. But she didn't." It had been a very exciting story, and the newspapers were full of it. But not of Miss Maud Silver. She mightn't have been there at all for all the notice she got. "She just goes back to her 15 Montague Mansions and keeps on knitting until another case turns up."

Susan couldn't think why she hadn't tumbled to it before. Of course Silver was quite a common name. Anyhow it wasn't until she saw the whole name and address on the envelope in Mrs. Alexander's hand that she thought of any possible link between Mrs. Ball's old family friend who looked so exactly like someone out of the Victorian novels she had been sorting and Ray Fortescue's marvellous detective. A faint but eager hope sprang up in her mind.

Chapter 32

"I DON'T KNOW HOW I DIDN'T THINK OF IT BEFORE, BUT I JUST didn't. Ray and I were at school together—she told me all about you. I was one of her bridesmaids, and I saw her just before I came down here."

Miss Silver beamed.

"They most kindly asked me to the wedding, but I was away on a case."

"Ray said there might never have been a wedding if it hadn't been for you. She and Bill are so happy."

Ruth Ball had left them together in the small comfortable morning-room. Miss Silver sat in the corner of the sofa and knitted. An infant's vest in a delicate shade of pink depended from the needles. She wore a dress of olive-green cashmere, with a high boned collar and modesty vest of cream-coloured net. An ancestral brooch of bog-oak in the form of a rose with an Irish pearl at its heart reposed upon her bosom. Her very neat ankles and feet were encased in black woollen stockings and slippers of glacé kid with beaded toes. Nobody could have looked less like a detective.

Susan said abruptly,

"Edward says the police are going to arrest him."

Miss Silver's eyes dwelt on her compassionately.

"Indeed? What makes you think so?"

Susan told her.

"You see, he says himself that the truth sounds silly. But it *is* the truth—it really is. He says they won't believe he put in all that time in the woods watching a fox. But it is just exactly the sort of thing he would do. It's the sort of thing we used to do together. I've known him all my life, you see. He's got a quick temper, and when he is angry he frowns and looks like thunder and his voice goes rough. But it doesn't mean anything—it doesn't really. He couldn't possibly plot against anyone or plan to kill them—he really, really couldn't. Besides, he hadn't got any reason to kill Clarice Dean. She was making a nuisance of herself running after him and trying to flirt, and wanting to talk to him about his uncle's will—and that's a thing Edward just won't talk about. You know, it must have been pretty horrid to come back and find that everything had gone. He cared a lot for his uncle, and the Hall had always been his home. He must have felt as if there was nothing left. Arnold Random wouldn't do anything about it, you know. Edward won't talk about any of it, not even to Emmeline. So you can imagine what he felt about Clarice trying to butt in. And she just hadn't got any tact at all. She went on pushing and hinting and ringing him up until it wasn't any wonder he was angry. But you don't kill people for that sort of thing."

Miss Silver neither agreed nor disagreed. She knew with what fatal suddenness a long strained self-control may break. She had traced the small beginnings of many a tragedy in human affairs. She turned her knitting and enquired,

"It did not occur to him that she might really know something about Mr. James Random's will?"

Susan looked surprised. She had thrown back her coat. The light shone down upon her bright hair and the smoky blue of the jumper and skirt which she wore. She said,

"But there isn't anything to know. How could there be? The will was proved months ago. Arnold came in for everything. James Random thought—everybody thought —that Edward was dead."

Miss Silver coughed gently.

"Suppose Mr. James Random had not believed his nephew to be dead?"

Susan stared.

"He wouldn't have cut him out of his will."

"If he had become convinced that he had made a mistake in supposing his nephew to be dead, what would you have expected him to do?"

"To make another will."

"If he had done so, who would be the most likely person to be aware of it?"

"Miss Silver, you don't mean——"

Miss Silver's needles clicked, the pale pink vest revolved.

"A nurse occupies a very privileged position. She can hardly fail to be aware of anything which affects her patient. I think it is a pity that Mr. Edward Random

should have so persistently refused to see Miss Dean and
hear what she had to say. If he had not done so, she might
have been alive to-day. I will not say any more than that.
If you have any influence with Mr. Edward, urge him to
be perfectly frank with the police. It is only a guilty person
who can afford to be silent. The investigation of a murder
is always handicapped by the fact that so many people
have something which they would prefer to hide."

Susan was only half listening. Her mind and all her
energies were set upon the idea which had come to her as
she walked towards the Vicarage. She leaned forward now,
her cheeks pale, her eyes very bright.

"Miss Silver—if you would help him—if you only
would——"

"My dear——"

"You do take cases, don't you? You took the Ivory
Dagger case. Ray told me about it."

"My services were retained by Lady Dryden. Her niece
was engaged to Sir Herbert Whitall who had been murdered. But I do not come into any case to procure a result
which will be agreeable to the person who employs me. I
can have but one object—the discovery of the truth. I
cannot undertake to prove any person innocent—or guilty."

Susan looked at her very straight.

"If you can find out the truth, it will prove that Edward
is innocent."

Miss Silver returned the look with a kind one.

"He has a very good friend," she said. And then, "I
would be very much interested to see Mr. Edward
Random. There is something which I think he should
know. If he then wishes me to come into the case, I will
do so."

Susan felt a little as if a cold shower had descended upon
her. It had not occurred to her that she was assuming a
responsibility for Edward, and that she had not the least
shadow of a right to do so. She wasn't his sister, or his
cousin, or his fiancée, or anything at all but Susan Wayne

who used to know him when she was a schoolgirl, and who happened just now to be staying with his stepmother. It came home to her with horrid force that Edward would think she was interfering in his affairs. Like Clarice—— A flood of burning colour rose to the roots of her fair hair. She caught her breath and said,

"I don't know. He might think—he won't talk about things—ever—I haven't got any right——"

She encountered a glance of bright intelligence.

"You have not his authority for coming to me?"

Susan shook her head.

"I never thought about it. I didn't know you were Miss Maud Silver. It was only when Mrs. Alexander asked me to bring you that letter and I saw your full name on the envelope——"

"I see. Then perhaps it would be better if I were to ring him up. I have been intending to do so, but was not sure if he would be at home. He is there now?"

"Oh, yes. But—you will remember that this is a party line, won't you? Anyone might be listening in."

Miss Silver smiled.

"I shall not forget." She laid her knitting aside and went over to Ruth Ball's writing-table. "So convenient to have an extension in here, and it saves disturbing the Vicar. Mrs. Ball has really made the house most comfortable in every way. She will not, I am sure, object to my using her telephone."

Susan sat with her hands clasped together in her lap. She had the most overpowering sense of dread. Suppose Edward had gone out. Suppose the police had already come and arrested him. Suppose he was so frightfully angry that he never spoke to her again. . . . Her feet got colder and colder. Just when she couldn't have borne it another moment she heard Miss Silver say,

"Is that Mr. Edward Random?"

There was a pause while a disembodied voice sounded on the line. Susan could not hear what it said. It gave her a giddy feeling. Edward's voice scratching and scrabbling to get in, and she couldn't hear what he said. . . . She came back to Miss Silver saying,

"I wonder whether you could come up to the Vicarage for a little. I have something to tell you which I think you might consider to be of interest. Miss Susan Wayne is here."

The voice said, "Has anything happened?" with so much vigour that the words reached Susan. Edward was certainly angry. She wondered if it was possibly because he thought that something might have happened to her. She heard Miss Silver make some suitable reply. Then the receiver was put back and the knitting resumed. Over the clicking needles Miss Silver said,

"He will come."

Chapter 33

EDWARD WAS CERTAINLY ANGRY. HIS DARK LOOK PASSED SUSAN by as if she no longer existed. Miss Silver encountered it with a faint smile and the reflection that men really had very little sense. If you are in danger of being arrested for a murder, it is extremely unwise to go about looking as if nothing would give you greater pleasure than to commit another at any moment. She said in a kind, grave voice,

"Won't you sit down? I need not detain you for more than a very short time. I happen to have some information which I think you should possess. It will be more comfortable if you will take a seat."

He did so with reluctance. There was a feeling of being shut in—an echo from his interview with the police. Other echoes, not faint but harsh and bitterly insistent.

He said abruptly, "I don't know——" and found himself quite gently but firmly interrupted.

"That, Mr. Random, is the trouble. There were things you should have known before, and which you should certainly know now. Miss Wayne can leave us if you would prefer it."

"Thank you—it doesn't matter."

Susan didn't matter. It made no difference to Edward whether she came or went. She was outside the place which he kept bolted and barred. It doesn't matter who goes by on the outside of your house. If she had had a scrap of proper pride she would have got up and walked out of the room and slammed the door. She was too cold to move—in front of Ruth Ball's comfortable, rosy fire she was too cold. And she had lost all interest in her pride.

Miss Silver was saying,

"I do not know if you are aware of my profession. I am a private enquiry agent. . . . No, Mr. Random, I am not here in my professional capacity, nor have I willingly intruded into your affairs. It just happened that Miss Dean knew of my occupation, and that she made me a very curious confidence."

"When?" The word shot out like a stone from a catapult.

"In town. Two days before her death. I should like to tell you what she said to me."

He listened with a set face whilst she told him of her interview with Clarice Dean. When she had finished he let the silence settle. Miss Silver made no attempt to break it. She had knitted all through her recital, and she continued to do so now.

When he spoke, it was to say sharply and suddenly,

"Do the police know about this?"

She inclined her head.

"Inspector Abbott is a very old friend. After seeing Miss Dean's death in the papers I had some conversation with him on the subject. Neither he nor I was then aware that

Scotland Yard would be called in. I merely felt that I could not keep the matter entirely to myself."

His eyes met hers with a look of singular directness.

"Of course this is why they have not arrested me—yet. They have quite a case, as Abbott has probably told you— I could see that. What I couldn't make out was why they didn't get on with it. They think I wrote the note which brought Clarice down to the splash. It was typed on the old machine up at the Church Room. I was up there on the Friday morning, and it was just the kind of note I might have written. I left Mr. Barr's house at a quarter-past nine that evening, and I didn't turn up at the Vicarage to say I had found Clarice drowned in the splash until ten o'clock, which leaves half an hour to be accounted for."

"And how do you account for it, Mr. Random?"

He gave quite a natural short laugh.

"Oh, I was watching a fox up in the woods. As one couldn't possibly expect a policeman to believe that, I could not imagine why they did not arrest me. But of course this story of yours would stick in their throats. If that is what Clarice was going to say to me, I was the last person on earth to want her dead. The motive must have been a bit dicky anyway, but on the top of this story it would be sheer, stark lunacy."

Susan listened in an amazement that was to deepen. The black look of anger was quite gone. He was talking with the quick zest which she had remembered and missed. The armour-plating which had warded off any touch upon his affairs had been discarded.

Edward himself could not have explained what had caused the change. It was simple, but like many simple things it was profound. If you are cold and you come into a warm room, you are presently not cold any more. You cannot say just how, or why, or even when the warmth invades you. He was not at all aware that he was sharing the experience of many other people whose troubles, difficulties, and danger had brought them into contact with

Miss Maud Silver. As she sat there knitting she diffused a quiet atmosphere of security and order. For a parallel you had to go back a long way—to the nursery and the schoolroom, to the pleasant fixed routine and ordered ways of childhood. He did not think of these things consciously. They had been in his life. They had been horribly wrenched away. In Miss Silver's presence they returned. The string of his tongue was loosed. He went on speaking.

"You see, if I had sent that note, it would have been because I really did think that it would be better to see Clarice and find out what she wanted to say. She kept on hinting things about my uncle, and I thought she just wanted to paw the whole thing over. Everyone seems to want to do that, and I wasn't going to have it. My uncle had a right to do what he liked with his property, and he thought I was dead. Arnold had a right to keep what was legally his. It wasn't anyone's business but mine. And I wasn't going to talk about it—why should I? But if I had got to the point where I thought it would be better to hear what Clarice had to say and be done with it, and had written her that note and met her at the watersplash, don't you see, the first thing she would do would be to come out with this yarn about my uncle making a second will. After that I don't see how anyone is going to believe I could possibly want to kill her."

Miss Silver inclined her head.

"That is a very lucid statement. The points you have mentioned will certainly have occurred to the police."

He had been leaning towards her. Now he straightened up.

"Did you think she was telling the truth about my uncle having that dream and changing his will?"

"Certainly I did. She had no possible motive for lying to me. She was under the impression that she had disguised the names, and she could have had no idea that I was in a position to identify them. She spoke to me because she was aware that she was playing a dangerous game.

William Jackson's death had frightened her. She was the only person left who knew that there had been a second will. She could have put herself in a position of safety by taking her evidence to your uncle's solicitor, but she wanted to make sure of securing some advantage for herself. She wished, in fact, to drive a bargain with you. I warned her very seriously that the kind of blackmail she was contemplating was not only criminal but dangerous. Unfortunately she did not take my warning."

He leaned towards her again.

"You don't think I killed her!"

Her ball of pale pink wool had rolled a little way upon the sofa. She reached for it and dropped it into her knitting-bag before she answered him.

"No, Mr. Edward—I have never thought so."

"Then who did?"

She replied with another question.

"Who would benefit by the death of a surviving witness to the missing will, and of the only other person who knew that this will had ever existed?"

An extraordinary look passed over his face. Anger, surprise, incredulity, sardonic amusement—there was a fleeting impression of all these things, culminating in a laugh.

"Arnold? Not on your life! He's a stuffed shirt—all window-dressing and nothing behind it. He's a dull, pompous version of all the family portraits—a kind of composite Random type minus the good points—and the bad. He's a set of features—and a tedious, intolerable bore. But he wouldn't do murder—it would be against the rules. He's not one of your bold independent thinkers, you know. He has his small inherited code, and I assure you he would rather die than depart from it. I don't like him—I never have. You have probably gathered as much. But he wouldn't murder anyone. And I don't think he would destroy a will. No, I really don't think so. His code wouldn't allow it."

She was watching him closely.

"You interest me very much."

He went on as if she had not spoken.

"No, I don't believe it would. Let's do a bit of supposing. Uncle James makes that will, and dies—did you say a week later?"

"Yes."

"He probably wouldn't say anything about the will to Arnold. That dream of his—he wouldn't want to talk about it. He believed in it, and he wouldn't want to have anyone bothering him and telling him it was all nonsense. No, I'm sure he wouldn't tell Arnold. Probably left a letter for him with the will. Well, Arnold finds the will, with or without a letter explaining that Uncle James has had a dream and thinks I am still alive. It would be a nasty shock, you know. Consider the legal position. Officially, I'm not dead, I'm just missing. They would have to wait —how long is it—five years—seven?—and then go to the Courts for leave to presume my death. I can't think of anything that would irritate Arnold more. He has one of those inveterately tidy minds. Imagine having to make up that sort of mind to years of delay, with all sorts of untidy ends lying about. And I was dead—quite certainly and positively I was dead. I can imagine Arnold's code allowing him just to put that upsetting will away and say nothing about it—I can even imagine that it might enjoin this course. If by any chance I ever did turn up, there would be no harm done—the will could be made to turn up too."

Miss Silver gave her gentle cough.

"But it has not turned up, Mr. Random."

"Not yet. He wouldn't want to rush things, you know. It wouldn't look well if the will turned up too soon. No use stretching a coincidence farther than you need. And then there are these murders—a really nasty complication. No wonder Arnold goes about looking like death——" He broke off. "I suppose you think this is all nonsense?"

"On the contrary I find it extremely interesting. There

is one thing that supports your belief in Mr. Arnold
Random's innocence—at least of William Jackson's death.
As you know, the unfortunate man left the Lamb before
closing time and was seen going in the direction of the
splash, which he was obliged to cross in order to reach his
home. Mr. Arnold Random was in the church playing
the organ, and Miss Blake states that she went over from
the Vicarage work-party to speak to him at about ten
o'clock. He afterwards accompanied her as far as her
home, by which time William Jackson must certainly have
reached the splash, and may already have been struck down
there, or have slipped or been pushed into the pool which
drowned him. If Miss Mildred's statement is to be believed, it gives Mr. Arnold Random a very good alibi."

Edward laughed.

"Rather a case of any port in a storm, I should say!"
Then, with a return to his frowning look, "Do you mind
if we go back to the beginning? You sent for me partly
because of what you had to tell me about Clarice and my
uncle's will, and partly because Susan had been talking to
you. I want to know what she said."

Miss Silver said,

"Had you not better ask her?"

He nodded.

"All right, I will. We seem to have got a bit beyond
the conventions anyhow." The frown came to rest on
Susan. "Well, what about it?"

She had never felt more defenceless in her life. She had
done what he was bound to resent, and she had to give an
account of it under the eyes of a stranger. She knew how
cold and enduring his resentment could be, and she had
always known that there was no surer way to arouse it than
to interfere in his private affairs. She sat up straight and
told him just what she had done and how it had come
about—the envelope dropped in Mrs. Alexander's shop; her
offer to take it up to the Vicarage; and Ray Fortescue's
story coming back with a rush when she read Miss Maud

Silver's name and address. She kept her eyes on his face
all the time—clear, serious grey eyes, darkened by the
effort she was making.

And then before she knew quite how it happened they
were all three talking about the Ivory Dagger, with the
burden of the conversation falling more and more upon
Miss Silver.

When she had done speaking Edward said,

"I was out of the country when it happened. Susan of
course read about it in the papers as well as getting the
inside story from Ray Fortescue. Then when she saw your
name on that envelope she came up here and asked you to
come in on this case."

Miss Silver said gravely,

"I can only come into any case in order to serve the ends
of justice. I think Miss Wayne understands that."

He gave her an odd crooked smile.

"In fact if I am guilty, you will have the greatest possible
pleasure in hanging me, but if I didn't do it after all, you
won't have any objection to establishing my innocence."

She smiled.

"It would give me very great pleasure to do so."

He leaned towards her.

"Then will you be so kind as to take the case."

Chapter 34

MISS SILVER LOOKED AT HER WATCH. IT WAS A LITTLE AFTER
nine o'clock at night. She was alone in the comfortable
room. Mrs. Ball had apologized for leaving her, but she
had promised to check over the accounts of the Boys' Club
with the Vicar.

"There seems to be a tiresome discrepancy, and you know how it is—once you have made a mistake you can pass over it again and again. John is even afraid he may have taken this one on last year when we came here. The late Vicar was an old man, you know, and things were in a shocking mess. The trouble is, we are neither of us really very good at figures, and John is so conscientious."

Miss Silver did a little quiet thinking.

When she had looked at her watch she went up to her room, changed into outdoor shoes, and put on her black cloth coat and the black felt hat reserved for dark or rainy days. After which she slipped quietly out of the front door.

At first it seemed to be quite dark. She had in her hand the powerful electric torch which she invariably took with her when paying a visit to the country, but she did not want to turn it on. Standing just beyond the faint glow which came through the curtained upper half of the door, everything was plunged in featureless obscurity, but after a moment or two the shapes of trees and bushes began to emerge, and she could distinguish the path which led to the churchyard. Following it, she came through a shrubbery shadowed by overhanging trees to a gate in the churchyard wall. A few steps farther and she was clear of the trees. Before her lay the black mass of the church and the line of the yew tunnel, overhead the soft deep grey of the clouded sky, and all around her the glimmering shapes of tomb, and cross, and headstone.

She went on a little way, came to the mouth of the tunnel, and there stood. The air was mild, with very little movement. Sometimes it would be altogether still, sometimes it seemed to pass amongst all these memorials like a sigh. It made a quiet background to the thoughts which were in her mind. Two people had been murdered within a stone's throw of this place. The murderer had come upon them by one of three ways—down the yew tunnel from the church, along the road from the village, or from the other side of the splash. The murders had been separated by no more than a week. They had both taken place on a Friday. They had both taken place in the dark. These were common factors. There were others. There was the knowledge shared by William Jackson and Clarice Dean. There was the fact that both were prepared to use that knowledge to their own advantage. In each case the scene had been set for murder in the space around the watersplash, with the church standing there above it.

When a stage has been set, the people come upon it to play their parts. The two victims, William and Clarice, and two other persons were known to have trodden that stage. At the time of both murders Arnold Random had been practising in the church, and Edward Random had come home by way of the splash. Edward admitted to having met William as he came up the rise. He said that he had spoken to him briefly and wished him good-night. He said that William was fuddled, but not drunk. There could have been more than that brief interchange. Edward could have turned, followed William down to the splash, and drowned him there.

He had no motive.

No motive had appeared.

Arnold Random had an alibi. Miss Blake had been at the church. He had walked back with her. They were old friends. Ruth Ball had not been in Greenings for a year without learning that there had been a time when the village, and perhaps Miss Mildred herself, had expected that she would become Mrs. Arnold Random. This and many other useful bits of information had been passed on in the confidential atmosphere of the Vicarage morning-room. The Vicar might disapprove of gossip, but if you live in the country and do not take an interest in your neighbours you might just as well be dead. Greenings took an interest, and so did Miss Silver. She did not feel any great respect for the alibi provided by Miss Mildred Blake. Arnold Random could have come down from the church to murder the servant whom he had dismissed, and who was certainly prepared to blackmail him. Edward Random could have turned and come back by the road. And by the third way, the dark rough track on the other side of the splash, someone else could have come—someone who knew that William must come this way, if indeed he meant to came home to her at all that night. A white-faced shaking woman with a bruise on the side of her head and fearful thoughts in her mind. She could have crossed by the stones, waited in the shadows by the lych gate, and followed him down to the pool which was to drown him.

There is no reason for murder, but even a crazy brain must think that it has a reason. Jealousy and fear and resentment could have pushed Annie Jackson into the murder of her husband. They are the oldest motives in the world. But why should she kill Clarice Dean? The answer came up quite clearly in Miss Silver's mind. Clarice might have been a witness of the murder. She knew that Edward Random came home by way of the splash. She had been ringing him up at all hours. On the night before her death she had waited for him down by the splash. There might have been other times when she had done the same thing. The note which brought her to her death, whether written by Edward Random or by someone else, had certainly implied as much. And the witness to a murder stands in no safe place.

When all these things were clear in her mind Miss Silver entered the yew tunnel and began to walk slowly down the incline. She was obliged to switch on her torch. Centuries of growth had locked branch and twig and leaf in an impenetrable mass. Even at midday the place was dark, and at this hour of a November evening the gloom was absolute. If the murderer of William Jackson had come from the church, he too would have needed a light. Or would he? She thought even the most accustomed feet might stumble on this winding path. And murder must go silently.

Her mind was now occupied with the question as to the

actual means by which William and Clarice had been killed. In Clarice's case the back of the head had been bruised. In the case of William Jackson the medical evidence was silent. He might have been pushed, or there might have been a bruise which had not been noticed. She had considered whether the murderer could have snatched up a stone or some broken piece of masonry, but a careful daylight examination had afforded no support for this. The church-yard was beautifully kept, and as far as the road was con-cerned the soil was a soft loamy clay upon both sides of the splash. As she followed this path from the church she was doing what the murderer must have done if he had come this way. Light and shadow play strange tricks. They are also sometimes unexpectedly revealing. Walking slowly down towards the road, she turned the ray of the torch here and there, her mind alert and clear, but the old yews gave up no secret. She came to the lych gate and found it empty under the timbers which had protected it for three hundred years. There was nothing here except deep shadow and the weathered oak.

She passed out on to the road. On either side of the gate there was a stretch of low stone wall. Since the village children had developed a tendency to play such games as King of the Castle upon the flat convenient top of this wall, the late Vicar had caused an iron railing to be set up on it. Mrs. Ball had been informative as to her husband's dislike of this addition.

"It's quite hideous, and John can't bear it. Like those dreadful little railings you used to see in the suburbs. John is only waiting until we have been here rather longer to have it taken away. He says he doesn't think it would be tactful until we have been here at least three years. Fortun-ately, the gilding *is* wearing off."

Miss Silver did not share the Vicar's repugnance. She considered the railings very neat and tasteful, the dark green of the paint harmonizing pleasantly with the grass in the churchyard beyond, and the touches of gilding really quite subdued. But it was not with its artistic merits or demerits that she was concerned as she turned the ray of her torch upon the series of arrow-heads which defended the wall. If one of these spikes was loose——

She was testing them with her free hand, when a voice said from behind her,

"Oh, no, it wasn't one of them."

If Miss Silver had come near to starting she showed no trace of it. She turned with her usual composure and spoke to the dark shape which stood on the grass verge between her and the road. Transferring the torch to her left hand and letting it hang down, she said,

"Was it not, Annie?"

The shape went back a little.

"Oh, no, it wasn't one of them."

"What makes you so sure about that?"

"What makes anyone sure about anything?"

"We can be sure of what we know." Miss Silver's voice was quiet.

For a moment everything was so quiet that they could hear the water moving down towards the splash. It had cut itself a channel below the slope of the churchyard before it widened out and shallowed to take the stepping-stones. It moved all the time, and the mild air moved above it. The sky was thick with cloud.

Annie said,

"What anyone knows is their own business."

"Not always. When murder has been done, everyone has a duty to tell whatever they know. Two people have been murdered."

Annie said, "Two——" on a caught breath. And then, "Things go in threes, don't they? Next time it might be you—or me——" Her voice was like a ghost's voice—weak, and worn, and with no feeling in it.

Miss Silver put out a hand towards her, and she stepped back. She had been a dark shape, but now she was so little distinguishable that she might have been part of the dark-

ness itself: Miss Silver made no attempt to follow her.
She drew her hand back again and said,

"I will not touch you, Annie, but I would like you to
listen to me. Your husband knew something. If he had
spoken of it to those who had a right to know he would
not now be dead. Miss Dean also knew something, but like
your husband she tried to use this knowledge for her
private advantage. I think that is why she died. If there
is something that you know, I beg you very earnestly to
consider that you are endangering your own safety by not
being frank with the police. I said this to Miss Dean, but
she did not take my advice. Now I say it to you. Pray
think about what I have said. And now let us go in. I do
not feel that you should come down here alone in the dark,
and I should like you to promise me that you will not do
so again."

Annie said on a grieving note,

"Time was I'd have been afraid. You get used to being
alone." Then, after a pause, "I heard you go, and I came
after you."

"Then we will go home together," said Miss Silver with
cheerful firmness.

Avoiding the yew tunnel, they took the open way of the
Vicarage drive. It was when they had almost reached the
house that Annie, a little way in front, turned her head
and spoke.

"You didn't find what you were looking for—nor you
won't."

Miss Silver let a moment go by before she said,

"How do you know that I did not find it, Annie?"

Chapter 35

ANNIE JACKSON MADE NO REPLY. SHE HAD BEEN A LITTLE WAY
ahead. Now she was gone, running quickly and lightly
along the path which led to the back door.

Miss Silver stood where she was and waited until a gleam
of light through the shrubbery informed her that the door
had been opened to let Annie in. She went on waiting until
she heard it close behind her. It was then, and not until
then, that she was aware of what seemed at first to be just
a vibration on the air, but which, as it swelled, she recognized to be the sound of organ music coming from the
church. With one of those quick decisions which sometimes made her actions unpredictable she turned from the
house and took her way along the churchyard path to the
side door of the church. She was, in fact, doing just what
Mildred Blake had done when she left the Vicarage work-
party on the night of William Jackson's death. Like her
she tried the door, found it unlocked, and passed quietly
within. As she did so, the music sounded in the empty
place like the rolling of drums, the crashing of a stormy
tide, the sound of wind, and the sound of thunder.

Miss Silver recognized this music. It was the *Dies Irae*.
"Day of wrath, day of mourning"—with its picture of the
Last Judgment—heaven and earth consumed in the burning wrath of the Judge. But she had never heard it played
like this before. If it was Arnold Random who was playing,
there must be something behind that grey, controlled
façade. She did not count herself to be musical, but she
could recognize that here was a musician, and, what mattered a good deal more, someone in an extremity of pain.

She came forward until she was level with the curtain.
It was not quite drawn. Arnold Random sat there in the

light. The sweat ran down his ravaged face. He looked like a man in torment, and he played as if he was possessed. She had no plan in her mind. She just stood there and watched him. The storm of sound died down. Very high and soft, a long wailing note came stealing upon the empty silence. Words from the old Latin hymn rose in Miss Silver's mind—" *Recordare Jesu pie*". Mercy after judgment? There were a few more of those soft mourning notes. Then Arnold Random dropped his hands from the keyboard with a groan. He spoke in a dead voice, as a man may speak to himself when he has come to a place where he can no longer go on.

"It's too late——"

As he spoke he turned with a kind of groan and saw Miss Silver standing there. She did not speak. They looked at one another. After quite a long time she said,

"You are very unhappy, Mr. Random."

"Yes—very——"

After another pause she spoke again.

"There is always a right thing to do, as well as a wrong one."

His hands had fallen upon his knees. He lifted one of them now and let it fall again.

"It is too late——"

"I do not believe it. We may not see the whole of the way, but it is always possible to take the first step."

Afterwards he was to look back upon this conversation and wonder how it had come about. He had been in extremity. His sleep had gone from him. He had thoughts which he could no longer control, and from which there was no escape. He saw himself slipping with an ever-increasing velocity into an abyss of loneliness and shame. And just when the whole nightmare had reached its unendurable climax, there was, as it were, a gleam from the daylight world which he had lost. And with this gleam a sense of assurance, of calm authority, a sense of goodness. He had known the presence of evil and been tortured by

·it. Now he knew the presence of good. It did not matter to him that it was a stranger who laid this tranquillizing touch upon the fever of his thoughts. If you are dying of thirst, it does not matter to you that it is a stranger who holds the cup of cool water to your lips.

He looked at her and said in a bewildered voice,

"What am I to do?"

Miss Silver shook her head.

"I cannot tell you that. You will know what it is your-... self. It is only the first step which is hard."

He went on looking at her. In the end he said,

"There are things I must do—I should have done them long ago. Good-bye."

She said, "Good-night, Mr. Random," and turned to go. His voice followed her.

"I don't know your name. You are staying with Mrs. Ball, are you not?"

"Yes. My name is Maud Silver."

.He came as far as the door and held it for her to pass out. A streak of light fell from it upon the gravel path and remained there until she had turned the corner of the church.

Chapter 36

THE OLD CHURCH CLOCK GAVE OUT THE TWELVE STROKES OF A cloudy midnight. As a rule, when Miss Silver had read a psalm or a chapter from the shabby Bible which was her constant companion she would put out the light, arrange her two pillows to her liking, and pass immediately into a state of tranquil repose. Upon the rare occasions when this did not happen it was because her mind was too pre-

occupied to relax. To-night her thoughts were very deeply
occupied indeed, and not only occupied, but burdened.
Annie Jackson's words stood out among them—"These
things go in threes". Two people had been murdered.
Two successive Fridays had seen a victim struck down. To-
morrow it would be Friday again. The Vicarage work-party
would assemble, Arnold Random would doubtless come to
his practising in the church, and the faint sounds of the
organ would steal out across the churchyard and hang in
the air above the watersplash.

There might be no reason for the murderer to strike
again. There might be a grave and insistent reason. Only
the murderer would know. And in murder, as in many
other things, it is the first step that is the difficult one. A
couple of homely proverbs reinforced this line of thought—
"In for a penny, in for a pound", and, "As well be hanged
for a sheep as for a lamb". And with each step into the
dark other world beyond stability, the strength of the
motive required would become progressively less, until in
the end there might hardly need to be a motive at all. In
the unbalanced mind the link between cause and effect may
be crazily wrenched, if not altogether broken.

When the church clock struck twelve Miss Silver folded
back the bed-clothes and went over to the window. Her
room looked towards the churchyard, very deeply covered
by the cloudy darkness, very sombre, mysterious and vague,
and the black church watching it, its steeple pointing to
heaven. The casement window stood partly open. She
loosened the catch, pushed it wide, and leaned out. The
house was two-storeyed and rambling. One of the windows
glowed faintly. The curtains were not drawn. The two
leaves of the casement jutted out, and between them the
darkness thinned away. She could discern the window-
frame, the sill, and those two jutting leaves. She knew the
room to be Annie's.

After some pause for reflection she put on her warm blue
dressing-gown with the hand-made crochet trimming which

had already completed years of useful service upon its red
flannel predecessor, and opening her door, stepped silently
into the passage. The landing was not far away, and a
faint light burned there. Every step towards Annie Jackson's room would take her farther away from it, but it
would serve. Her feet, in black felt slippers lined with
lamb's wool and adorned by neat blue bows, made no sound
on the rather worn carpeting.

Standing before Annie's door, a hand upon the knob, she
heard a deep choking breath, and then a gasping cry; "No
—no—*no*!"

Before the third "No!" was uttered she was in the room
and the door shut behind her. She wanted neither Ruth
nor the Vicar to be a witness to what might be going to
take place between herself and Annie Jackson. The glow
which she had seen from her window proceeded from an
old-fashioned night-light stuck on a saucer and set very
prudently in the basin upon Annie's washstand. There
was even a little water in the basin. Miss Lucy Wayne had
evidently trained her maidservants well.

The light slanting up out of the basin threw all the
shadows high. The bed, an old-fashioned single four-poster,
was bare of the curtains for which it had been designed.
The posts, and the rods which connected them, stood up
stark like the bars of a cage. And in the middle of the bed
Annie sat up straight, her hands clasped to her breast, her
eyes wide, and fixed, and sightless. She was asleep, but not
at rest. She walked in a dreadful dream and cried out
against it.

Miss Silver stood at the bed foot and watched her. There
was sweat on the face. The hair was pushed back in a dis-
ordered tangle. The mark of the bruise showed plain. She
was speaking now in a rapid mutter where the words were
lost. Hurry and fear, hurry and fear—they rode her, and
needed no words to make themselves plain.

And then the words began to come through.

"Dark—dark—dark——" The voice was no more than

a whisper at the first, but it rose to a thin trembling scream.
And then the muttering——

Miss Silver made no move. She stood and watched.

Slowly and painfully, words were thrown up.

"Dark. . . . In dark—of night——" Then, with a convulsive shudder, "Dreadful—sin—dreadful—dreadful sin——"

Somewhere in Annie Jackson's mind there walked the ghost of Christopher Hale, drowned in the watersplash more than a hundred years ago. The words which came from her on those difficult gasping breaths were part of the verse which she and Miss Silver had read together upon the tombstone set up by his wife.

> "In dark of night and dreadful sin
> The heart conceives its plan."

Was it really the ghost of Christopher Hale who walked ·in Annie's dream, or was it the ghost of William Jackson?

Miss Silver leaned forward from where she stood at the foot of the bed and said,

"Annie!"

There was a change at once. The hands which had been clenched at the thin chest were flung out as if to ward a blow.

"I didn't tell—I didn't—I didn't! No one can say I did! There isn't no one can say I was there! There isn't no one——" On the last word her voice faltered and dropped. Her hands dropped too. She looked about her as if she had waked in a strange place—wardrobe on the right—chest of drawers and washstand on the left, with the jug lifted out of the basin and the night-light burning.

Her troubled gaze came to rest upon Miss Silver in her blue dressing-gown, her hair very neatly controlled by the strong brown net which she wore at night.

"What—is it?"

"You have had a bad dream. You cried out."

Annie closed her eyes. The dream still lay behind them.

"It won't let me be——" The tears began to run down over her pinched face. "It won't let me be. Soon as ever I lie down it's there again. I dursn't go to sleep but I'm down there in the dark—and the water drowning him." Her eyes flew open suddenly. "I didn't say it—oh—I didn't say it!"

Miss Silver came round to the side of the bed. She sat down there.

"Annie, won't you tell me what happened on the night your husband was drowned? If you did, I think that the dream would go away, and that you would not be troubled with it again."

Annie stared at her with dilated eyes.

"And have them—hang me?" she said.

Miss Silver took one of the bony hands.

"Have you done anything for which they could hang you?"

The hand jerked in hers. The whole frail body jerked.

"And who's going to believe I didn't? Who's going to believe me against them whose word 'ud be taken afore mine? If my Miss Lucy was here she'd speak for me. Twenty-four years is a long time to be living with anyone, and you'd know they wasn't the kind to do murder. But she's gone—and there's no one now. They'd find out about the girl in Embank—and how I said I wished I was dead before I married him. And they'd see how he bruised me. It didn't show so much at first—but they couldn't help but see it now—not if they looked. And they'll think I did it!"

"And did you do it, Annie?"

She was holding the hand in a firm but gentle clasp. This time there was no jerk. It closed a little upon hers and was still. Annie looked at her and said,

"Oh, no, miss. I've wished myself dead many's the time —but not him."

"But you went to the watersplash the night that he was drowned?"

Annie took a heavy sobbing breath.

"I've gone there most nights lately come closing time—
to see if he was coming home. Sometimes he'd come—and
sometimes he wouldn't. Then I'd know he'd gone off to
that girl."

"You went every night?"

"Mostly. Mr. Edward could have told them that—if
he'd a mind. There's two or three times he's gone by me
—walking quick—coming back from Mr. Barr's he'd be—
and he'd go past me and say good-night. He might
have spoke of it—but he wouldn't want to get me into
trouble."

After the loneliness, the coldness, and the dark secret on
her heart, Annie was feeling a quite extraordinary sense of
relief. There was an easing of her whole mind and body.
The words which had come with so much effort now flowed
like water. In some strange unreasoning way she recognized the presence of kindness and authority and responded
to them.

Miss Silver held her hand and said gently,

"Then you went down to the splash on the night your
husband was drowned——"

Annie repeated the words in an uncertain voice.

"I—went—down——"

"What time was it?"

"It was—getting on—for ten——"

"Did you see Mr. Edward Random?"

"He'd gone past me—just before I come to the splash."

"Where was he when you came to it?"

"He was going up the slope—and William was coming
down. They said a word or two, and I heard him call out,
'Good-night, Willy!' They'd known each other from
boys."

"What happened after that?"

"I went back—up the other side of the rise. I didn't want
William—to see me. I waited to hear him—come over the
splash——" She gave a sudden violent shudder. "But he
never."

" Why? "

The answer came in a shaking whisper.

" He was done in——"

" By whom? "

Annie's eyes met hers in a fixed stare. The flow of words had stopped. Fear had come down and cut them off like the closing of a dam.

" Annie, what did you see, or hear? "

She just stared.

" Did you go down to the splash again? "

" When—he—didn't come——" The stumbling answer was so faint that it was hardly to be heard.

" And then? "

" He—came——"

" Yes, Annie? "

She pulled away her hand with great suddenness.

" I went away home. Do you think I wanted him to catch me? I ran most part of the way. I see them come down the rise, and I ran for it."

Miss Silver picked out a single word and presented it with gravity.

" Them? "

The breath caught in Annie's throat.

" What do you think I'm going to say—that there was someone coming down there after him? It was dark, wasn't it? How could I see in the dark? And if I could, what do you think I'm going to do—put up my word against them that would set their hand on the Bible and swear they saw me push William in? And stand by and see me hanged— and never lose a good night's sleep over it neither! Who's going to credit my word against them that would do that? Not if I·was to take my Bible oath that I ran home the fastest I could go! "

" Why did you do that? "

Annie was sobbing, a hand at her throat. Her words came out between the sobs.

" I thought—he'd have—my life. He was drunk—and

he was angry. I could hear him—talking—to himself. 'I'll get it out of him!' he said—and a lot of bad words—and, 'I'll be even with him!' And I didn't wait to hear no more —I took and ran."

There was a pause. Faint steady light in the room, and a soft air coming in from the mild November night. Miss Silver said,

"Someone was following your husband?"

There was a slight movement of the bruised head.

"Who was it?"

Annie caught her breath painfully.

"It—was—dark——"

"Shall I tell you who it was?"

The sobs ceased. The troubled breathing ceased. Everything seemed to wait and listen.

Miss Silver leaned forward and spoke a name.

Chapter 37

SUSAN WENT UP TO THE HALL IN THE MORNING. IT WAS difficult to go, but it would have been difficult to stay. They had come to a point where there was no easy path. If the police had made up their minds to arrest Edward, they would do it whether Susan Wayne was there or not. And he would hate it more if she was there. It was all that she could do to walk away up the drive and not look back. He meant to go over and see Mr. Barr, but not until later. He would give the police their chance before he went. And every step away from him felt like a long, hard mile. Older and stronger than logic was the instinct which has survived from the beginnings of the race. Nothing will go wrong if I am there. But out of sight, what enemies, what pitfalls, what ambushes? Stay where you can cover the creature you love, if need be with your own shrinking flesh. It is when he is alone that the evil thing may creep up close and strike.

Susan did not formulate these things, but they were there under the reasoned thought which told her that the best way to help Edward was to go about her business as if this was just a day like any other day. She would come back at one, and Edward would be there—unless Mr. Barr had kept him.

Doris had lighted a fire in the library. Susan had not really thought about it before, but the sight of the blazing logs reminded her that it was colder. She stood to warm her hands for a minute before putting on her overall and getting down to the eighteenth-century books. She had reached the uppermost shelves by now, which meant climbing almost to the top of the ladder.

She was half-way up, when the door opened and Arnold Random came in. As she answered his "Good morning", she thought how ill he looked. He went over to the fire and stood there with his back to her, warming himself. After waiting a little to see whether he would speak she went up the remaining steps and began her work.

The first book she took out was a volume of her great-grandfather's sermons with a long-winded and ornate dedication to Edward Random Esquire. That would be Edward's great-grandfather. The sermons were long, and appeared to be quite intolerably dull. The parish had doubtless been obliged to listen to them week by week, but she wondered whether anyone had ever had the urge to read them in print. Great-grandpapa had certainly been born in the eighteenth century, though only in its last decade, and she was trying to make up her mind whether to leave him there or to transfer him to the early nineteenth century, when Arnold spoke from the hearth.

"You are getting on."

"Oh, yes. I'm afraid it must seem a bit slow——"

"Not at all—I didn't mean that. I was just wondering——"

"Yes, Mr. Random?"

He stooped down to put a log on the fire and said with a sudden fretfulness,

"It's very cold this morning—really very cold indeed. You must keep up a good fire."

Looking back over her shoulder, she saw him shiver. He went on speaking.

"Dreadfully cold. What was I saying?"

"You were wondering——"

"Yes, it was about my brother's prayer-book. It was mislaid after his death, and I thought perhaps it had got pushed into one of these shelves. He used this room a good deal, you know. I wondered whether you had come across the book. Perhaps I should have mentioned it before—I just thought——"

He had both hands on the edge of the wide mantelshelf, gripping it. The knuckles stood up white. She could not see his face. She said, "No, I haven't come across it. I will let you know at once if I do," and reached up to put her great-grandfather back upon the shelf.

Arnold Random straightened up and went out of the room.

With her hands still touching the book of sermons, it came to Susan that she knew beyond any shadow of doubt just why she had been given this job—that she might find James Random's prayer-book. It was the reason why she was here at this moment putting her great-grandfather's sermons back upon the eighteenth-century shelf to which he was not lawfully entitled. Arnold Random wouldn't care whether he or anyone else was a couple of centuries out of his proper place. He cared for one thing, and for one thing only—that there should be an accidental discovery of his brother's prayer-book. It was to be found by someone who could have no interest in the finding. It was to be found by Susan Wayne. It was for this purpose that

she had been engaged. And she was being too slow. At
first it had not mattered, but now the thing was so urgent
that he had been driven to a more or less direct approach.
If the prayer-book contained what she thought it did, he
must have been very hard pressed to do that. She believed
that he was very hard pressed. He looked like a man who
is driven by the Furies. She had a sudden picture of
Mildred Blake as one of them. Odd, irrelevant, and
horrifying!

A prick of remorse assailed her. You mustn't have
thoughts like that about people just because they happen
to be rather tiresome and unattractive. Emmeline would
never have had a thought like that about anyone.

She turned from it to the thing which she had shut away,
just knowing that it was there but not letting herself look at
it or think about it, because if she did, it might take to
itself wings and be gone.

When she came out of the Vicarage with Edward last
night she had the dazed feeling that anything might be
going to happen. He might be so angry that all the friend-
ship between them would go down in the storm. He might
be quite dreadfully, witheringly polite, or he might just
go into one of those silences which made you feel about a
million miles away and out of sight. At first she thought
it was going to be that way, because he didn't say a word
until they emerged from the drive. And then he laughed
suddenly and slipped a hand inside her arm. Odd that just
a laugh and a touch should make you feel as if the sun had
come out and all the birds were singing. When the last
house in the village had been left behind them, his arm
came round her shoulders without a word spoken. They
walked on like that until they came to the south lodge and
were going up the path to the house. Something soft and
furry brushed between them, purring. Edward's arm
tightened a little. He laid his face against hers for a
moment, laughed again, and said,

"Interfering creature, aren't you?"

Then they went in.

It didn't mean anything, it couldn't mean anything. But he wasn't angry, and he hadn't gone right away by himself. He was near, and kind.

It was about half an hour later that she found the prayer-book. It was behind some more sermons, those of a still older Vicar, the Reverend Nathaniel Spragge, 1745 to 1785. There were three volumes, "Printed by Subscription", and the prayer-book was wedged behind them. Susan looked at it with something approaching dismay. If Arnold Random couldn't be more convincing than this, he had really better stick to being honest. Who on earth was going to believe that a dying man had climbed to the top of a book-ladder and taken out three heavy volumes in order to hide something which he had no possible reason for wanting to hide? She wouldn't put it past Arnold to have left his finger-prints on the leather cover. Why on earth hadn't he just poked the prayer-book in amongst the Victorian novels? The answer, of course, was that it might have been found. And it was only lately that he had wanted it to be found.

These thoughts raced through her mind as she opened the prayer-book and shook it. There fell out an envelope addressed, "To my brother Arnold. My last Will and Testament. James Random."

Susan had known it would be there, but actually to see it, to hold it in her hand, gave her a horrid giddy feeling. It was Edward's inheritance that she was holding—the Hall and its surroundings, its woods and fields and farms, its cottages and hedgerows, and the village of Greenings—all in one light sheet of paper which would have burned away in an instant at the touch of a spark.

Arnold hadn't burned it. He had waited to see what would happen. And in the end he had wanted the will to be found. There would be a lot of talk of course. Edward was going to hate that. Whatever happened between him and Arnold would happen privately.

She went on thinking. In the end she wiped the shelf

and the volumes of Nathaniel Spragge, and she wiped the
prayer-book and the envelope. After a little more thought
she took out the enclosure and wiped that too. Now there
wouldn't be any fingerprints but hers, and the fresh ones
which Arnold would make when he took it from her. If
anyone asked any questions, she was quite ready to do the
idiot child and say she was so sorry if it was wrong, but
there was such a lot of dust.

She came down from the ladder and went along to the
study.

Arnold Random turned round from the window as she
came in. The outlook was accounted a pleasant one. A
shrub with scarlet berries on either side of the bay, a gravel
path, and beyond it gently sloping grass, with here and
there a group of trees. The kind of view, in fact, which
may be seen almost anywhere in rural England. Arnold
had been looking at it, but he had not seen it. All that he
saw was a cold grey day too much akin to his own mood.

He turned, and saw Susan Wayne with the prayer-book
in her hand. She held it out to him and said,

"Is this what you wanted me to look for?"

"Let me see. . . . Yes, I think it is. Where was it?"

The real answer was, "Where you put it," but of course
she couldn't say that. But her colour rose.

"On the top shelf behind some sermons by the Reverend
Nathaniel Spragge."

"The top shelf? What an extraordinary thing!"

He was holding the book. He hadn't opened it. He came
up to the writing-table and put it down. His hand shook.
He stood there looking at it. She thought, "He can't make
up his mind. He wanted it found, but now he can't make
up his mind. He doesn't know whether to go on or go
back. He doesn't know whether I've seen the will." She
said quickly,

"There's a paper inside it, Mr. Random. I think you
ought to see it."

He drew a long breath. She wondered if it was a breath

of relief. When you have carried a secret like this for a year, it might be a relief to let it go, no matter what would come of it.

He rested one hand on the table and opened the prayer-book. The leaves fell apart where the envelope divided them. Susan watched whilst he looked down at it and read the words which she knew were there:

"To my brother Arnold. My last Will and Testament. James Random."

It was a minute before he opened his dry lips to say,

"It's a will——"

"Yes."

"My brother James' will——"

"Hadn't you better open it?"

He started.

"Yes, yes—of course——"

He took the enclosure out of the envelope and unfolded it. Just an ordinary sheet of paper written on in a shaky hand, signed at the foot by James Random and witnessed by William Jackson and William Stokes. When he had stared at it for quite a long time he said,

"My brother's will. Dated a week before he died. It leaves everything to Edward."

Chapter 38

MISS SILVER HAD VOLUNTEERED TO DO ANY SHOPPING THAT might be required for the Vicarage.

"You will be having your work-party this evening, and that will mean more to do in the house, to say nothing of the cutting-out, at which you are, I am told, most proficient. Your dear mother was just the same. I remember that she won the sewing prize at school. So if there is any little thing I can do for you in the village, I should really enjoy having an object."

Ruth remembered that they were short of custard powder, and cook had planned to make some of her celebrated cream-custard biscuits.

"She thinks they are wasted on the work-party, but she can't resist showing them off. Everyone in Greenings has asked for the recipe and been refused. And if Mrs. Alexander has any of her home-made apple-ginger left, do find out if she can spare me a pot. John is so fond of it. And I can cut out a whole batch of children's frocks and be sure that they will be some kind of a human shape."

As Miss Silver took her way down the drive she had a thought to spare for her old friend's daughter. Such a pity that she had no children—a pity and, she was afraid, an abiding grief. But instead of letting it embitter her she allowed it to flow out in service to the desolate children who needed it most. She thought that Mary had brought up her daughter well.

She found Miss Sims at the counter in Mrs. Alexander's shop. She was commenting unfavourably and at great length upon an imported cauliflower, each word carefully separated from its neighbour and coming out with slow deliberation. "Sinful!" she was saying as Miss Silver came in. "Two shillings for a cauliflower! And Mr. Pomfret had to plough in I dunno how many hundreds in the spring! 'Wilful waste makes woeful want', is what my father would have said!"

Mrs. Alexander opined that times had changed, and did she want the cauliflower?

Miss Sims gave a sigh that was almost a groan.

"Seems I'll have to take it. The doctor's so fond of them he'd eat them day in, day out all the year round if they was to be had, which thank goodness they're not, for there's nothing smells so strong when it's cooking as a cauliflower."

Miss Silver entered the conversation with a bright smile

and the remark that a piece of bread in the saucepan would often do wonders in reducing the disagreeable odour.

Mrs. Alexander said her mother always put a bit of bread in with the greens, but Miss Sims merely shook her head and gave it as her opinion that what was all very well for a good English cauliflower grown in your own garden was neither here nor there when it came to this foreign stuff.

It was while Mrs. Sims was producing her purse and counting out five threepenny bits, three coppers, and a sixpence that Mrs. Alexander leaned over the counter and asked Miss Silver whether she could tell her how poor Annie Jackson was.

"If you'll excuse me asking, but I saw her yesterday just for a minute going past, and I thought she looked dreadful, poor thing. We all know there's nobody would be kinder to her than Mrs. Ball, but I did think she looked dreadful, and I couldn't get it from my mind. They say she goes down to the splash and looks at the water, and she didn't ought to do that."

Miss Silver shook her head gravely.

"It is very difficult to stop her. She slips down there in the dark. I found her there myself last night. I am afraid the place has a morbid attraction for her, especially about the time her husband must have been drowned. Of course, it is exceedingly bad for her, as you say."

"She didn't ought to do it," said Miss Sims in a tone almost as disapproving as if she had just found out that the fish was high.

Mrs. Alexander was disapproving too.

"She doesn't go along to that cottage of hers, not by herself, does she? I did hear the Hodges hadn't moved in yet. Seems her mother's been ill and they're bound to stay till she's better."

Miss Silver coughed in a hesitating manner.

"I am afraid I cannot say. Of course you are quite right. She ought not to do these things, but it is extremely difficult to prevent her. So easy to slip out, especially whilst a work-party is going on."

Miss Sims began to stow away the cauliflower in her shopping-bag.

"I wouldn't go down to the splash in the dark if you were to pay me."

"Oh, well," said Mrs. Alexander, "Annie is used to it. There's a lot in being used to things."

They had talked about Annie Jackson for a quarter of an hour before Miss Silver found an opportunity of mentioning either custard powder or apple-ginger.

The conversation might have gone on a good deal longer if it had not been for the sudden irruption of Cyril Croft in search of batteries for his bicycle lamp. It appeared that he had been away visiting an aunt, and had come back with two batteries that were completely dud.

"I had a frightful time there—there wasn't a piano in the house! And I missed everything that was going on here. Clarice—and poor old William Jackson! It must have been a homicidal maniac—mustn't it? And that's a grim thought, because he's probably still somewhere about!"

Miss Silver left him talking and proceeded on her way. Approaching the Miss Blakes' house, she was waved and nodded to by Miss Ora, whose sofa had been pushed even farther into the bay than usual. Regardless of the colder day, a window was opened. Greetings were exchanged, and a pressing invitation extended to come up and have a cup of tea and a chat. Remembering the horrid fluid which had passed under that name, Miss Silver might have been forgiven for finding some excuse, yet she accepted with smiling alacrity and was invited to walk in.

Miss Ora's best shawl had been put away for another tea-party, but she was wearing a very nice one with a pale blue border, and ribbons of the same shade in the lace trifle which passed as a cap. She received Miss Silver with great affability, designated a hand-bell, and asked if she would

be so kind as to ring it just outside the door, explaining that
it would bring Mrs. Deacon, which it presently did.

"Miss Silver is being kind enough to pay me a visit, and
we will have tea, and the cake that was not cut yesterday."

Mrs. Deacon looked uncertain, seemed about to speak,
checked herself, and retreated. Just before the door closed
upon her she remarked that Miss Mildred was turning out
the kitchen cupboard. It was obvious that the prospect of
seeing yesterday's cake had been dimmed. Miss Ora made
a small vexed sound, clutched fretfully at her shawl, and
only began to brighten when it became apparent that, un-
like Ruth Ball, Miss Silver was by no means averse from
talking about the murders.

They had reached some interesting speculations as to the
possibility of Annie knowing more about her husband's
death than she had hitherto been induced to divulge, when
the door was first unlatched, and then pushed open by the
thrust of a bony elbow. It was Miss Mildred, who had
brought up the tea. And not even in a pot—just three
cups, one of them chipped, with a drop or two of milk
added to the pale brew, and no sugar. Instead of the cake
so optimistically suggested there were two very plain biscuits on a cracked plate.

Miss Ora's colour deepened. But this was no moment to
quarrel with Mildred. She swallowed her annoyance and
exclaimed,

"Do you know, Miss Silver says that poor Annie Jackson
just can't keep away from the splash—not even at night.
You'd think she'd be frightened—wouldn't you?"

Mildred Blake set down the tray. She stared at her sister
across it.

"What has she got to be frightened about?"

The white curls were tossed. The blue ribbons fluttered.

"Well, *really*—when two people have been murdered
there!"

Miss Mildred's voice was coldly disapproving as she said,

"You are taking a good deal for granted, Ora." She

turned to Miss Silver. "My sister is prone to exaggeration.
There is no proof that anyone has been murdered. William
Jackson was drunk, and he fell into a pool and was drowned.
No one had any reason for wanting to get rid of him—
except his wife. Miss Dean was an excitable young woman,
and she had been crossed in love. I find it much easier to
believe that she took her own life than that anyone else
should have had the slightest desire to do so."

Miss Ora was now very much flushed.

"Really, Mildred—you might just as well say I tell lies!
And you don't know what Miss Silver has just been telling
me about Annie Jackson. She goes down to the splash
between half-past nine and ten and stands there talking
and muttering to herself—and why should she do that if
she hasn't got something on her mind? It's my belief she
went to meet poor William, and pushed him in, which
wouldn't have been hard to do if he was drunk. You know
Mrs. Deacon always says it never did take much to go to
his head. It would have been quite easy for Annie to have
pushed him in, and it's my belief it is just what she did.
And Clarice Dean too. You see, if Clarice was hanging
about there on the chance of meeting Edward Random,
well, she might have seen more than she was meant to see
on the night that William was drowned. And then Annie
would have had a motive for pushing her in too. You can't
deny that."

Mildred Blake said in a slow, cold voice,

"My dear Ora, you should write a novel. It would give
you something to do." She took up the third cup and
sipped from it. "I prefer to leave these conjectures to the
police. But Annie should really not be allowed to go down
to the splash in the way you describe. It is most unsuitable.
Mrs. Ball should look after her better."

Miss Silver coughed in a deprecating manner.

"I think she does her best. But it is quite an obsession—
she just slips out and goes down there. It does make one
wonder whether she could have seen something on the

night her husband was drowned. I have heard her say things that would seem to point that way. And she cannot keep away from the splash."

"Most unsuitable," said Miss Mildred coldly. "And I should have thought Mrs. Ball would have expected her to stay in on a Friday night. She always offers quite elaborate refreshments. Most unnecessary and extravagant, as I have told her, but I believe they have money and can afford a rather pretentious standard."

"I am quite looking forward to it," said Miss Silver. "I hope you will be there."

Miss Mildred shook her head.

"I do not often miss, but when my sister is without a nurse I do not care to leave her alone in the house. There is also a great deal extra to do, and I shall be glad to get to bed early."

Miss Ora threw her a fleeting sideways look and sighed.

"I am a sad trouble," she said.

As she emerged upon the street again Miss Silver looked at her watch. She had spent nearly three-quarters of an hour beside Miss Ora's couch, but there would still be time for one more call.

She walked on up the road and turned in at the south lodge.

Emmeline took her visitor into a room littered with cats. Amina and her kittens occupied a basket in front of the fire. Scheherazade and the ill-favoured Toby were sharing the window-seat, while Lucifer, black and beautiful, lay in an attitude of profound repose along the back of the sofa from which Emmeline had just risen. When Miss Silver sat down in the other corner he opened one tawny eye, let it rest upon her in a negligent manner, yawned slightly, and plunged again into slumber. A pleasant impression that the stranger was praising him for his beauty went with him into a delightful dream in which he stalked and caught enormous mice.

Beginning with her tribute to Lucifer, Miss Silver found

herself launched upon a conversation during which Emmeline told her all about his ancestry.

"Of course, on Scheherazade's side he is pure Persian with four champions in his pedigree, but I am afraid I shall not be able to show him as a Persian because I really can't be sure about his father. Scheherazade always has such pretty kittens, only this time they were nice healthy little things but quite plain. There were four, another brother and two sisters, and I was able to find good homes for three of them. And then suddenly Lucifer began to turn into quite a beauty. It was really most extraordinary. I don't think I have ever known a case quite like it."

It was not until they had talked about cats for quite twenty minutes that Miss Silver found an opportunity of turning the conversation in the direction of Annie Jackson.

They were still talking about her when the telephone bell rang from the small back room, and a minute later Edward Random opened the door, began to speak, broke off to say how do you do to Miss Silver, and then went back to what he had been about to say.

"I'm going up to the Hall. Arnold wants to see me—I can't think why. So if anyone asks for me, you can tell them where I am."

"Anyone?" Emmeline looked at him in a puzzled manner.

Edward said grimly, "The police, darling," and was gone. Miss Silver went on talking about Annie Jackson.

Chapter 39

SUSAN ALWAYS LOOKED BACK UPON THE REALLY SHORT TIME during which she and Arnold Random waited for Edward in the library as one of the most uncomfortable she had

ever spent. As if it wasn't enough to have her mind in a
black turmoil about Edward being arrested and wondering
whether the finding of this will was going to make things
better for him or worse, there was Arnold looking as if
he had every crime in the Decalogue on his conscience and
walking up and down the room like a panther in a cage!.
The state of her mind may be indicated by the fact that she
was definitely conscious of being thankful that they were on
the ground floor. If Arnold chose to plunge out of the end
window, there would not be more than a matter of six
inches between him and some nice soft garden mould.
There didn't seem to be anything else of a lethal nature he
could do before Edward got here, but she found herself
counting the lengthening minutes.

Edward walked in unheralded. He gave her a quick
surprised glance as he came up to the table and said,

"Well?"

Arnold's last prowl had taken him over to the hearth. He
straightened himself now and said,

"Thank you for coming. I asked you to do so because
something has happened. I could not talk about it on the
telephone. James made a later will than the one that has
been proved. Susan has just found it."

He was doing it well. After all, there is something in
breeding. The nerve-ridden creature of a few minutes ago
was gone. This was Arnold Random as both Edward and
Susan had always known him—rather dry, rather formal,
not very interesting, but a member of an old and honour-
able family, well bolstered up by tradition and a certain
code of behaviour. As Edward looked at him in silence, he
added,

"She will tell you."

Susan said her piece. It could hardly have been briefer.
"His prayer-book was pushed in behind some books.
The will was inside it. I brought it to Mr. Random, and
he rang you up."

Edward too had reverted to the family mould. There

was not a trace of expression in either face or voice as he said,

"What books? On what shelf?"

Susan found it difficult to come by any words at all. She felt as if she was digging up stones with her bare hands as she said,

"Nathaniel Spragge. Three volumes. On the top shelf."

His eyebrows rose slightly.

"An odd place for Uncle James to keep his will. May I ask the date?"

Arnold Random said,

"A week before he died."

"Curiouser and curiouser, my dear Arnold. However. . . . Am I to understand that I have an interest in this will?"

"It leaves you everything."

Edward sat down on the corner of the writing-table. He could not have seemed more casual or completely at home, yet Susan found herself wincing. It was as if at that moment the Hall and all that it stood for had changed hands.

Sitting there at his ease, Edward said,

"Well, I think this is where we ask Susan to leave us. It's going to flutter the legal dovecotes a bit, isn't it?"

"I would rather she stayed."

Edward shook his head.

"Oh, no, I don't think so. She can go back to her sorting, but she had better not find any more wills." Then, when she had most thankfully escaped, "That's better! Now it's between you and me. Was there a letter with the will—anything to show why he did it?"

Arnold came over to the table. The envelope with its enclosure lay there across the blotting-pad. He took it up and gave it to Edward. The envelope dropped back upon the pad. The will dropped.

It was James Random's letter that Edward took over to the window to read. A short letter to take up so much time.

"I am altering my will, because I am quite sure that my boy is alive. I saw him in a dream last night, and he told me that he was coming home. So I have altered my will."

There was a shaky signature—a very shaky signature. Edward stared at it until it disappeared in a momentary clouding of his sight. With the outer vision darkened, he had an astonishingly vivid picture in his mind—an old man sitting there writing at that table behind him—a very tired old man—writing in the faith and hope of a dream. And it touched him to the depths. It was a little time before he could turn round and say,

"Well, he took a chance."

Arnold had moved to watch him.

"You haven't read the will," he said in a kind of dull surprise.

Edward came up to the table again and stood there reading it. Simple, comprehensive. "Everything to my nephew, Edward Random." He looked over his shoulder at Arnold and said,

"I see both the witnesses are dead."

"Yes."

"In fact there would have been no questions asked if the will had never turned up."

"I suppose not."

"But Susan found it. Very inconvenient of her—from your point of view. I feel that I ought to apologize. Only it wasn't I who brought her down here to rummage in the library, which has done very well without being catalogued for all these years. It looks almost as if you thought she might find something. It even looks as if you wanted her to find it."

Arnold had gone back to staring down upon the blazing logs. He said stiffly,

"You cannot imagine——" and heard Edward laugh.

"My dear Arnold, I can imagine anything—I've always been quite good at it. I can imagine, for instance, that a will like this turning up when you were perfectly sure that

I was dead must have presented you with a horrid vista of legal obstacles and delays. It might be years before my death could be presumed, and meanwhile a minor state of chaos! I can imagine its appearing in an extremely unattractive light. What I can not imagine, and what I hope you are not going to ask me to believe, is that Uncle James climbed to the top of the library ladder in the last week of his life and hid the will he had been at so much trouble to make behind old Nathaniel Spragge's ditchwater sermons. After all, why should he?"

Arnold said nothing. The firelight showed that there was sweat on his face.

Edward stood now with his back to the table, leaning against it. It came to him that it was his table, and that the room was his room. And a lot of good it would do him if he lay in Embank jail on a charge of murder. But the production of the will—how was that going to affect the prospect? Not very greatly, he thought. The police already knew from Miss Silver's account of her conversation with Clarice that William Jackson had witnessed a will and was proposing to blackmail Arnold on the strength of it. They knew that James Random had told Clarice about the will, and about the dream which had induced him to make it. All that the actual production of the will could do would be to provide strong corroboration of what Clarice had told Miss Silver. It left him no motive at all for the murder of William Jackson, and the merest thread of a motive for the murder of Clarice Dean. After all, you don't bump girls off because they drop hints that they know something to your advantage, or even because they throw themselves rather assiduously at your head. On the whole, then, his position would be improved. But Arnold's wouldn't. If the police got the idea that he had been suppressing the will, they might begin to think very seriously indeed about the possibility that William Jackson had actually made some blackmailing attempt, and that Clarice was following it up. And if Arnold showed the police the same sweating mask that he was now turning to the fire, they would probably arrest him at sight.

He said in a voice which had lost its ironic edge,

"It seems to me that we have got to be extremely careful what we do next. The family wash strictly in private, and a convincingly united front. I think the best thing will be for you to take the initiative. Drive over to Embank this afternoon and show this will to the solicitors there. You can take Susan along if you like. But no, on the whole better not. You don't want to appear to need any backing up. You've been having the library catalogued, and this will has turned up behind some old books. I shouldn't mention the top shelf or anything like that. Just say it was behind some early nineteenth-century sermons. And of course nobody is better pleased about it than you are." He smiled, and the ironic flavour returned for a moment as he added, "Do you know, curiously enough, I've really got a feeling that's the truth."

Chapter 40

"I SIMPLY WILL NOT HEAR OF IT," SAID FRANK ABBOTT.

Miss Silver gazed at him across the last of the pink vests.
"My dear Frank!"

"My dear ma'am, it's no use—I simply will not lend myself to any such thing. And you know very well that you ought not to ask me to take such a responsibility."

The mildness of her aspect remained quite unchanged.

"Then perhaps you will tell me what you propose to do about it."

The time was just after lunch, and they were in Ruth Ball's comfortable morning-room. Two empty coffee-cups testified to the fact that her hospitality had not been lacking. Outside, a November murk had begun to gather between the hedgerows and along the course of the stream. It would be early dark to-night, and there would be no moon. But within all was cosy and bright. The standard lamp behind the sofa had been switched on and shed a warm glow over Miss Silver and her knitting. A fire burned cheerfully upon the hearth, and in front of it stood Detective Inspector Abbott, extremely polished and elegant, in the immemorial attitude of the man who is laying down the law to his women folk. He said,

"I shall do what I should have done this morning if Bury hadn't taken me off on a wild goose chase. It seems the girl William Jackson was running after at Embank has a husband, and when it was suggested that we had better find out what he was doing on the night that William was drowned, I naturally had to agree. He is said to be a man of violent temper, and there is some evidence of his having been heard to utter threats—the quite commonplace sort— like breaking every bone in William's body if he ever found him speaking to his wife. He works for a contractor over at Hanmere, and Bury couldn't get hold of him till he came off the job for his dinner. Well, he said he and his wife were visiting her parents at Littleton on both those Friday nights. He says it's a regular thing—they bicycle over, have supper, and get back about eleven. Bury has gone to check up on it. The chap says half a dozen people can speak to their having been there. Well, according as that pans out, we either go on and arrest Edward Random—or we don't. As for your plan, it is absolutely out of the question, and it is no use your asking me to have any hand in it."

He received an indulgent smile.

"Then, my dear Frank, I must make other arrangements."

"And just what do you mean by that?"

She reached for her knitting-bag and loosened some

strands of the pale pink wool. Her smile persisted, and so did her silence.

Frank Abbot said with an edge on his voice,

"You cannot intend to carry out this impracticable scheme by yourself!"

Miss Silver coughed.

"I should naturally prefer not to be obliged to do so."

"Miss Silver!"

"Yes, Frank?"

"You are the most obstinate woman that ever breathed!"

"Men always say that, I believe, when they cannot succeed in inducing a woman to change her mind."

He looked at her in an exasperated manner.

"What do you intend to do?"

"I shall carry out the plan of which I gave you an outline just now."

"Alone?"

"If you leave me under that necessity."

"You know very well I can't allow any such thing!"

"Well, what will you do, my dear Frank? You cannot very well arrest me, and I assure you that unless I am put under physical restraint I do most certainly intend to carry out my plan. It is simple, and I believe that it will prove effective. If nothing comes of it, you are in no worse a position than you are at present."

His tone changed.

"You really believe that something will come of it?"

"I think there is a reasonable chance. The ground has been carefully prepared. I shall be much surprised if by this evening there is anyone in Greenings who is not aware of Annie's distressing state of mind and the morbid attraction which the splash seems to exert upon her."

"And you expect that to produce results?"

"I think so. You must consider the murderer's frame of mind. Two people have already been killed because of something they knew. Annie has made it patent to everyone that she knows more than she has told. I made three useful contacts this morning. Then the old cook here is an intimate friend of the housekeeper at the Hall—they see each other nearly every day. I think we may conclude that Annie's behaviour would not go unmentioned."

The corner of his mouth twitched.

"I should say that would be an understatement."

She inclined her head.

"Look here," he said—"as man to man, or words to that effect, just how sure are you about all this?"

She laid her knitting down upon her lap and looked at him very seriously indeed.

"I cannot tell you that I am sure, because I do not think that this is a case in which anyone could be sure. When I mentioned a name to Annie she burst into hysterical tears and repeatedly denied that she had ever said anything at all. She would not even admit that she believed her husband to have been murdered. She was, in fact, in a state of panic, and very much afraid that she had already said too much for her own safety. Do you really believe that a murderer who has killed twice will wait for this fear to subside and take the risk of what Annie may be persuaded to disclose?"

He frowned.

"I suppose not. But if you are going to talk about risks—an attack upon Annie wouldn't be exactly safe."

"Was there no risk in the case of William Jackson and of Clarice Dean? Yet it was taken. And each success will have heightened the murderer's sense of immunity. The criminal becomes persuaded of his own power to override the law and evade it. In the end he arrives at a stage where he believes that he can do anything."

He nodded.

"You are right of course—you always are."

She shook her head.

"That is a dangerous attitude of mind, Frank, and one which would greatly shock Chief Inspector Lamb."

He threw up a hand in protest.

"If this plan of yours comes off, I shall get his longest homily about Wind in the Head, its Deleterious Effect on the Morale of the Junior Police Officer. And if it doesn't come off——" He paused, gave her a really brilliant smile, and continued, "he won't be told anything about it. And, as you were doubtless about to remark, what the eye doesn't see the heart doesn't grieve over."

Chapter 41

THE FRIDAY EVENING WORK-PARTY WAS IN FULL SWING.

"Such a pity neither Miss Susan nor Mrs. Random could get away, but there are a good few of us here all the same. And of course though it's only a step, anyone might have their reasons for not wanting to go along the dark piece between the village and the south lodge. Only you'd think Mr. Edward might have stepped over to see the ladies safe home—unless maybe he's working late with Mr. Barr again."

Mrs. Deacon shook her head. By virtue of Doris' position at the Hall and her own with the Miss Blakes she always knew rather more than anyone else. On this occasion she knew more than Mrs. Alexander.

"Mr. Edward hasn't been over to Mr. Barr's to-day. If he had, Miss Ora would have seen him go by. I go in evenings now to help her to bed, and she told me particular he hadn't been by. I could have told her he'd been up at the Hall getting on for three-quarters of an hour just before lunch, but it wasn't my business——" She paused to bite off a thread, and added with emphasis, "*nor hers.*"

Mrs. Alexander nodded assent. She considered this amazing news in silence. Everybody in Greenings was

aware that Mr. Edward hadn't set foot in the Hall since he
came home, and that he and Mr. Arnold didn't meet, nor
wouldn't speak if they did.

She and Mrs. Deacon were both working on warm
woollen frocks for Displaced Children. Hers was blue, and
Mrs. Deacon's was green. She took time to reflect that her
sewing had been better than Ada Deacon's before she
said,

"Mr. Edward was up at the Hall?"

Mrs. Deacon restrained her legitimate pride.

"Doris saw him—from the big landing window. Coming
out of the drive, and across the sweep, and in at the front
door. She could hear it shut after him, so she ran to look
over the banisters, and there he was, going through to the
study just as if he hadn't been gone a day."

Miss Sims was putting the sleeves into a rather dull brown
dress. Good warm stuff, but not what you would choose
for a child. Manufacturer's remnants, that was what these
pieces were, Mrs. Ball having some kind of a relation in the
trade. She began to brood upon the fact that everyone else
seemed to have a prettier colour, but was able to rouse herself at the mention of Annie Jackson's name. It was Mrs.
Pomfret who brought it up with an enquiry as to how she
was getting on. Miss Sims, very deliberately tacking the
right sleeve into the left armhole, was able to tell her all
about Annie.

"Right down melancholy she is, poor thing, and no
wonder. She'd a sister that went wrong in the head, and I
shouldn't wonder if Annie didn't go the same way—hanging round the splash the way she does, and going backwards
and forwards to that cottage of hers. I'm sure I wouldn't
have lived there, not if I was paid."

Old Mrs. Stone was listening with all her ears. She liked
a bit of company, and she liked the Vicarage cake. She
could usually manage to put a piece in her pocket as well
as the slice which Mrs. Ball always cut for her to take to
Betsey. Sometimes Betsey was obstinate about being left,

making such remarks as, how would her mother like it if she was to come home and find her murdered in her bed, and once in a way there would be hysterics. But as a rule the slices of cake could be trusted to smooth her down. Of course she would have to get off early, before the others. She went on listening to all that was being said about Annie Jackson.

Tea and cake were brought in at half-past nine, the usual pleasant anticipation being heightened by the fact that everyone was expecting to get a glimpse of Annie Jackson. But it was Mrs. Ball who had slipped out of the room and now appeared with the tray. In response to enquiries she explained that Annie was not very well, and since she began at once to pour out tea and cut slices of cake, the attention of the ladies was diverted, especially as Mrs. Deacon chose this moment to point out to Miss Sims that she was putting her sleeves in the wrong way round. The point was doggedly contested and Mrs. Deacon provoked into asserting her claim to know what she was talking about on the ground of being a mother.

"So I suppose I do know which side of a frock a child puts its arm through, and you may say what you like, but you've got them in wrong."

Miss Sims held up the small brown garment and gazed at it.

"I don't know what they want to make them different for," she said. "There's two arm-holes and two sleeves, and I suppose the child will have two arms same as other children. I don't know what more anyone wants. And as to being a mother, Mrs. Deacon, that's not what I call a suitable remark, not at a Vicarage work-party. Not what I'd call very refined. But of course we've all been brought up different, and I hope I know how to make allowances for those that haven't had the same advantages that I've had myself."

Coming out in a very deliberate manner but on a rising note, this speech could hardly have failed to induce recriminations if it had not been for Ruth Ball's timely intervention. Arriving with a cup of tea in each hand, she asked Mrs. Deacon to be so very kind as to hand the cake, and warfare was averted. It is really not at all easy to partake of rich fruit cake and conduct a quarrel at one and the same moment. One or the other must be dispensed with, and when it came to competition the cake could be trusted to win. The fascinating topic of just what gave it that moist consistency, that inimitable flavour, superseded all others.

Old Mrs. Stone was having a very successful evening. She had not only had a second slice of cake herself, but she had managed to slide two more slices into her rather distressing work-bag. And now here was Mrs. Ball cutting her a piece for Betsey.

"And most kind, I'm sure, ma'am, but she's a sad sufferer as you know. And I'll be getting along if you'll excuse me, for she don't like being left, and that's a fact. Nervous, that's what she is, and no wonder, seeing as how she lays helpless there in her bed, and no one in call. So I'll be going now, and thank you kindly, Mrs. Ball."

"Well, whoever is nervous, she isn't," said Mrs. Pomfret in her decided voice. "Of course it's only a little way, but I don't mind saying if I hadn't got my car I'd just as soon have company! There's something about those two people being knocked on the head that gives me the creeps, and if I was to hear a footstep behind me in the dark I really shouldn't like it at all." She looked round, gave her jolly laugh, and added, "I hope I'm not frightening anyone— but the rest of you can all see each other home, can't you?"

It was a little after this that the side door of the Vicarage was softly opened and a dark figure slipped out. The air was mild, with a south wind blowing and a sky full of cloud. It was so dark that the woman who had left the house was obliged to switch on a small electric torch before going down the drive. She walked in a slow, hesitating manner and let the torch swing aimlessly to and fro. Her head was bent, and seemed to be covered by a scarf. She went down the drive and turned out into the road.

Chapter 42

DETECTIVE INSPECTOR ABBOTT STOOD IN THE DARK AND listened. He would not have admitted it to anyone else— he barely admitted it to himself—but he was just about as nervous as a cat on hot bricks. Miss Silver's plan, which had sounded so simple in the cosy atmosphere of the Vicarage morning-room with lamplight and firelight and a modicum of daylight to keep the off chance from pushing in, was now, in the darkness, exposed to every kind of doubt. He ought never to have consented to it. That had been his original standpoint, and he ought to have stuck to it. And so what? If he could stick to a plan, why, so could she. And not only could, but would. He had known his Miss Silver for a good many years now, and he was perfectly well aware that when she had made up her mind to a course of action she would pursue it. All that he could do was to remonstrate, which he had done this afternoon, and remonstrance having failed, take what precautions he could to ensure her safety.

He had done what he could. He hoped that he had done enough. There was a plain-clothes man in the bushes at the bottom of the Vicarage drive. Inspector Bury was on the other side of the splash. He himself stood just inside the lych gate. If anyone came down the yew tunnel, he would have ample warning. The softest-footed creature that ever walked could not come that way without the crack of a twig underfoot or the rustle of a leaf. The old dry

droppings of the years were there at the roots of the immemorial yews, and for all the sexton's sweepings, the wind
drifted them across the path again. If anyone came from
the Vicarage and turned towards the splash, he himself
was here, not half a dozen yards from the water and to all
intents and purposes invisible. If anyone came from the
village and passed the Vicarage gate, Grey would follow
soft-foot.

He glanced at the dial of his luminous watch, and found
that the time was a quarter to ten. Only half an hour since
they had taken up their positions, and speaking for himself,
it might have been half the night. Long enough anyhow
to think of a hundred ways in which precaution might fail.
The lych gate was very old. The lych gate—the lyke gate
—the corpse gate—the German *leiche*, a dead body. . . .
They rested the coffin here before a funeral. . . . The
thought came up in his mind, and faded under a flash of
sardonic humour. What a superstitious creature man was!
Civilized? The veneer was pitifully thin. He had only to
be alone in a dark place, and all the old bogies would squeak
and gibber from the shadows.

The church clock startled him with its three ringing
strokes. He looked at his watch again. A minute past the
quarter. Then the church clock was slow by just that
minute. The air seemed still to vibrate under the last
stroke when, lifting his eyes from the illuminated dial, he
thought that something moved. It was one of those im-
pressions without substance. He had just been looking at a
bright object. He looked away from it, and his eyes
dazzled against the dark. If there had been a movement,
he could not have seen it then. Between the lych gate and
the entrance to the Vicarage drive the road sloped upwards.
It was as black as a black cat's fur.

He stood leaning forward, every sense at its fullest stretch,
and he thought someone breathed in the blackness. The
wind blew, and the water ran—a light soft wind, a slowly
moving stream. Impossible that he should have heard the

sound of human breath. His ears strained towards the
sound. His mind strained. And he heard it again. He
heard it because it was so near. Someone else's foot took
the wide, shallow step of the lych gate. If he had not been
in his stocking feet he would have been heard as he stepped
back. But he was not heard. It was the other who had
been heard, soft and crafty as that tell-tale foot had been.
There was no further movement, only now and again that
deep betraying breath. There was no other sound, but
there was a growing sense of tension, of urgency, of a purpose from which there would be no turning back.

And then, away up the rise where the Vicarage drive
came out, there was a flicker of light. From where he stood
it came just within his line of vision before the solid oak
of the lych gate cut it off. The flicker showed and was
gone, and came wavering into sight again low down upon
the ground. He could see what it was now, the small weak
ray of a torch whose battery had come near to petering
out. The hand which held it hung down and swung loose.
It was a woman's hand. If the torch was meant to light
her way it failed wretchedly, since it produced a mere con-
·fusion of sliding shadows. If it served any purpose at all, it
was to make her visible, or partly visible, to those who were
watching the road. She came slowly down the rise, seeming
to drift rather than walk, now at one side of the road, and
then on a wavering course towards the other. She gave the
lych gate a wide berth and passed down beyond it to the
watersplash.

Inside the lych gate something stirred. Someone went
by. Standing rigidly controlled and still, Frank Abbott was
aware that he was alone again. He had hardly dared to
draw his natural breath, had hardly even dared to think,
lest that someone should discern an alien presence. Now
he leaned forward and saw the flicker of light blotted out
by a moving shape. With every sense alert, he followed.
Cold, damp ground under foot, the wet of it striking
through a pair of socks that would probably never be quite

the same again—light moving air that went by with a scatter of rain—the lulling flow of the stream—and two shadows ahead of him. There was one of them now, right down at the edge of the splash where the water took the flicker of the torch. The small, weak ray went out across the stream and swung back again, to go sliding to and fro upon wet grass and oozing clay. The second shadow was very close, and Frank no more than a yard behind. It had all been without any sound except the soft going of wind and water. But now there was a human sound, the sound of a voice kept low.

" Annie! "

The figure at the edge of the splash did not turn. The torch shook in her hand, the ray went wide. She said in a whispering way,

" What—is—it? "

" You ought not to be down here by the splash. Why do you come? "

This time Frank caught only the two words,

" William—drowned—— "

Then the deep voice again,

" What do you know—about his being drowned? What did you see? What have you told? "

There was no audible answer this time, only a slow shaking of the head with its enveloping scarf.

" What did you see? "

The whisper came again.

" I—saw—— "

There was movement then, sudden and violent, an upward swing and a sudden flailing blow. The figure at the edge of the splash fell forward. The torch hit the water and went out. Frank battled in the dark with a hard bony strength which was beyond anything he had expected. He shouted, and the plain-clothes man came running. Bury came running from across the splash, sliding off the last stepping-stone and getting wet up to the knees. The three of them grappled in the dark until the whirling, twisting

limbs were pinioned and the crazed fury broke up in a
hurry of words. The whole thing was a kind of nightmare
where time was suspended and the impossible was happening. The harsh voice screamed in the dark.

Frank Abbott emerged from the mêlée to find himself
calling Miss Silver's name.

"Where are you? Are you all right? For God's sake!"

He groped where he had seen her fall, and heard a
familiar and most welcome cough.

"I am rather wet, and I shall be glad of your hand. This
clay is extremely slippery."

He helped her to her feet, and stood there with his arm
round her, breathing hard.

"I'll never forgive myself!"

The water dripped from her skirts, but her voice was
perfectly composed.

"My dear Frank, there is no need to distress yourself. I
heard her arm go up, and I thought it best to drop forward
into the water. I think you will find that the weapon was
one of those heavy torches, in which case it should be somewhere about here, unless it has rolled. We need some light.
Ah—I see Inspector Bury has a torch!"

He said,

"So have I, but I was in such a damned flap that I forgot
it."

He had never supposed that he would swear in front of
Miss Silver and go unreproved, yet it happened. Her "My
dear Frank!" breathed nothing but affection.

They moved on together to where Inspector Bury's torch
had been turned upon the dreadful draggled figure of
Mildred Blake.

Chapter 43

"NO, MY DEAR FRANK, I AM NONE THE WORSE, I AM THANKFUL to say. Such a mild night, and the hot water supply at the Vicarage quite unusually good. I was able to have a most refreshing bath, and Mrs. Ball insisted upon my remaining in bed for breakfast this morning, though I assured her that it was quite unnecessary."

He was looking at her with an expression which very few people had ever seen upon his face—moved, affectionate, concerned.

"I shan't easily forgive myself."

She returned his look with a very serious one.

"What else was there to do? Poor Annie's behaviour was betraying her. To the unbalanced watchful mind of the murderer it was obvious that she knew something, and this being the case, she was a potential danger. The person who had already killed twice would not scruple to kill again. From the time of my meeting with Annie at the grave of Christopher Hale it was evident to me that her mental health was giving way under the pressure of some terrible secret, and that this secret concerned the death of her husband. It seemed necessary to consider whether she herself had had any hand in his death. He had married her for her money, treated her with neglect and violence, and was being unfaithful to her. I considered whether she might not have come up behind him as he crossed the splash and pushed him into the pool where he was drowned. But then there was the case of Clarice Dean. You will remember, in the evidence at the inquest, that the last person known to have spoken with William Jackson was Edward Random. This is confirmed by Annie, who says Mr. Edward went by her and over the splash. He met William

Jackson on the rise, and she heard him say; 'Good-night, Willy', as he passed. I had to consider whether Clarice Dean might have been waiting inside the lych gate for the chance of a word with Edward Random. We know of two other occasions when she did this—the occasion on which Mrs. Stone saw them together, and the other and more tragic one when she went down to the splash to meet her death."

"You think she may have seen or heard something suspicious on the night that Jackson was drowned?"

"I do not think so. I had to consider it as a possible motive for her removal by Annie, but I almost immediately rejected it. For one thing, Annie herself had seen Edward Random go on up the rise after saying good-night to her husband. If Clarice had come to meet him, what was there to keep her in the neighbourhood of the splash? She had only to follow him and link her arm with his, as we know she did on a subsequent occasion. I found it impossible to believe that she could have witnessed the murder of William Jackson. If she had done so, there would be no reason for her to hold her tongue. So far from attempting to disguise her interest in Edward Random, she took every opportunity of proclaiming it. I really could find no motive for her murder by Annie Jackson. My second reason for rejecting the idea that it was Annie who was responsible for the two deaths lay in her own mental state, which was one of acute fear. At times it became so acute as to make her court the very danger which she felt to be impending. She believed that she was doomed, and there were moments when the strain of waiting for the blow to fall became too much for her, and she would go down to the splash and hope for death."

He smiled.

"I've always said that you see right through us all and out at the other side. It is a solemn thought, and I give you fair warning that when I really have something to hide I shall start avoiding you like the plague. Well, you saw through Annie, and decided that she wasn't the murderer but only the next prospective victim. And now perhaps you will tell me how you arrived at Mildred Blake."

She coughed in a gently hesitating manner.

"It was when I was considering the possibility that Mr. Arnold Random was the murderer. It was he who stood to lose if his brother had made a later will. It was he who was threatened with blackmail both by William Jackson and, indirectly, by Clarice Dean. It was he who more than anyone else could be said to have an interest in their deaths. And all that stood between him and the gravest suspicion was the alibi given him by Miss Mildred Blake. If she was speaking the truth, he could not have murdered William Jackson. If she was lying in order to provide him with an alibi, what was her motive for doing so? Local gossip had informed me that Mr. Arnold Random had at one time paid her some attentions which were expected to result in marriage. If I had had no personal acquaintance with Miss Blake I might have entertained the idea that she was actuated by this memory of a past romance, but after meeting her on a number of occasions I found myself quite unable to believe in any such thing. All the local talk— even Mrs. Ball's not uncharitable comments—served to confirm my impression of her as a hard, self-centred, grasping person whose ruling passion was the love of money. There was even some faint indication of other possibilities. Mrs. Ball and the Vicar were in some concern over the accounts of the Boys' Club. The late incumbent was a very old man. He and Miss Mildred ran all the funds. Ruth Ball appeared to be more distressed about the matter than would be warranted if it were merely the case of a nonogenarian's lapse of memory."

Frank whistled.

"A very unpleasant position."

Miss Silver inclined her head.

"As you say. My attention became more and more closely focused upon Miss Mildred Blake. Though enjoy-

ing a comfortable income, she appeared in garments really
suitable only for a scarecrow. When the murders were discussed in her presence she not only evinced no pity for a
young man whom she must have known since he was an
infant, or for the girl who was a member of her own house-
hold, but I could actually discern traces of satisfaction, even
of sadistic enjoyment. In a person of this kind the memory
of an abortive romance would be far more likely to produce
resentment than any softer feeling."

Frank was looking at her intently.

"Do you know, you are being very interesting indeed."

There was a hint of reproof in her voice as she continued.

"I went back over the events of that Friday night on
which William Jackson was murdered. Mr. Arnold
Random was practising in the church. The Vicarage
work-party was going on, and did not break up until a
quarter-past ten. At a little before ten, when the strains of
the organ could still be distinctly heard, Miss Mildred Blake
got up and said she wanted to have a word with him about
taking his duty. Mrs. Ball says it is her impression that
the organ had stopped playing and the church clock had
struck ten before Miss Mildred actually left. The latest
testimony we have as to the whereabouts of William Jackson is that of his wife Annie, and of Edward Random.
Edward Random says he passed William on the rise and
said good-night to him, and he thinks he heard the clock
strike some time later when he was already in the village
street. Annie heard Edward Random say good-night to
her husband and go on up the rise, and she too says that
the clock struck after that. Knowing that William Jackson
had it in his mind to blackmail his employer, I considered
whether William would have let slip such an excellent
chance. The sound of the organ would inform him that
Mr. Arnold Random was in the church, and he had taken
enough drink to embolden him. Even before Annie disclosed the whole of what she saw that night I thought it
very probable that William had gone up to the church."

He gave her a sharp glance.

"So Annie has spoken?"

"Yes. I will tell you about that presently. You were asking me how I arrived at my conclusions with regard to Miss Blake. It will be simpler if we take that first. Mildred Blake's story was that she went across to the church, found Mr. Random putting his music away, and had a few words with him, after which he saw her home and went on in the direction of the Hall. This gave him an alibi, but it gave her one too. On the other hand, unless she had some guilty knowledge, it would not occur to her that she could possibly require an alibi, and the more I knew of her, the less could I believe it possible that she should have been swayed by sentiment."

Frank cocked an eyebrow.

"It could have happened just as she said, you know—a few minutes' talk in the church, and Arnold seeing her home."

She shook her head.

"I found myself unable to believe in that alibi. Annie was on the far side of the splash, and, whatever she admitted or concealed, I was quite sure that she had not seen her husband cross the splash. And if he did not cross it, where was he while she stood waiting for him on the other side? He must have gone up to the church. And if he went up to the church, Mildred Blake must have found him there when she went across to speak to Arnold Random. Let us go back to the moment when she got up and announced her intention of doing so. There would be work to be put away, farewells to be said, an outdoor coat to be assumed, and, as I know from my own experience, after leaving the house a little time to accustom her eyes to the change from light to darkness. The clock has now struck and the organ ceased, but she knows that there is no need for her to hurry, because Arnold Random will be putting his music away. She takes the path to the churchyard, comes to the side door, and hears voices inside. I believe most firmly that

that is what she did hear. She would certainly want to know what was going on. I have myself been in the church when Arnold Random was at the organ. If he had not broken off he would have had no idea that I was there. Mildred Blake could have stood and listened, as I believe she did stand and listen, to William Jackson's clumsy attempt at blackmail. The will would have been mentioned, and an angry scene would follow. In the end William Jackson must have gone off, stupid and angry. And Miss Mildred Blake conceives her plan. She knows Arnold Random too well to suppose that he will face disgrace rather than pay blackmail. But why should the proceeds of this blackmail go into the pockets of William Jackson? He will certainly bungle the affair—has probably already bungled it. But in her hands, what a weapon, what a source of income! She knows Arnold Random's every weakness and how best it may be played upon. I believe most firmly that she saw her whole wicked plan in a flash and hurried away to put it into execution."

Frank had a startled look.

"You don't mean she bumped William off in order to blackmail Arnold on her own!"

A slight cough reproved his choice of words, but she replied with firmness.

"I do indeed. And to obtain a still more effective hold upon him. You will recall Lord Tennyson's words about 'The lust of gain in the heart of Cain'. They exactly describe what I believe to have been that unhappy woman's frame of mind. She hurried after William Jackson, caught up with him before he reached the splash, and was able either to stun him with her torch—it is an unusually large and heavy one—or to push him into the pool and hold him down there until he lost consciousness. He was, you must remember, in an extremely fuddled condition. The whole thing would take only a very few minutes. Next day, as I have learned from Mrs. Deacon whose daughter Doris admitted her, Miss Mildred called upon Arnold Random at the Hall. She was carrying with her the black collecting-book with which everyone in the village was familiar. Can you be in any doubt as to the nature of the collection which she had come to make? Just consider the strength of her position. She has only to come forward at the inquest and say that she had overheard an attempt on the part of William Jackson to blackmail Mr. Arnold Random on the ground that he had fraudulently concealed a will to which Jackson was a witness, and there could be very little doubt that there would be a verdict of wilful murder against him. Only a very stupid man could fail to see the danger in which he stood. There was no way out but to pay whatever she asked. In return she offered him her silence as to the quarrel with William Jackson, and an alibi which also protected herself. I really do not think, my dear Frank, that in the whole course of my experience I have ever come across a cleverer or more shockingly inhuman plan."

He nodded.

"And the Clarice Dean business? Mildred Blake typed the note of course."

"Oh, yes. She was up at the Church Room that morning. Edward Random told me he saw her coming and made his escape."

"Why did she try to put the murder on him? She did, you know."

"He would be a convenient scapegoat. There had been a good deal of gossip about his long absence, and it would not have suited her at all if Arnold Random had been suspected. She did just stop short of directly accusing Edward, though Miss Ora did not."

He said quickly,

"You don't think she was in it!"

"Oh, no. She is just a foolish woman with a love of gossip and no sense of responsibility."

Frank looked at her oddly.

"If you had said all this to me a day or two ago, or even yesterday, I should of course have listened to you with profound respect, but I'm afraid I should have remained rather obstinately unbelieving. But you know, that is just how it happened—as regards Arnold Random at any rate. He has made a statement, and you are right all along the line. William Jackson did come up to the church and accuse him of suppressing his brother's will. Of course he says he didn't—says he never knew of its existence until Susan Wayne came across it yesterday behind some of the old books she has been cataloguing in his library. Well, that seems to me to be a pretty tall story, but he and Edward Random stand together on it, and as Edward is the sole beneficiary and the will is already in the hands of the family solicitors, it has really got nothing to do with us. Arnold's statement goes on to say that Mildred Blake approached him after the death of Jackson—that he agreed to pay her the blackmail she demanded, and that she made a further demand upon him after the death of Clarice Dean. So you were right, but I still don't know how you got there. You know, the Chief really does suspect you of at least white witchcraft. I don't think it would surprise him if you were to fly out of the window on a broomstick. So if you don't want me to share his views, perhaps you will tell me just what it was that made you sure enough to take the risk I ought never have allowed you to take last night."

She had been knitting steadily, but now she laid the small pink garment down and rested her hands upon it.

"It was a little thing," she said, "but it convinced me. I went in yesterday morning to see Miss Ora Blake. She rang for tea, and it was Miss Mildred who brought it up. As she sat there pouring out, I noticed the condition of her skirt. It was not the one which she had worn when Mrs. Ball and I took tea with them on a previous afternoon. It was of the same dark grey colour, but the material was not the same. What I noticed was that this skirt had recently been very wet. The stuff had cockled, and there were traces of clay upon it. An attempt had been made to remove them, but, as you probably know, the task would be by no

means an easy one. Miss Mildred's natural indifference
to her personal appearance had doubtless prevented her
giving the matter the attention it merited. No one in the
village would notice whether there were a few more stains
on her garments. If I had not been a stranger I might not
have noticed them myself, but having done so, I became
more and more convinced that Miss Mildred had stained
and wetted her skirt on the clay bank and the stepping-
stones of the watersplash. After that everything fitted into
its own place. I had already considered Miss Mildred to be
a person who might be capable of murder. When I mentioned her name to Annie her reaction was one of extreme
distress. She would not speak, and she was shaken by
terror."

"Will she speak now?"

"When she heard that Mildred Blake had been arrested
she burst into tears and told me all she knew. It does not
add very much to what she has said already, but what it
does add is of the highest importance. You will remember
that she was waiting on the far side of the splash to see if
her husband would come home. The night was dark and
cloudy, but there was an occasional gleam of moonlight.
After Edward Random went by her and over the splash she
heard him wish her husband good-night and go on again.
William Jackson then came down a few steps towards the
splash. She could hear the sound of the organ being played
in the church, and so of course could he. She says he turned
round, ran back to the lych gate, and disappeared. He had
been dropping hints that Mr. Arnold wouldn't dare to discharge him, and she was very much upset, because she was
afraid he was going to do something against the law. I do
not know how much he had really told her—I just give you
her own words. She waited where she was. The church
clock struck, and the organ stopped playing. Some time
after that William came down the yew tunnel and out by
the lych gate. She says he was very angry. He stumbled
in his walk and kept muttering to himself and cursing.

He came about half-way down to the splash, and then turned and went back. But before he got to the lych gate he seemed to change his mind. He stood for a minute or two, and then came slowly down the rise. Just as he reached the edge of the water, someone else came out of the lych gate in a hurry. Annie's eyes were sufficiently accustomed to the darkness to see the movement of the figures and to discern that the second one was a woman, but she could not tell who it was until she heard her call, 'William —William Jackson!' and then she knew that it was Miss Mildred Blake. She says she could not be mistaken—there was no one else with a deep voice like hers."

"And then?"

"William stood still, and she came down the rest of the way and stood beside him. They began to talk. At least she says Miss Mildred was talking and William was shrugging it off. She may have been talking about the will—I suppose we shall never know—but all at once William began to come over the splash, and Annie was afraid to stay any longer. She turned round and ran. She looked back once, and she says she saw Miss Mildred on the first stepping-stone. There was a gleam of moonlight, and she is quite sure Miss Mildred was not on the bank. She could see the water, and the first stepping-stone and Miss Mildred standing on it, and William two stones ahead. She says she was more frightened than she had ever been in all her life, but she didn't know why. It just came over her and she ran all the way home."

Chapter 44

"DO YOU WANT TO LIVE AT THE HALL?" SAID EDWARD RANDOM.
He was kneeling on the hearth-rug, drawing up the neg-
lected fire with a couple of sheets of newspaper.

Susan, on the window-seat with a book in her lap which
she was not attempting to read, could only suppose that
he had not noticed Emmeline's withdrawal. She said in
her clear voice,

"She's gone to feed the cats."

"Emmeline?"

"Of course."

A small bright flame was creeping up behind the paper.
He regarded it with approval, and said,

"But why? I wasn't talking to her—and anyhow she
much prefers this cat-ridden cottage. I was talking to
you."

He snatched the paper back as he spoke, and the flame
followed it. There was a whoosh and a few damns before
he got the whole blazing mass crammed back amongst the
now reviving logs. Susan dropped her book and said,

"*Really——*"

He sat back on his heels and surveyed his handiwork complacently.

"Well, that's got it going anyhow. If it weren't for the
cats, I don't believe Emmeline would ever know whether
she had a fire or not." He got up and dusted his hands.
"You know, I was talking to you. I was asking you whether
you would like to live at the Hall."

Susan said, "I should hate it."

"Why?"

She was frowning and rather pale.

"Oh, secret wills—and family quarrels—and big draughty

rooms that never get really warm—and the furniture all in dust-sheets——"

He shook his head.

"There aren't any draughts—Uncle James saw to that. And there aren't any more wills—at least I hope not. And the family hatchets are beautifully and decorously buried. So what about it?"

He was standing and looking at her. She did not know whether he was serious or not. If he was, then he was asking her to marry him, and it wasn't any sort of way to do it. Anger came up in her. It put colour into her cheeks and made her eyes shine. She held her head up high and said,

"What about what?"

She was in the middle of the window-seat, and there really wasn't room for anyone else, but all at once he was there, sliding in beside her and pushing her along to make room. She felt his hand come down on her shoulder as he said,

"You know perfectly well. I couldn't ask you when I was just going to be arrested, but I'm asking you now. Are you going to marry me?"

She moved as far away from him as the window-seat allowed. It was not very far, but she did what she could and turned to face him.

"Why do you want me to—if you really do?"

"I really do."

She could make nothing of the words or of his face. He might have been asking her to go for a walk. She had let him kiss her, and she had kissed him back. Aunt Lucy's training had been very emphatic on the subject of easy kissing—it made a man think less of you. Away from Greenings, she had been able to consider this rather old-fashioned. But she wasn't away from Greenings now, and whether it was old-fashioned or not, it was horribly and convincingly true. Edward was asking her to marry him without even bothering to pretend that he cared for her.

She had given herself away so completely that he didn't have to pretend. He just wanted to settle down and get married, and she was the sensible domestic kind of girl who would never provide him with any surprises. She did not feel either sensible or domestic. She felt like the bright burning flame of anger itself.

"You are not in love with me!"

His hand dropped from her shoulder. He too leaned back.

"It depends what you mean by being in love."

"You know perfectly well what I mean!"

He said lightly,

"The gilt on the gingerbread—the icing on the cake?"

"No, I don't mean that."

"A lot of people do. What *do* you mean then? Spring fever? The feeling that you've got seven-league boots and can go racing off to the ends of the earth to bring back some entire and perfect chrysolite for the beloved one? The magnificent and ridiculous ecstasy of eighteen? It doesn't last, you know, my dear—it doesn't last."

She thought, "He felt that for Verona Grey. He will never feel it for me."

His hand touched hers and withdrew again.

"The chrysolite doesn't keep the home fires burning, and you can't live by moonshine or the cosmic rays."

The anger went out of Susan. She was dimmed and extinguished. She felt quite intolerably flat and middle-aged. Only when you are really middle-aged there are not so many dull, lean years stretching out before you as there are at twenty-two.

"I can't marry anyone who doesn't love me. And you don't. I suppose you are fond of me, but you don't love me."

He leaned forward and took her hands. She despised herself quite a lot for feeling that it was comfortable to have them held. He said,

"Now that is where you are entirely wrong. I love you

quite a lot. If it isn't the way you want, well that's just
too bad. I think it's quite a good way myself, because it's
got roots in the things that matter, and that means it will
go on growing. It has grown quite a lot in the last few
days. It mayn't sound romantic, but that depends on what
you think about romance. I don't see why it shouldn't be
like charity and begin at home. You know, if I had to
choose one word to tell you what you stand for, it would
be that. I can't think of having a home without you. It
mayn't mean anything to you, but to me it does mean
everything I thought I was never going to have—everything
that seemed to have dried up in me—everything that you've
brought back and called to life again."

All the cool, deliberate control was gone. His eyes were
wet, and his voice stumbled and broke. There didn't seem
to be any moment in which she moved towards him, there
was certainly no moment in which she spoke, but she found
that she was in his arms, and that it was the only right and
happy place for her to be.

She took up his word and made it her own. She had come
home.

THE END

LORD PETER VIEWS THE BODY

Dorothy L. Sayers

Written in the inimitable style of her best
novels, here is another collection of Lord
Peter Wimsey stories, equalling the STRIDING
FOLLY volume.

Lord Peter here puzzles his way through such
mysteries as 'The Abominable History of the
Man with Copper Fingers' and 'The Fantastic
Horror of the Cat in the Bag', besides many
others.

Without doubt Lord Peter Wimsey is one of
the greatest fiction detectives of this century,
and this fascinating collection only further
demonstrates the fact. This book is a
necessity for both established readers, and
newcomers.

NEW ENGLISH LIBRARY

DOROTHY L. SAYERS
AVAILABLE FROM NEL